The Misadvent
Reluctant Cou

It is 1803, and Great Britain is at war with France. James Farrant, a naval lieutenant, is enjoying the comforts of home while his ship is being repaired. Coerced into Intelligence by a friend of his father's, his adventures lead him into many situations where his inexperience is more of an aid than a hindrance. An adventure story in the finest tradition, our 'hero' saves the day, and finds his future wife in the concluding chapters.

The Misadventures of a Reluctant Counterspy

A. R. Dismorr

A.R. Dismorr

DRUM PUBLISHING

All characters in this book are fictitious and any resemblance to actual persons, living or dead, is purely coincidental.

A catalogue record for this book is available from the British Library

Published by Drum Publishing,
P.O. Box 199, Wallingford, OX10 9XR

ISBN 0 9534713 2 2

Typeset by Galleon Photosetting, Ipswich
Printed and bound in Great Britain by Biddles Limited
Guildford and King's Lynn

Chapter I

It was my wife, I think, who first suggested that I ought to set down some account of it all.

We were seated by the fire one winter's evening and, some chance remark happening to recall those far-off days, we were having a good laugh over one of the more absurd incidents that had befallen me during the course of those fateful few weeks.

"Now that you've retired it will give you something to do," she had cheerfully declared. "And besides it should make a good story. . . . Anyway the grandchildren will be amused by it I am sure."

So in obedience to her wishes I duly closeted myself in my study one morning and, with a sheaf of paper before me, commenced to imagine myself back some forty years or so, it must be now, and live over again that sequence of grotesque misadventures of which, as it chanced, I had been such a hapless and reluctant victim.

How long ago it all seems now and yet I find that I am able to recapture most of it clearly enough. Albeit that there are times, I must confess, when the whole experience seems more like some well-remembered dream and Nathaniel Cruden, Joseph Leckley, Dr Argent and the rest to have been simply the shadowy figments thereof. But they were real enough of course. And, anyway, I have only to feel up to my neck for the long white scar to be reminded that it all actually happened.

It was a September evening, the year being as I must quickly tell you, 1803, that my story should, I suppose, rightly begin.

Those autumn days were, as you may remember, singularly anxious ones for the old country. It was but a few months since we had once again broken with France, following the hollow peace of the Treaty of Amiens, and Napoleon and his armies, fresh from easily gained victories on the Continent, were threatening our peace and security from across the channel.

That an invasion was imminent few, I think, at the time seriously doubted. Indeed that the French were in earnest I could bear witness, having recently returned home from service with the blockading fleet off Boulogne, when I had had ample opportunity of observing something of their vast armies and the congregation of flat-bottomed barges, which, for several months past, had been assembling along that stretch of coast.

My ship the *Sirius*, a 28-gun frigate, had chanced to drag her anchor and coming too close inshore, had fallen foul of the enemy's batteries, the damage to her superstructure being so severe that she had only just managed to limp back to Portsmouth.

That it would be some while before she could be made seaworthy again seemed assured, and I was thus gleefully looking forward to a few weeks' respite from the discomforts and tedium of life aboard ship, which to be honest with you, especially as I was such a martyr to *mal de mer*, I had always found peculiarly irksome.

To be truthful, in spite of a family tradition of naval service stretching back over three generations, it had been with considerable reluctance that I had, some ten years previously, and at the tender age of twelve, first gone to sea.

I would have much preferred some more reclusive vocation. But my father for all my tearful protestations had remained sternly insistent. And my mother being of the same persuasion, I had, like my three brothers before me, duly succumbed to the parental will.

So, as you may imagine, it was with feelings of no little satisfaction that I was contemplating the weeks that lay ahead of me, when I would be able, for a while at least, to indulge in the comforts of home life and enjoy some of the pleasures that London had to offer.

Such then were my agreeable expectations and little did I realise, as I dressed for dinner on the second evening of my arrival back home, that they were soon to be shattered.

Not that that evening held out much promise of enjoyment, for Lord and Lady St Vincent had been invited to join our small family gathering. The former, I should mention, had been a close friend of my father's since their midshipman days and had consequently been a visitor to the house as far back as I could remember.

As you will recall, his career had been a most distinguished one. Ennobled some five or six years previously, following the battle after which he had taken his title, he was at the time of which I am writing First Lord of the Admiralty.

I had for a term served under him in the West Indies and so had experienced something of the harsh discipline for which he was renowned and which had done little to endear him to either officers or crew.

I certainly had always found him a most forbidding personage, for whatever the social circumstances he never seemed to unbend. Even as a child I had dreaded his coming to the house when, if given the chance, he would never lose an opportunity of catechising me about my doings. A habit which, I might add, he had continued to pursue with even greater assiduity now that I was a serving officer.

So for all that we had at that time a most excellent cook, who tended to excel herself upon such occasions, it was one from which I would certainly have contrived to absent myself had not my father made it firmly to be understood that I would be present.

So there was nothing for it, I decided, but to see the evening through with as much forbearance as I was able, when, having attired myself in my best tailcoat and knee-breeches, I set off downstairs to join the rest of the company in the drawing-room.

For a while the evening passed pleasantly enough. At dinner the conversation, as it must have done over many similar tables that evening, soon turned upon discussion of the 'if', 'where' and 'when' of the expected invasion.

"My opinion is he'll never hazard the attempt. He's got too much respect for our navy, as he's every reason to have of course," declared Lord St Vincent emphatically. "And, if he does, I promise you that those barges of his will be smashed to smithereens before they're even half-way across."

"Well I'm not so sure Johnny," responded my father doubtfully, although with a deference he always accorded his old friend.

"The prevailing weather conditions might make things tricky for us don't you think? Given a couple of days of high winds or fog I would allow them a sporting chance of making some sort of a landing, especially now that the spring tides are approaching. . . . Whether they make much progress after that, well that of course is quite another matter."

"I agree fog might make things awkward for us but, as for high winds, that surely would hamper them as much as us," retorted his lordship as he continued to gulp down the excellent turtle soup with which the meal had begun.

"You may be right," responded my father, "but after all the trouble he's gone to I'm pretty sure Old Boney's going to make some sort of an attempt."

"Possibly, James, possibly," interposed Lord St Vincent doubtfully. "He's certainly always been something of a gambler, I grant you, and never too mindful of casualties I understand, so I suppose he might be foolhardy enough to chance his arm."

My opinion not being sought and Lady Vincent and my mother being happily absorbed in the interchange of family news I was able to give my undivided attention to a plate of boiled turbot and lobster sauce, which Chivers the footman had just placed before me. The pleasures of the table, for as I have said we had an excellent cook at that time, being something to which I particularly looked forward when coming home on leave.

A roast partridge having followed the turbot, the talk then proceeded to a discussion of which sector of our coastline the French were likely to aim for.

Here again there appeared to be some disagreement, Lord St Vincent declaring for the stretch opposite the Romney marshes, while my father was of the opinion that further round the Sussex coast, close by the Pevensey levels, was a more likely landing site.

My own view, which I tentatively interposed, that the Thanet coast north of Margate, where the flat terrain for several miles inland and a readier approach to London might perhaps be considered, was received with the curtest of dismissals, a response which, no doubt, it deserved.

"Anyway wherever they may attempt to land, and as I said I don't believe for a moment that they'll get that far, you can rest assured Ma'am," declared Lord St Vincent addressing my mother, "that Sir David Dundas and his troops will be more than a match for them."

"Well I sincerely hope so," responded my mother feelingly.

And with this and the meal having been concluded with apple pie and cream, as I remember, my mother and Lady St Vincent rose to leave, while Lord St Vincent, my father and I remained at the table to circulate the port and nibble away at the dessert.

For several minutes the two of them exchanged naval gossip while I sat a little way apart quietly sipping my port and thinking my own thoughts, scarcely heeding what they were saying.

Then of a sudden Lord St Vincent turned to me and said, "I was sorry to hear about your ship, David. The *Sirius* wasn't it?"

"Er, yes Sir. That's correct," I replied, all at once shaken out of my reverie.

"She was knocked about quite a bit I understand," went on his lordship.

"Yes that's right, Sir. The damage was pretty extensive. Her mizzenmast was shot away and . . ."

"Ah! Yes. Yelland of course. Well I'm not surprised," he added sardonically. An aspersion which, as I knew, was quite unwarranted. "So it looks David as if you are going to be at a loose end for a while," continued Lord St Vincent after a pause.

"I'm afraid it seems rather like it, Sir," I agreed, trusting that the sigh I gave was not too obviously simulated.

"Well we must try to find something for you to do," he then said, as my heart sank within me. "Don't you think so James?" he then added, turning to my father. "We can't have our young officers sitting idly by in these perilous times can we?"

"You're right Johnny. Much better than twiddling his thumbs at home for the next month or so. As I am sure he would agree," exclaimed my father, eyeing me sternly as he did so, for he was only too aware of my real sentiments.

"Well now what do you think my boy? I'll warrant you'll be much happier being usefully employed in some way or another, instead of idling your time away in London," said Lord St Vincent eyeing me severely.

"Yes, er, of course," I said lamely as I grabbed hold of the nutcrackers and a walnut in an attempt to conceal my dismay.

For several moments nothing further was said and I had begun to hope that, although my father would later doubtless continue to press his friend to find me some temporary posting or other, there was just a chance that nothing might come of it after all.

Unhappily my thoughts of a reprieve were, I fear, to be short-lived, for after pausing to refill his glass from the decanter, Lord St Vincent then went on, "I don't know James whether you know anything of this new Intelligence Department that's just been set up. Anyway, it seems that they are having the greatest difficulty in finding the right sort of recruit. In fact they've made an approach to the Admiralty to see if we might be able to help – officers on half-pay who for some reason or other were not fit for active service or who were temporarily unengaged. That's what they had in mind, I imagine. Now this might be just the sort of thing for David, don't you think?"

"It's a splendid notion, I'm sure he'd be delighted!" interposed my father with alacrity, and an enthusiasm that I certainly did not share.

"Come now David, you know you would," he then added derisively, as I sat there too stunned by the implications of what Lord St Vincent had been suggesting to say anything.

"You appear hesitant David. I must say you surprise me," interjected his lordship coldly. "Why if I were your age I would have jumped at such an opportunity."

"But I've never had any experience of that kind of thing," I blurted out at last in desperation.

"Oh! I don't think that need worry you. All that is required, I imagine, is some common nous and a spark of enterprise, that's all," asserted his lordship lightly. "Of course I can't pretend to know exactly what might be required of you, but you'll be able to manage perfectly well I am quite sure. At least it'll be a welcome change from the monotony of blockade duty, eh?" he then added, with a heavy attempt at jocularity, which I was in no mood to share, I can tell you.

Indeed far from any feelings of exhilaration, so horrified was I by what was being proposed that I must, I fear, have looked the very picture of dejection as I sat there distractedly fiddling with the nutcrackers, and was only too thankful for the dimness of the candle-light which must, partially at least, have obscured my discomfiture.

I could I suppose have simply declined to have anything to do with the whole proposition, for it was certainly an irregular one and scarcely within an officer's terms of duty. But I knew full well that I could not do so. For quite apart from the humiliation of refusing, any chance of future promotion I might have would assuredly be jeopardised.

"So then David, how do you feel about it?" put in my father impatiently, as I continued to hesitate.

"I'm willing to give it a try, I suppose," I murmured doubtfully at last. "But I don't really . . ."

"Come now David, we want no 'buts'," cut in my father with finality. "As

Lord St Vincent says we only wish that we were your age. Why I'd have given my right hand for such an opportunity."

So it was all decided then, I reflected bitterly, as the three of us rose to rejoin Lady St Vincent and my mother in the drawing-room. For knowing my father's obduracy there was, I was quite sure, to be no evading the commitment.

Thus instead of the cosy few weeks at home, which I had been so fondly cherishing, here I was, destined to some 'cloak and dagger' assignment or other. A sphere of activity in which I had absolutely no experience or indeed aptitude for. Let alone, as you will have gathered, any inclination. It really was altogether heartrending.

And you can imagine, I am sure, with what feelings of desolation, not unmixed with a certain grim foreboding, that I set off for my bed later that evening.

Chapter II

When I awoke the following morning, after a night of broken sleep and disturbing dreams, and the events of the previous evening began to drift back into my half-conscious thoughts, I was inclined to imagine, at first, that they had been nothing more than the fantasies of a nightmare.

Unhappily the delusion was of the briefest, as a further moment's consideration was quickly to determine.

As the realisation burst in upon me and I continued to lie there, gloomily speculating upon the wretched course which events had taken, all manner of intimidating fancies started to present themselves to my mind.

For although, as I have said, I had had no experience of intelligence work or indeed any real idea of what might be expected of me, I knew that any such undertaking was certain to be a hazardous one, and also that anyone apprehended by the opposition in the performance of it could expect nothing but the shortest of shrifts. Not that I was likely to be posted to France I imagined. My unfamiliarity with the language would surely preclude me from an assignment over there. Still if they were as desperate for recruits, as they apparently were, anything was possible I dolefully supposed!

Whatever the case I had little opportunity for further disconsolate reflection just then for I had, as I discovered, overslept, and knowing my father's insistence upon punctuality at meals I had barely time to make a hurried shave and to dress in order to reach the breakfast room somewhere near the stipulated hour of eight o'clock.

My father was already at the table when I arrived and my mother, as was her custom, breakfasting alone in her room, we were the sole occupants.

"You're late David," he greeted me severely, taking out his watch as he did so and giving it a fixed look.

"I'm sorry Father, I'm afraid I overslept," I said blandly as I moved over to the sideboard, where I helped myself to a plateful of kidneys, eggs and bacon.

"I must see that Chivers calls you in future. For as you well know I won't abide unpunctuality. I'd have thought the service would have taught you better ways," he exclaimed, giving me a long-suffering look.

"Er, yes father," I mumbled as I reached for some toast.

"You'll be seeing those intelligence people this morning of course. You'd better get around there as soon as you can for these are no times for any sort of dilly-dallying," added my father after an interval. "I don't know exactly where their headquarters are. Somewhere at the back of Whitehall I believe. But if you look in at the Admiralty they'll tell you where to go and to whom to report I imagine."

"Right father," I said absently.

"I really wish David that you would sometimes show a little more enthusiasm," cried my father suddenly in exasperation. "This is a splendid opportunity you've been afforded. All kinds of advantages could well spring from it. Why there's no telling, that if you make a success of it, it might even lead to a command."

There was of course, as I reflected to myself ruefully, the obverse side of the coin, and that if I did not come out of it well, gone would be any such hope.

Anyway, with this my father had taken up *The Times* so the remainder of the meal was thankfully passed in silence, while I continued to do full justice to the toast and marmalade before quietly slipping away to my room.

There I continued to dawdle about for an hour or so, endeavouring to pluck up the necessary resolution, until at last I decided that I could postpone the moment of truth no longer. And so having attired myself in my lieutenant's uniform with cocked hat and sword I set off from our house in Hanover Square and made for the direction of the Admiralty.

After a good deal of trouble I eventually obtained the necessary information and, moving on and around to the back of Whitehall, eventually came upon a house which, despite its mean and dilapidated exterior, I thought must be the headquarters of the Department of Intelligence, tallying as it did with the directions I had been given.

In response to my tug at the creaking bell-pull, there shortly emerged a tousled-haired youth of such unkempt appearance as would have done no sort of credit to a poor-house, let alone a government department.

"What do you want?" surlily enquired this unprepossessing doorkeeper.

"I've come to see a Mr Atterbury," I said.

"I'll see if 'e's in," responded the youth listlessly and so saying he disappeared into the dim interior of the hallway.

Some moments later there came a shout from the stairway above.

"'E says, who is it?"

"Tell him it's a Mr Farrant. I've been sent along by the Admiralty," I cried back. After disappearing again for a moment, the youth then reappeared.

"'E says as you've to go up."

In deference to this unceremonious request I proceeded to the far end of the hallway, and then up a narrow flight of stairs, to be met at the top by a dapper little man of some fifty years, whose dandified appearance seemed strangely at odds with the dinginess of his surroundings.

"I must apologise for our young Cerberus. I fear that he doesn't exactly grace the department, does he? But our regular fellow's away and the lad's all we have available at the moment," he said as he conducted me down a narrow corridor.

"Our premises, as you will have observed, are hardly what you might call stylish, I'm afraid," he added as he threw open a door at the far end. "All very different from what you must be used to at the Admiralty. I'm continually pressing the powers that be for something more commodious, but they never take any notice of course. It's really becoming quite impossible, especially with all this additional work we've got on our hands just now."

"You certainly don't seem to have much elbow room," I sympathised as we entered his sanctum which was, indeed, scarcely spacious. It had been furnished nonetheless with a certain elegance. The floor was sumptuously carpeted, under the window at the far end had been placed a small but very fine 'Carlton House' desk, and the two armchairs which stood back and front of it were of fine craftsmanship, as was the bookcase which lined one of the walls, the opposing one being covered with an array of charts and maps of various kinds.

"You mustn't imagine that the government provided the furniture," he said as I glanced about admiringly. "These are some of my own things I brought in to make the place a little more habitable. And it's not only the wretchedly inadequate accommodation we are obliged to put up with," he went on in the same long-suffering tone, as he led the way in, twirling all the while a large gold seal, which hung from his waist.

"You've no idea of the pinch-penny way they treat us. How they expect us to finance a department like this on nothing more than a shoestring, heaven alone knows. It's really quite monstrous! And then they wonder why we have so much difficulty in attracting the right sort of agents. However, you haven't come here Mr Farrant to be plagued with my little problems," he concluded with a sudden decisiveness as, returning the seal to its fob, he seated himself behind his desk.

"Well now, so you've agreed to work for us. That is why you are here, I take it?" he said, giving me as he spoke a look of searching appraisal as I took the chair opposite him.

"I'm willing to do what I can," I said uncertainly. "But I'm not sure that I'm going to be of much use to you. I've had absolutely no experience of this kind of thing."

"Oh, I don't think that need concern you," responded Mr Atterbury cheerfully. "In this game a completely fresh approach can be something of an advantage. In fact, it's been my experience that it's the new recruits who get the best results. The way some of the older hands shirk their responsibilities is really quite appalling. Some of them I would scarcely trust from here to the door, I can tell you. Not above working for the other side even, if it suits their pockets, the scoundrels! No, the first quality I look for is integrity. Given that, and a modicum of resourcefulness; really, that's about as much as I've learnt to expect, I'm afraid. And with the funds at our disposal, such commodities are not so easily come by, I can assure you," he added bitterly. "So you can imagine how grateful we are to be given the opportunity of having one or two young serving officers like yourself working for us."

Little did he know, I thought, how flattering the inference was.

"As it happens Mr Farrant you couldn't have called in at a more opportune moment," continued Mr Atterbury. "For one of my agents has just let me down over an assignment. He says he's got some fever or other. Just an excuse I shouldn't wonder. The truth is, I'll warrant, that he's simply too scared to take it on."

"Oh! I see," I said with mounting alarm.

"So, now then, you will be impatient to know something about the commission which I have in mind for you." And so saying he unlocked a drawer beside him and removed a folder, the contents of which he then proceeded to scrutinise for a minute or two whilst I, in no little suspense I can tell you, sat there waiting to hear what it was that he was going to disclose.

"Yes, I think that you could well be just the sort of fellow we need here," he said at last, as sitting back in his chair he held an open gold snuff box over towards me.

"I don't know whether you indulge?"

"No thank you I don't," I said.

"Sensible fellow. It's a noxious habit, I suppose, but I find it helps to get me through the day," he added deprecatingly, as he took a couple of elegant sniffs himself before proceeding.

"There's one thing anyway. You won't have far to travel. To the place where you'll be operating I mean. It's the port of Gravesend. Some twenty-five miles or so down river from here, it would be I suppose. You may know it."

"I've heard of it of course. But I've never been there," I said.

As ominous-sounding a ring as the name of the place had, it was a relief, anyway, to hear that I was not, as I had feared, to be posted to France.

"From which it naturally follows," he went on, "that the mission I wish you to take on is essentially a counter-intelligence one. It's to do, of course, as you will have surmised, with this invasion business and the infiltration of enemy spies into the country. Not that they've been having it all their own way by any means. Indeed, I think I can fairly claim that we're wise to a good deal of what they're up to. However, there's still a lot going on that we don't know much about and there can, I fear, be no doubt that much invaluable information is getting across the Channel from one source or another. And, we have good reason to believe," he went on after withdrawing a silk handkerchief from his sleeve and making a show of blowing his nose, "that one such source is a spy ring located in or about Gravesend. How long they've been active there we don't know. In fact, it was only last month that we came to have any suspicion of what was going on and then it was only by the merest chance. An outward-bound Dutch merchantman happened to strike some wreckage out in the Nore and foundered. Several of the crew unhappily were drowned and upon one of the bodies that was washed ashore was discovered a package containing some coded script. Fortunately the excise people realised its significance and sent it on to us here." Here he paused to partake of some further snuff, whilst I sat there fearfully wondering what was to come next.

"The code was a pretty ingenious one I don't mind telling you," he then continued. "However, we eventually managed to decipher it, and when we did, it at once became clear that we had, indeed, hit upon something. For what was disclosed was a detailed account, and an uncomfortably accurate one it was too, of an important sector of our coastal defences. We had no idea, of course, from where the agent might be operating. What we did find out, however, was that the merchantman had been on a regular run between Gravesend and Rotterdam. It wasn't much to go on, but it did provide us with something of a lead, albeit a very slender one. Nevertheless, we decided that it was worth following up, so we sent one of our best agents down to Gravesend to see if he could discover anything. A week later the poor fellow was found in a ditch with his throat cut which, if nothing else, at least seemed to suggest that we could well be on the right track," he said giving me a meaningful glance.

"Er, yes, I suppose it did," I gulped, already beginning as I did so, with his talk of 'bodies in ditches' and 'throats being cut', fervently to wish, I don't mind telling you, that I had, from the outset, firmly declined to have anything to do with the whole proposition, whatever the consequences to my career.

"I should have asked you this before and I hope you won't think it impertinent of me. But, you are not married, I trust?" he then added, giving me an anxious look.

"N-no," I affirmed with an increasing sense of dismay.

"You're not! Well, perhaps it's just as well. . . . Now as to what we have already managed to discover," continued Mr Atterbury, "which isn't a great deal I must tell you. For poor Thornton, I'm afraid, hadn't made much progress. There was one thing he seemed to be pretty sure about though, that a certain Nathaniel Cruden was, somehow, mixed up in it all. He's the landlord of an inn down there apparently. Now, let me see, what was the name of it? Ah, yes, here it is," he went on, after referring to the document in front of him. "The 'Three Daws', that's the place. It backs on to the river, I believe. Anyway, this innkeeper, I gather, is the fellow to watch. From the account Thornton gave of him he's an uncouth, illiterate sort of creature, with a pretty black reputation in those parts. But he'd certainly be no more than a pawn in the scheme of things, I would imagine. Oh! he's also something of a pugilist, I gather, and has acquired a certain amount of fame by his achievements in the local prize ring. And that, I'm afraid, is about as much as I can tell you Farrant," he then concluded.

He must have noticed my look of consternation as he did so for he then quickly added:

"It's not a lot, I agree, but you'd be surprised how much can develop from a lead of that kind. Now as to the arrangements I have made for you," he went on quickly. "You will be staying with Sir George Thurlow at Parrock Manor, which lies a little way out of Gravesend. Sir George is an old acquaintance of mine. He's a likeable old fellow and a most generous host, as I know, so I'm sure you'll be comfortable there. They're bound to become suspicious, the opposition I mean, of any new arrival in the neighbourhood, especially as they will know by now that we're wise to what they're up to; so it would be best, I think, if you had some plausible reason for being there. Now, it so happens that Sir George has a large library, which he has often talked of having catalogued, and it occurred to me that this would suit your purpose admirably. I have, in fact, already put the idea to Sir George and he is perfectly willing to go along with it. You shouldn't find that too difficult a role to play I would imagine?"

"No, I suppose not," I replied doubtfully. "Not that I'm really much of a bookish sort of person."

"Oh! I don't think that need concern you," put in Mr Atterbury cheerfully. "You won't be expected to do more than potter about the library a bit, that's all. You'll have to dress the part though. Be sure to wear nothing too prosperous-looking mind. But I can leave all that safely to you, I am sure."

"Yes, of course," I said blithely. Indeed, so bemused had I become by the preposterous unreality of it all that I would, I am sure, have consented to anything, however bizarre it might be.

"That's all settled then. Now, as to the question of how you are to communicate with us. This we find is usually best done through an intermediary, especially as you'll be new to it all. Now there's a retired naval officer, a Captain Wakeley, who lives in Gravesend and has, on occasion, been of help to us in the past. He's already aware of what's going on, so he'll be expecting you. When you have something to report he's the fellow I want you to contact and he'll see to it that the information gets to us with the minimum of delay. You may well, of course, find him useful to you in other ways, so it might be as well to look him up soon after you get down there. He lives quite alone, by the way, close by the river in a little court named Barnard's Yard. His lodging, from what I can remember, hasn't a number or anything, but there's an old ship's figure-head of a dolphin over the entrance so you shouldn't have any difficulty finding him. As I say, if you have anything to report, be sure to let him know as quickly as possible. That's most important just in case anything should, er, happen to. . . . Well I'm sure you know what I mean," he said, giving me a pointed look, the significance of which, I need hardly add, was all too uncomfortably obvious.

"So, there we are Mr Farrant. I don't think there's anything more I can usefully tell you. I'm sorry we haven't anything more substantial for you to go on, but that's so often the way it is in this game, I fear," he said throwing out his arms in a gesture of resignation. "However, if there's anything that you are not quite clear about . . .?"

"No, I don't think so," I said blankly. For what there was to clarify I really could not see, so little that was likely to be of much help to me had he been able to impart.

"You are quite sure? Well then, I don't think that there's much more I can say. As you can imagine, we haven't any time to lose, so I shall want you to get down there as soon as possible. I should like you to leave tomorrow, in fact, if you don't think that'll be rushing things too much. The Dover coach stops off on the high road above Gravesend just by the manor, so that'll be your best means of getting there. There's one that leaves the 'Bricklayer's Arms' at ten o'clock, I believe, which should get you down there in good time enough. So, do you think you could manage to be ready by then?"

"Yes, I suppose so," I said.

"Splendid. I'll see to it that a place is booked for you so you won't have to bother with that and, as I say, Sir George will be expecting you. Well, Mr Farrant, I don't think there's really anything more I can say," he said with a brisk finality, as he rose from his chair. "Except to tell you how grateful we are to you for agreeing to help us out like this. It's really most handsome of you and it only remains for me to wish you every success. Now, you're sure you've got the name of that innkeeper?" he added as he accompanied me to the door.

"Cruden, wasn't it?" I said.

"Yes, that's right, Nathaniel Cruden. He's the fellow that you've got to watch. At the 'Three Daws' remember. And don't forget Captain Wakeley at Barnard's Yard. Oh! And it would be wise, I think, to take a pistol with you. Not that I want you to take any unnecessary risks of course, but it's always reassuring to have one about you. Grierson's in Bond Street are the people to go to if you haven't got one already."

And with this parting advice, I made my way down to the street below and, in a tread heavy with foreboding, set off back homewards to Hanover Square.

Chapter III

With all the preparations for my departure on the morrow to see to, I had, during the remainder of that day, happily little opportunity to brood over what lay ahead of me.

First there were a number of personal affairs which needed to be settled, engagements to be cancelled and certain monetary affairs to attend to. In particular, the drawing up of a will which, in the circumstances, seemed only prudent, I had decided.

Then there was the visit to Grierson's for the purchase of a suitable pistol; the one I possessed being, I deemed, too large and clumsy for such purposes as I might need it. I had, as well, to hunt out the sort of attire which would be in keeping with the role of an impecunious bibliophile which, as you may remember, I was having to assume.

Among my own belongings I could find nothing shabby enough to suit, but fortunately my eldest brother, who was of much the same build as I, had ever a disinclination to discard outworn clothing and, secretly rummaging through his wardrobe, I was able to discover what was required. An old, shiny, brown tailcoat, more to the purpose for being a little old-fashioned, knee-breeches to match, a much worn greatcoat and a beaver hat, which I was able to knock into some semblance of shape. To complete the dissimulation I hit upon the idea of some plain-glass spectacles which I found, together with a shagreen case, at a theatrical traders.

So, what with one thing and another, the rest of that day was, as I say, so fully occupied for there to be much time for anxious soul searching.

Deciding that it would be wisest to divulge as little as possible to my parents I acquainted them in only the vaguest terms with what I was embarking upon.

Not that they seemed much interested or indeed to be concerned over the nature of the undertaking, being only too pleased, I imagined, to have me out of the house for whatever reason.

To avoid the mutual embarrassment of appearing before them in my strange apparel I also thought it best to be off and away from the house before they were likely to be about, so I had let it be understood that I would be catching an earlier coach than the one upon which I was booked.

I had, therefore, to ensure that I was awake long before my accustomed hour. However, as is not unusual on such occasions, I slept only fitfully, and was alert, I remember, much earlier than I need have been.

Still the sooner I was away from the house the better, I thought, especially as I was anxious to avoid the servants. And so, having shaved and then dressed myself in my makeshift garb, I crept cautiously downstairs. And a bizarre sight I must have looked, anyway to those who knew me, as with the old grandfather clock in the hall striking the hour of five behind me, I stealthily opened the front door, and was soon down the steps and away across the square.

It was still quite dark of course, and, with nowhere in which to take refuge so early in the day, I was obliged, I remember, to spend a cheerless hour or so wandering aimlessly about with my portmanteau. Happily, however, I knew of a coffee house which opened betimes and there I was able to while away a further hour or so over breakfast and the daily papers.

With still some time in hand before the Dover coach was due to leave and mindful of the role I was to assume, I then decided, it being upon my way, that I would make for Paternoster Row by St Paul's, where I knew a number of booksellers to be located.

I have never, I fear, been what you would call a bookish sort of person. I had received, I suppose, a fair enough grounding in the classical authors when I was at school and I was familiar with the novelists and essayists of the previous century, notably Goldsmith, who has always been a particular favourite of mine.

There were, as well, one or two subjects in which I had an especial interest. My family being a naval one, I had been reared upon tales of old sea voyagers, and a boyhood spent among the countryside of Norfolk had prompted an interest in natural pursuits, in particular to acquiring some knowledge of birds and their habits.

So, one way and another, I was able to discover enough to absorb me as I continued to poke among the bookshelves. Although confronted as I was by so much of which I was in total ignorance, the browsing among the books did little I fear to encourage me in my ability to play the part I was shortly to dissemble.

Anyway, it was too late to worry about that. Indeed, with the hour of the coach's departure fast approaching, it was high time, I decided, that I went off in search of a hackney cab to convey me to the "Bricklayer's Arms".

Not that I need have hurried, for when I arrived, the horses were only just being led out so I had time enough to repair to the taproom where, in an attempt to restore my flagging spirits, I proceeded to gulp down, I remember, a couple of pints of their strongest brew.

Thus suitably refreshed, and with the guard shortly sounding us to our places, I joined my fellow passengers on the rear of the coach where, in accordance with Mr Atterbury's promise, an outside seat had, duly, been booked for me.

Scarcely was I settled down than there came the guard's "All right!", and then, with a further blast on his horn, the ostlers whipped away the quarter cloths and off we trotted out of the yard and into the roadway beyond. Filled with dire forebodings enough as I already was, I yet little imagined to what desperate perils I was in fact heading. Indeed, had I done so, I am quite certain that I would have leapt from the coach forthwith.

Howsoever, with the team soon settling into a fast trot, it was not long before we had left the hurly-burly of London behind us and, having crossed Blackheath Common, had come among the fields and orchards of the Kentish countryside.

It was a lovely day, I remember. The mist had just begun to clear, leaving a cloudless sky, from which a bright sun shone to reflect the brilliance of an early morning frost.

Not that I was in any sort of humour to relish it, as I sat there huddled up in my corner, gloomily reflecting upon the intimidating implications of what I had committed myself to.

The more I did so, the more weighed down did I become with the utter hopelessness of it all. What could I, the veriest tyro, possibly be expected to achieve, I really could not see, especially where another with, no doubt, a wealth of experience behind him, had been so tragically unsuccessful.

The probability was, I thought glumly, that my own endeavours were to end as summarily, and at no distant date withal!

In truth, to such a state of dejection had I sunk by the time we reached Dartford, where our journey was broken for lunch and a change of horses at the old "Bull", that I came very near, I remember, to abandoning the whole venture and making the best of my way back to London.

I would like to think that my resolve to continue was occasioned by a natural plucking up of courage; but it was, I fear I must own, more likely to have been the comforting influence of some further tankards of ale, laced this time with generous tots of rum which, in the event, persuaded me to rejoin the coach, and go through with it come what may.

Indeed, when some little while later I was put down on the high road above Gravesend, my spirits had so revived, that I began to view my prospects if not with confidence, at least with a certain fatuous cheerfulness.

It was nothing more than pot-valiance of course. Nevertheless, so intoxicated with a sense of well-being had I for the moment become, that I decided that I would postpone my arrival at Parrock Manor until later that evening, and meanwhile spend the afternoon exploring the river port and while I was about it, take the 'bull by the horns' as it were, and pay a visit to the "Three Daws" to see for myself what sort of a fellow this Nathaniel Cruden was.

The coach, as I have said, had dropped me down at a point well above the river, which now lay in full view below me, as it meandered upon its course towards the sea.

Nestling beside the water, at a couple of miles or so from where I had alighted, I could see a huddle of dwellings surmounted by a church spire, which must, I presumed, be my destination, and so having deposited my small belongings at the coach-house, I proceeded, at once, to set forth thither.

Although a thin mist lay over the valley, it was still a glorious day, and with the sun beginning to set directly upstream, the whole river and everything upon it was, at that moment, bathed in a golden shimmering light. Indeed, as I hesitated briefly to gaze down upon the scene, I could almost have believed myself to have been transported to some far eastern station or other, so startlingly brilliant was it.

In mid river several seagoing vessels lay at anchor. Most conspicuous among them being a fine East Indiaman in full canvas, as it awaited a favourable wind. Then further downstream I espied, not without a pang of nostalgia, a naval frigate with sails furled. While among their larger brethren, there busily scurried a great variety of smaller craft, engaged in the myriad activities of which the little port was the focus.

The terrain bordering the port on each side, appeared, as I observed, to be quite flat and featureless. That eastwards of it, as I was later to discover, being nothing but marshland, which extended back some way, and continued to flank the river as far as the eye could see. And, with a low mist hovering over it, a bleak and uninviting locality it looked, I remember thinking. An opinion which was to receive no little vindication, I might add, by a perilous encounter which was subsequently to befall me out there in the solitude of its marshy depths.

But that is anticipating for, exhilarated as I still was by my ale-induced sense of well-being, all such presageful thoughts had, for the while, been quite obliterated.

Indeed, it was with almost a carefree step that I continued to stride on my way down towards the river.

And, as I was soon to discover as I reached the port, a more rollicking, seafaring sort of a place you could not have wished for, with almost every sight, sound and smell that one encountered smacking somehow of the sea and its affairs. To the accompaniment of a continuous chorus of shrieking gulls could be heard the creaking of derricks, the dull thud of carpenters' hammers and the constant cries of the watermen in search of fares. Whilst, everywhere one went, the heavy odour of pitch and tar clung about one's nostrils. There appeared, in fact, to be scarcely any trade that was not being pursued without some nautical association or other. Blockmakers jostled shoulders with sailmakers, rope and tackle vendors with chandlers, whilst every street seemed to have a boatbuilder's yard leading from it, their masts dizzily projecting above the house tops.

For some minutes, and not without a certain grim fascination, I stopped, I remember, to lean over an open hatchway where, from within, ship's biscuits, or 'seabread' as it is called, were being shovelled into great sacks to provide the staple diet for some wretched crew or other for a voyage as long, perhaps, as a year or more.

For most of that afternoon I was thus happy to divert myself in aimless exploration. However, with dusk beginning to fall, and anxious as I was to arrive at the manor in good time for dinner, I had better soon, I decided, search out the whereabouts of the "Three Daws".

As I already had had occasion to observe, Gravesend was certainly not wanting for taverns. Indeed, every building by the riverside appeared to have a sign swinging from it.

There was an "Amsterdam", a "Pope's Head", a "Christopher" and many another besides but not, as far as I could discover, a "Three Daws" and I was beginning to wonder whether Mr Atterbury had not, perhaps, confused the name when I came upon an old weather-boarded house with bottle-glass windows and a sign so begrimed with age that its features had been almost obliterated.

After scanning it attentively for some while I was, however, able dimly to distinguish upon it the outlines of three birds which could, I supposed, pass for jackdaws quite as well as any feathered species, and so concluded that this must, in fact, be the inn I was seeking.

By this time my Dutch courage had largely deserted me and I continued for some while, I remember, to dither about on the cobbles outside, trying to screw up what little resolution I had left, before I was able to bring myself to take hold of the latch and peer cautiously within.

So clouded with smoke was everything that I had difficulty, at first, in making much out. Although even through the haze there could be no mistaking mine host, whom I could see towering massively above a long, shining bar counter at the far end of the parlour.

"Close that bloody door! Unless you want the perishin' candles out on us, that is!" he bellowed across at me, as I continued to hesitate on the threshold.

Having quickly secured the latch behind me in response to his rough request, I stood there for a moment or two blinking about me. As the candles flickered up again I could see that the parlour was well thronged. Close by me at a table by the window I was concerned to notice a party of English sailors, the sight of whom prompted me to move hurriedly towards the bar. A precaution which was, however, scarcely warranted, for had, in fact, any one of them, by some chance, served with me, it would surely have been long odds his associating the acquaintance with the shabbily attired, bespectacled figure I must then have presented.

"Well, what'll you be wanting?" came the surly greeting as I approached the bar.

"A pint of your best ale," I said as firmly as I could, although my heart was beating nineteen to the dozen within me, I can tell you. So this then was

Nathaniel Cruden. From Mr Atterbury's account of him I had formed a mind's image of the fellow and it was, at least in outline, not much divorced from reality.

He was, in truth, a most villainous-looking creature with a swarthy square-boned head, from which glowered a pair of bloodshot, closely set eyes surmounted by a great shock of tar-black hair which grew, I noticed, almost to his brows. To add to his general repulsiveness his mouth was twisted into a perpetual leer by a thick white scar, which disfigured one side of his face.

It was, however, the size of him which most impressed me. He really was a giant of a man. In stature not far off seven feet, he must indeed have been, with great square shoulders in proportion, and arms like battering rams.

That he would be a match for anyone in the ring I could certainly believe.

"You're a stranger hereabouts, ain't yer?" he observed bluntly, as he thrust a tankard down in front of me and giving me, as he spoke, a dark look of suspicion, I noticed.

"Y-yes, that's right," I stammered in reply. "I arrived by the London coach but an hour or so ago."

"So, you're from London are yer? Stayin' long?" he then added; this in an offhand sort of way, which did nothing to belie his blatant curiosity.

Raising my tankard I took a long draught of its contents before replying. "Yes, it's likely I shall be in Gravesend some few weeks," I said. For all the casualness of my reply, my heart was, nevertheless, beating like a water-hammer.

To my relief he moved away just then to serve another customer, and I was afforded an opportunity to look about me. It was a cosy enough parlour with a shining, pewter-covered bar counter, a rough-boarded, uneven, sanded floor and a low oak-beamed ceiling, into the centre of which had been set an old ship's compass. High-backed settles and small trestle tables occupied the perimeter, whilst the walls were adorned with prints of celebrated pugilists of the day.

As one would have expected, the bulk of the patrons appeared to be of a seafaring stamp, sailors, longshoremen, watermen and the like; most of whom, as was apparent from the hilarious atmosphere which prevailed, being already more than half-seas-over. And I could not but feel for the sensibilities of the young serving girl, who, as she darted among them in attendance upon their demands, was obliged to endure a constant stream of ribaldry.

Anyway, just then Cruden came over to rejoin me.

"Can I get yer another pint?"

"No, thank you," I said.

"You got business in Gravesend?" This again carelessly like, and said without looking up from a pewter tankard which he was making a pretence of polishing.

"Well, no, not exactly," I replied evasively. That he was piqued by my closeness I could tell. For the moment, he said nothing further, and I had turned away to finish the remainder of my drink when he suddenly observed:

"Maybe you've come to join the volunteers, and help chase Old Boney away when he comes. For we could do with some strappin' young fellows like you!"

This was said in such a sneering tone, and in a voice so raised as to be clearly intended for the ears of some of his cronies, who were standing close by and who dutifully responded with a chorus of laughter at my expense.

Stung as I was, I thought it best to ignore the slight and so forbore replying.

In fact, upon reflection, I was not a little reassured by his apparent estimation of the sort of figure I must be cutting, for having sensed his initial suspicion of me, I had begun to persuade myself that he was already fully aware of the true purpose of my coming to Gravesend, and being so, had marked me down for an early dispatch.

In fact, all in all, I was inclined to feel not too displeased with my opening move. I had not only discovered for myself what sort of a fellow this Nathaniel Cruden was, but I had, at the same time, done something perhaps (or so I believed), to allay the suspicion which my arrival in the neighbourhood would have aroused.

With my object thus achieved, it was time, I decided, that I took my leave and went off in search of Parrock Manor, and addressing Cruden I requested directions thither.

"So, it's for the manor you're bound," he said half to himself. "You've come out of yer way a bit, 'aven't yer? The coach would 'ave set yer down no more 'an a couple of 'undred yards from the gates. Any'ow, if yer goes straight up the road opposite and turns left as yer comes to the 'ill, you'll come to it," he then added, his manner becoming almost respectful all at once, I noticed.

"Thank you," I said, as I made to leave.

"But if yer cares to wait a bit Joe Leckley 'ere would likely show yer the way," Cruden then interposed, nodding his head towards a table by the window as he spoke.

"What's that, Nat?" responded the person thus alluded to.

"I was jus' tellin' this gentleman 'ere that yer might like to accompany 'im to the manor seein' as 'e's a stranger 'ereabouts," reaffirmed Cruden gruffly.

"Only too pleased to oblige yer, Sir," said this Joe Leckley cheerfully, as he leapt from his seat and skipped over towards me.

He was, perhaps, a year or two older than myself. A diminutive little fellow with a quick darting manner and a most engaging, broad-grinning countenance. His whole demeanour having, as I remember thinking at this, our first meeting, something of an elfin-like quality as it might best be described. An impression to which, doubtless, the colourful nature of his attire not a little contributed, composed as it was of a jauntily angled moleskin cap, yellow nankeen breeches and a loose-fitting 'pepper-and-salt' tailcoat, which garment, as he was later to inform me, had been worn by both his father and grandfather before him.

"But won't it be taking you out of your way?" I said.

"Oh! No Sir, not at all. I works at the manor yer see. Any odd job. Cleanin' boots, snuffin' candles, drivin' the chaise, 'elpin' at table when there's a bit of company. Anythin' yer like," he happily declared, as he recited his menial accomplishments.

"You seem to be something of a general factotum," I commented with a smile.

"I don't know about that, Sir, but I can set me 'and to most anything, 'cept read and write that is, for I'm no scholard, I can tell yer."

"Well, Mr Leckley, I think that perhaps we ought to be going. If you're quite ready that is," I then said. And with a rough "Good-night" from Cruden, we made to depart.

We could not have taken more than three or four steps, however, when the parlour door was suddenly thrust open and around the corner there appeared the head of a small boy who piped, "The gang's a comin'! The gang's a comin'!" And then, as suddenly, vanished again.

Chapter IV

No sooner had the boy sounded the alarm than all was pandemonium. The whole parlour seemed suddenly to have erupted as all about me tables were overturned, bottles and tankards were sent crashing to the floor, and candles extinguished in the frantic struggle to escape before the press-gang arrived.

Of the ways of such bodies I was only too familiar having, upon occasions, led one myself. And knowing full well that little mercy would be granted to anyone unfortunate enough to be seized, I could certainly appreciate the panic that had been excited.

That I, myself, could be in any danger had, for the moment, not occurred to me. Indeed, with the disappearance of my companion I had, to avoid the general stampede, simply withdrawn to one side of the parlour where I was calmly waiting for the furore to subside when I was all at once reminded of the shabby way in which I was attired and my consequent lack of any stamp of gentility. And, as I did so, the thought struck me that I might not be as safe from the gang's attentions as I had imagined. That there was, in fact, a real possibility that I would be seized upon and, my immediate protestations being ignored, would find myself being manhandled away and aboard ship before I had opportunity to establish my credentials.

Overtaken with alarm at such a prospect, my first impulse was to join the others and make a run for it. I was tolerably fleet of foot and I might, with luck I thought, manage to get away.

The intention had, however, scarcely been formulated and I had reached no further than the door, when it became clear from the clamour without that the gang was almost upon us and that I would be too late.

At a loss what to do I looked desperately around the now deserted parlour for some conceivable place of concealment. But none offered itself, and I had decided that there was nothing for it but to remain where I was in the hope that I might somehow be able to brazen it out, when I felt a hand at my elbow and a breathless voice say, "Unless you've a fancy for sea breezes, Sir, you'd best follow me."

No sooner had the words been uttered than I was hot upon the heels of Joe Leckley, for he it was, as we sped to the back of the parlour, thence down a flight of steps into a kitchen and then on downwards into a cellar, across which we hurriedly stumbled our way between stacks of barrels to the far corner.

Three or four others, I discovered, were already there before us, one of whom was frantically applying his weight against the stone wall.

"Quickly mate!" urged Joe Leckley. "Or it'll be salt beef and weevily biscuits for the lot of us."

"The cursed thing must be stuck, I can't shift it," gasped the other. At this another tried his strength with no more success, and I was beginning to fear that all would be up with us, for I could already hear the gang searching the rooms above and knew that it would not be many moments before they were into the cellar.

"'Ere let me 'ave a try," intervened Joe Leckley anxiously. "Maybe I 'ave the trick of it." As we all stood aside he bent down and leant his small body against the wall. For an agonising moment or two he appeared to elicit no response, but then, of a sudden, there came a harsh grating sound, and to the accompaniment of subdued exclamations of relief from us all, I became dimly aware that a portion of the stonework had given way.

"Sharp lads and we'll give those sea louts the slip yet," whispered Joe as one by one we slipped through the narrow aperture. And none too soon for as the stone swung back into place again I could hear the gang tumbling down the steps and into the cellar behind us.

As we crouched there huddled together in the darkness, none moved or spoke, and with good reason as some of the searchers were by now within a few feet of us. I could hear the scraping of the barrels as they were being hurled aside, and also the impatient exhortations of the officer in command as he urged his men on.

One of the gang actually drummed his fist against the wall of our hiding-place I remember, and for one sickening moment it seemed that we might be discovered.

Nothing came of it however, and after a while the commotion subsided, as the gang eventually gave up the search and withdrew.

Even then it was not deemed safe to stir and wisely so, for of the existence of such secret hiding-places press-gangs were fully aware, as I well knew; it being the custom for an ambush to be posted in readiness to seize the fugitives upon their reappearance.

That my companions were equally alive to such a danger soon became apparent, for after a further minute or two had elapsed, instead of returning to the cellar as I had imagined we would, at a whispered directive from Joe Leckley, we all proceeded to make off down a narrow tunnel to which our place of concealment had, as I now realised, been but the entrance.

With an entreaty from Joe Leckley to "'old close and keep yer 'ead down," I dutifully followed him. And an uncomfortable business it was for everything was as black as pitch, of course, and the tunnel, no wider than a carpenter's walk, was so confined that we were obliged to bend double. To make things more uncomfortable, its floor was awash with a foot or more of water, indicating, I imagined, that the tunnel must be below water level, anyway at high tide.

For some hundred yards or so we must thus have crawled and groped our way before we eventually came to a halt.

"Not a sound, mind," whispered Joe Leckley anxiously. "For they won't be far away remember." And as he spoke I could see that the darkness had given way to a grey light ahead of us, as the exit to the tunnel was swung aside and a moment later we had emerged on to what appeared to be a small jetty against the steps of which I could hear the tide lapping just beneath us.

Here we paused for a while with our backs against the jetty wall, for we were still not out of danger, as was plain by the hullabaloo still echoing from the street overhead, and to make a move, as yet, would be sure, I thought, to bring the gang upon our heels again.

That I was participating in a preconceived plan to which my companions were by no means strangers, had, of course, by now become evident to me. And that they had, in fact, no intention of returning to the street I was soon to discover.

"It ought to be safe to make shift now lads," whispered Joe. And so saying he moved across to the edge of the jetty and taking hold of a tethering rope, proceeded to haul alongside some kind of river craft, a wherry, I think it is called, and into this we all embarked.

"Well mates, we're landlubbers yet," said Joe Leckley, giving expression to the relief of us all as we pulled out into midstream.

"Ay, by all that's merciful!" rejoined another. "But god's truth, it was a close run thing. When I 'eard 'em coming down those cellar steps, it looked a ship-o'-the-line to a pint of shrimps we'd be taken. Why, it's more than yer liberty's worth to stir out o'nights these times, blimey if it ain't! That's the third time they've raided the 'Daws' this for'night and only yesterday they 'ad 'alf a dozen poor wretches from the 'Christopher', or so I 'eard."

As I sat there crouched in the stern I could not but inwardly sympathise with their sentiments of relief and bitterness, for there could be no denying that, as a method of recruitment, the press-gang was a cruel and ruthless business. For once the unfortunate victim was seized there was little chance of an appeal, and without even so much as a farewell to his family, he would be bundled aboard, henceforth to endure for, perhaps, many a long year, the privations, brutality and hardship, which, at that time were, as I knew only too well, commonly the lot of our ordinary seamen.

"Roundabout way to the manor, you'll be thinkin', Sir?" ventured Joe Leckley suddenly interrupting my thoughts.

"Yes, indeed!" I laughed.

"But you can't afford to take chances when our naval friends are on the prowl, can yer mates?" exclaimed Joe Leckley bitterly.

"Ay. That yer can't," put in another. "Why, even out 'ere I hardly feels safe now they've started usin' that cutter o' theirs. They went after a bawley boat only last week, I 'eard, and 'ad two poor blighters. And would 'ave 'ad the rest if they 'adn't swum for it."

By this time we had pulled over to the Essex shore, and had come under the shadow of old Tilbury fort. There we stood against the tide for a while keeping a wary eye out for the cutter, but thankfully, I could see no sign of it. Nevertheless my companions were, as yet, plainly in no mind to take any chances, for having shipped oars, we then continued to drift downstream on the ebb for some further while.

And an uncomfortable time of it we were soon having, with a bitter north-easterly wind now blowing across from the Tilbury flats, and our clothes continuously awash with spray as it showered over our low-lying craft. I for one anyway, as much as I appreciated that it would be foolhardy to take any chances, was soon beginning fervently to wish that it would not be too long before they decided to make for the shore again.

It had, after all, been a good hour or more since we had left the jetty and the press-gang would surely, I imagined, have given up the hunt by now.

That my feelings were not unshared was evident, for just then one of the others exclaimed, "I don't know about the rest of yer, but I'm fair perished and near enough drownded, and if we stays out 'ere much longer you can forget about the gang for it's me maker that's goin' to 'ave me of a chill, and that's the truth!"

"Ay, you're right enough there," agreed Joe Leckley bitterly. "It's no sort of an evenin' for a jaunt, that it ain't. Well, what do yer say lads, don't yer reckon it'd be safe to turn back now?"

To this proposal, thankfully no dissenting voice was raised, and taking up the oars, we forthwith made about and steered for shore. Not however, back to Gravesend as I had anticipated, but instead to a landing-stage which stood out from the river bank, a mile or so downstream from where we had embarked. To this we tethered the boat – and then having clambered out, proceeded to make our separate ways. The others setting off back to Gravesend along the river bank, whilst Joe Leckley and I struck inland over the sea wall and on to a narrow track skirting the edge of the marsh which, as I have said, stretched away for some miles on that side.

"'Fraid yer clothes must 'ave got messed up a bit Sir!" said my companion, as we strode off together into the darkness.

"Oh! Don't worry, they'll soon dry off," I replied cheerfully. "Anyway, that's of small account considering what might have befallen us. You must forgive me for not thanking you before, but I am most grateful to you for coming to my rescue the way you did. I really don't know what I should have done if you hadn't," I added feelingly. Indeed, considering that I was a virtual stranger to him, it had certainly been a most unselfish act on his part. For, thinking back, I realised that he must already have been some way to the cellar when, at considerable risk to his own liberty, he had thought to come back for me.

"Please don't mention it, Sir. We're only too 'appy, I can tell yer, to put anyone in the way o'escaping their clutches. Any'ow, I dare say they wouldn't 'ave touched the likes o' you."

"I wouldn't be too sure of that!" I responded.

"It's the watermen and the like they're mainly after. Those that 'ave already got a bit o' the sea about 'em. Still, they're gettin' less choosey than they were, so I reckon yer may be right, for no one's safe these days from what I 'ears," he rejoined wryly.

As I have said, the path we were taking lay alongside the marsh, and in the light of a half moon, a singularly eerie and desolate locality it looked, I thought, as I gazed across the flat, grey expanse which stretched away into the far distance.

"Not a very cheerful spot this, is it Sir?" said Joe Leckley suddenly, as if reading my thoughts.

"It certainly doesn't appear so," I agreed.

"Nor 'ealthy either, Sir," added Joe grimly. "There's many as 'ave died of the ague as 'ave bin caught from the vapours and such like that comes off of it. It fair gets into yer nostrils at times, 'specially after there's been much rain about. 'Aunted it is as well, Sir, 'orribly 'aunted," he added darkly.

"By ghosts do you mean?" I said.

"That's right, Sir. By the spirits o' them that are buried out there."

"Are there graves out there then?"

"'Undreds of 'em Sir. Though not marked mind yer. Bodies o'those that 'ave died at sea, o' the pox and the like. There's not many, I can tell yer Sir, as'll tread the marshes alone after dark, that there ain't!"

"Have you actually seen them yourself, the ghosts I mean?" I asked doing my best not to sound too incredulous.

"Well, no, I can't say as I 'ave meself, I never set foot on 'em any more than I can 'elp, leastways after dark that is. But there are plenty that 'ave, and awful stories they 'ad to tell," went on Joe Leckley, with a perceptible increase of step, I noticed.

"Nobody lives out there then?" I asked.

"Lor' no Sir! The farmers keep a few 'ead o' cattle, cows and sheep an' that, but that's all."

"But those lights I can see in the distance. Isn't that a house?"

"Why, yes, you're right, Sir. I'd quite forgotten about 'im. That's where old Mr Fenton lives. But 'e's a queer'n and no mistake. Mad enough for Moorfields they say. A very odd gentleman 'e is, though a rare scholard, I've 'eard tell. 'E comes to the manor sometimes after a book out o' the library. I met 'im there once and a fair turn it gave me, I can tell yer Sir."

"Oh! How was that?" I interposed.

"'Cos o' is shape, yer see, Sir. 'Is body bein' all bent and twisted like and

’is face so ’orribly torn about as you’d ’ardly know it was one. Yer see ’e was ’ad by a tiger in India, or so Sir George ’as it. ’E only comes out at night, on account of ’is terrifyin’ people by ’is looks.”

“Does he live quite alone then?”

“Oh, yes Sir, all by ’isself, ’cept for ’is servants o’ course, and they’re all misshapen like ’im. Regular show of monsters ’e ’as. One of ’em ’e took from a travellin’ fair when it came. ’Uge ’ead ’e ’ad, and tiny arms and legs like a child’s. I ’ad to go there once for Sir George. Fair gave me the creeps it did, I don’t mind tellin’ yer!”

“It certainly sounds an unusual household,” I said.

“That it is Sir!”

By this time we had left the river well behind us and, turning away from the marsh, had climbed up above Gravesend and on to a high road. The very one it must be, I imagined, along which the coach had dropped me earlier in the day.

It was by now quite dark. Indeed, by sounding the repeater of my watch, I discovered, to my consternation, that it was already well past seven o’clock so there was no chance, I thought ruefully, of my reaching the manor in time for dinner.

“Have we far to go now?” I asked my companion anxiously.

“Bit above a mile, I’d say, that’s all. See them clump o’ trees just this side o’ the ’ill? That’s where it is.”

On the rising ground ahead, and to the right of us, I could see the trees he had indicated, and among them I could dimly perceive the outlines of a large squarish building. Just beyond, the ground rose sharply to a hillock upon the summit of which, as I had already noticed, stood a windmill.

“’Scuse me askin’, Sir, but you must be the gentleman Sir George told me about as was comin’ to see to the books?” interposed my companion after we had continued in silence for a while.

“Yes, that’s right,” I said. “I’ve come to catalogue the library. Sir George has quite a collection of books I understand?”

“’Undreds, Sir. Shelves full of ’em. I ’as to dust ’em every week, so I gets to know ’em well enough. You’ve got a job listin’ that lot, Sir!”

“Yes, I imagine I shall have,” I said.

“You was expected for dinner as I ’eard, Sir.”

“Yes, I believe I was.”

“’Fraid you’re goin’ to be a bit late. They always dines at six and Sir George’ll never be kept waitin’. Kicks up an awful fuss even when they’re no more’n a minute late. And ’e’s bin out with the Yeomanry today, so ’e’ll be more’n particular ’ungry, but they’ll ’ave put something by for you as you’re expected, you can be sure o’ that. Anyway, it’s not far now, Sir. The gates are along o’ this road and then there’s only a bit of a driveway up to the ’ouse.”

“Do you live at the manor yourself?” I then asked.

"Yes, Sir. 'Ave done since I was a boy. Mother was cook there until she died and I just stayed on. 'Ave sometimes thought o' leavin' and doin' somethin' on the river. But I've no complaints, for I can't say as they 'aven't bin good to me."

"Is it a large household?" I then ventured.

"No, not really, Sir. There's Sir George o'course and Miss Catherine, and then there's 'er ladyship's sister. Master William's away with 'is regiment, and 'er ladyship's not at 'ome at the moment either. Oh! and I forgot, there's a military gentleman; a major or somethin' stayin' too. Can't rightly remember 'is name. 'E's there to help with the recruits, volunteers and that, ready for when Old Boney comes, and I reckon it won't be long now either afore 'e does, and they'll be settin' light to them beacons up there."

"Beacons?" I queried.

"Yes, Sir, up there along o'the old windmill," he went on, pointing up to the hillock. Looking up I could just make out, against the darkness, two cone-shaped masses, one beyond the other on either side of the windmill. Such readily combustible stacks had, I should mention, been erected upon suitable promontories at regular intervals across the length of southern England in readiness to spread the alarm in the event of a French landing.

"They'll make a fair old blaze too, I can tell yer," he then added with relish.

And with this, we came up to the entrance to the manor grounds where, having once again thanked him for his kind assistance, I left my companion to seek a humbler way in, whilst I, after first retrieving my small luggage from the coach-house, turned in through the great wrought iron gates and hurriedly made my way up the driveway.

Chapter V

As well as I could see in the dim light, the manor was of no great proportions. A square house of a date some hundred or so years earlier, I would have thought, with its sash windows and an imposing, porticoed entrance. Fronting it was a small area of parkland with groups of oak and elm, the whole being surrounded by a high brick wall.

In such total darkness did everything appear to be, as I came up to the entrance and climbed the steps to the front door, that I feared Sir George, despairing of my arrival, may already have taken to his bed.

Awkward as this would be, I hoped there would be someone or other still about to receive me, and so taking hold of the great, lion-headed knocker, I gave it a couple of sharp raps.

For a while there was no response, and I was wondering whether I should not, perhaps, try the bell-pull when a dull glow appeared through the fanlight overhead, and a moment later the door was cautiously opened by an old man, who, after regarding me suspiciously by the light of his candle, inquired impatiently if I was the person who was expected.

"Yes, that's right," I said, stepping sharply backwards as I did so, for he had thrust the candle so close to my face, as to be in danger of singeing my eyebrows.

"I fear I'm rather late," I then added apologetically.

"You are!" responded the old menial bluntly. "Sir George 'as been expectin' you these three hours or more. Well, come in, come in," he then added irritably, as I continued to hesitate on the threshold. At which surly request I followed him into the hall where, after I had removed my besodden hat and greatcoat, I was conducted to a door further along.

"The person as you was expectin' Sir, is 'ere at last," announced the old servant as he ushered me in.

"Is that you Craddock? What is it?" Responded a sleepy voice from an armchair by the hearth.

"It's the young man, Sir, as is to do with the library. 'E's arrived!" repeated the old servant.

"Has he? Well, then show him in Craddock! Show him in!" replied the voice with sudden animation. "So you found us all right, Mr er . . ." he then added, as he rose from his chair to greet me.

"Farrant, David Farrant," I said as we shook hands.

"Yes, of course. No relation of Sir James Farrant, I suppose? We were at Eton together. Remember him well. Headstrong young fellow. Always up to some lark or other. An admiral now, I believe."

Intrigued as I would have been to hear something of my father's youthful exploits, although scarcely in character as they sounded, I thought it advisable, in the circumstances, to deny the relationship.

"Anyway, come along over and warm yourself. You must be cold for it's a prodigious raw night," added the old baronet amiably.

Having seated myself in one of the two high-backed, winged chairs, which stood on either side of a blazing log fire, I proceeded at once to apologise for my unpardonable lateness, and then went on to relate something of the cause of it; taking the opportunity as I did so, to make an appraisal of my host.

He was somewhat past middle age, I supposed. A broad figure of a man, with a round, jolly face, which was good humour itself, and a manner, which for all its breezy affability, concealed, I sensed, an underlying shyness. He was dressed, in a sky-blue tailcoat with ample buttons, and of a length longer than was the mode by that time; which together with his yellowing, voluminous wig, gave him a decidedly old-fashioned appearance.

"So, you've had His Majesty's Navy after you, have you?" he chuckled, when I had finished.

"They've been as active as ferrets down in Gravesend these past few weeks and none too choosy who they take either. Why, I've been almost afeared to venture down there meself, the way things are going," he added with a laugh. "But forgive me, I ought to have mentioned it before, you must be famished after all that chasing about. What have we got to offer our guest, Craddock?" he said, addressing the old servant who had remained standing by the door.

"There's some cold pheasant, I believe, Sir, and the 'am 'o course," replied the old butler, although with no great enthusiasm, I thought.

"What about that excellent venison pie we had for dinner? I suppose you've been having a dig at that yourself, eh?" returned Sir George slyly.

"The venison pie! . . . Why, if you recollect, Sir, you finished that yourself," responded Craddock indignantly.

"Bless me! Did I? I'd quite forgot. I've been on horseback all day," he added, turning to me with a show of apology. "And that always makes me as peckish as a hawk."

"Really, it's quite all right," I said. "It's very good of you, but I had something on my way down."

"One of those coaching dinners, you mean. That's no sort of a meal. I've had 'em meself. Miserable, ill-cooked fare and the damned horn a-blowin' before you've scarce swallowed the soup," he expostulated indignantly.

The luncheon, of which I had partaken had, indeed, been much as he described, and I would certainly have welcomed some of the ham; but the old servant was giving me such a discouraging look that, in view of the lateness of the hour, I had not the heart to put him to any more trouble, and so I reluctantly insisted that I had, in fact, been well satisfied.

"In that case, Craddock, I suppose you had better be getting off to your bed. I'll show Mr Farrant to his room meself. . . . Anyway, if we can't persuade you to eat something, I am sure a glass or two of Madeira won't come amiss, eh?" said Sir George, as the old servant departed.

"No, it certainly wouldn't," I said.

"He's been with the family since I was a boy and still tends to treat me like one," said Sir George as he filled two ample glasses from a decanter. "He's as faithful as a hound, even if he does tend to get a bit tetchy these days, I'm afraid."

"I must say that he certainly seemed somewhat out of humour when I arrived," I ventured laughingly.

"Did he, the old rascal? He's usually abed before this and doubtless doesn't like to be kept from it. But he really ought to behave more respectfully. I shall have to speak to him about it."

"Oh, please don't do so on my account. It gave me no offence, I assure you," I put in hurriedly; for my position in the household was, I felt, likely to be an awkward one, and I certainly did not wish to do anything to alienate the servants. At this we relapsed into silence for a while, and as I continued to sip Sir George's excellent Madeira, I was offered an opportunity of taking in something of the room. It was larger than I had at first imagined; the further recesses being only just discernible in the dim light, for the windows were closely shuttered, and apart from the glow of the fire, and the light from the single candelabra which stood upon a table between us, the room was in darkness. I could, however, make out something of the fine panelling with which the walls were adorned, as well as an immense glass chandelier which hung from the centre of the ceiling. Above the fireplace was emblazoned the family's coat of arms, and on each side of it horse racing prints. The impression I gained was one of homely comfort rather than elegance however, for the covering of the chairs was badly worn, and the Oriental carpet, which lay before the hearth, had begun to unthread at the edges.

"I am sorry my daughter was not still up to receive you," said Sir George as he bent over to refill my glass. "But with her mother being away, all the household affairs have fallen upon her shoulders, and she's finding it all rather wearisome, I fear. She hoped you would excuse her."

"Yes, of course," I said.

"As you no doubt must have heard, Lady Thurlow is a prisoner in France and . . ."

"In France!" I interrupted in astonishment.

"You hadn't heard then? Yes, I'm afraid the poor old thing was touring the country with her friend Lady Cooper when hostilities were renewed, and they were unable to get away in time."

"But how terrible for her!" I broke in.

"Yes, it really is most unfortunate. Still, we had all warned her that something of the kind might happen, but she would go. It's just one of the hazards of war, I suppose, and we must bear it as best we can," he added with a sigh which, as deep as it was, did not, it seemed to me, carry much stamp of sincerity.

"Is there no hope then of obtaining her release?" I interposed anxiously.

"I fear not," responded Sir George, shaking his head in mock solemnity. "Not that I haven't done everything in my power of course," he added quickly. "But as you can imagine it's all very difficult the way things are. However, I don't imagine she'll come to any great harm, but there it is. Well, Farrant, what's the news from London, eh?" he then exclaimed after a decent pause. "They say the Government's likely to fall any day now, is that true?"

I replied that I had heard something of the kind, and that the general opinion seemed to be that Addington would shortly be resigning in favour of Pitt.

"I should hope so too!" interjected Sir George with sudden heat. "How such a chicken-hearted incompetent as Addington was ever elected in the first place, I can never understand. I really don't know what the country's coming to. It's perfectly monstrous the way he's mismanaged things." He then went on to inveigh at length against the Government's handling of the nation's affairs, and as he did so, worked himself up into such a passion of furious indignation, that I had difficulty in keeping a straight face. He eventually simmered down again, however, and with a couple of gulps at his Madeira, was all at once his genial self again.

"You must forgive me," he said with a smile of embarrassment. "I don't know how it is, but the mere mention of that dreadful creature's name is enough to set me blood aboil."

"You're not alone there," I agreed, with a laugh.

Our talk, as you might have expected, then turned to the subject of the expected invasion. Sir George, to my surprise, seemed to be quite convinced that it was all just a scare. "A lot of damned nonsense. A devilish trick of the Government's to divert attention from their incompetent bungling of affairs at home, that's all."

Being quite certain in my own mind that the French were indeed about to invade, I was tempted, in view of what I had personally observed of the enemy's preparations, to refute him. But I prudently decided, that even with Sir George, the less I disclosed about myself the better, and so refrained from dissenting.

Anyway, whatever his opinion, it was quite evident from what he then went on to say, that he was doing everything he could to secure the defence of his own locality. That, in fact, for several weeks past, his days had been very largely expended in organising bands of militiamen, as well as a troop of yeomanry, of which he had appointed himself the commander.

"Well, I suppose we must be ready for the feller should he be foolish enough to chance his hand," he said in conclusion, as he excused his undoubted enthusiasm for it all.

By this time the candles were almost spent, so that the room was now more shadowy than ever, and what with my having been up so early, together with all the exertions of the day, not to mention the influence of three ample glasses of my host's excellent Madeira, my head was starting to nod. Although Sir George, as much as our talk had languished, had given no hint of being so disposed, I must admit that I was beginning to hanker after my bed. Indeed, I was on the point of making such a plea when it occurred to me that, of course, he was just itching to know what had brought me to Gravesend.

However, I had already decided that even to Sir George, the least divulged the wisest, and was thus in no mind to satisfy his curiosity.

Nevertheless, the sooner this was made plain the sooner I should get to bed. And so by way of broaching the subject I said:

"I am really most obliged to you, Sir, for having me to stay with you while I am down here. I trust it doesn't inconvenience you too much."

"Why of course not my dear fellow! Of course not! I am only too pleased to help in any way I can. I don't know what it's all about mind you. Atterbury didn't say much; but I imagine it's all to do with this damned invasion business, eh?" he added, giving me an inquisitive look.

"Well, yes, it is in a way," I replied evasively. "More than that I'm not in a position to say, I'm afraid. I'm sure you'll understand."

"Yes, of course, quite right, quite right," he quickly responded, although I could see that he was disappointed by my closeness.

"I gather that while I am here, I am to catalogue your library," I then said. "Mr Atterbury seemed to think that it might help to allay any suspicion, which my being here might arouse. I trust this meets with your approval?"

"Dear me, I'd quite forgotten. Yes, of course it's a splendid idea. It couldn't be better," exclaimed Sir George enthusiastically. "In fact, I have often talked of having it done, so it won't come as a surprise to anyone. You can rest assured, Farrant, that no one, apart from myself, will have any reason to believe that you are here for any other purpose."

"I'm afraid I'm unlikely to make a very professional job of it though," I interposed. "For I've no sort of experience of that kind of thing you must understand."

"Oh, I don't think that need worry you. Anyway, I don't imagine you'll be spending too much time there. But you're going to find them a pretty dry lot, I'm afraid, though. Most of 'em were collected by my grandfather who was a clergyman, and the bulk of them are sermons and the like. I'm not much of a reader meself. *The Times* and the *Turf Register* satisfy my wants. The library's not much used in fact. Dr Argent sometimes spends an evening there and old Mr Fenton, another neighbour, looks in for a book occasionally. However, you might, I suppose, unearth some rare folio or other," he added, jokingly.

"I should doubtless be unaware of it if I did," I responded with a laugh.

"Not that I think it very likely that you will," added Sir George. "For if there had been, Dr Argent, I'm sure, would have spotted it. He's really pretty knowledgeable about such things, I understand, and someone you'll have to be on your guard against if you are not going to be rumbled. . . . But dear me! Is it really as late as that! I had no idea," cried Sir George as he extracted a heavy gold watch from his waistcoat. "You really must forgive me Farrant, for keeping you up like this. For what with your journey and all that chasing about down in Gravesend, you must be pretty fatigued and won't be sorry to get to your bed, I'll wager."

"No, I don't think I shall," I agreed. And with this we both rose.

"The rest of the household you'll be meeting at breakfast," said Sir George, as taking up the candelabra he led me from the room. "Apart from me daughter Catherine, there's only Miss Beauchamp, me wife's sister. Oh! And there's also a military fellow, a Major Fripp, who's staying with us just now. However, he's out all day exercising the local militia, so you won't be seeing much of him," he went on, as he led me up a great curving stairway and thence along a narrow corridor.

"I trust you'll find this comfortable enough?" he said as he threw open a door at the far end of it, to reveal a spacious room containing a large, heavily curtained four-poster and, I was relieved to see, an ample coal fire blazing away in the hearth.

"I am quite sure I shall," I said.

"The bed anyway, I can vouch for, for I've slept in it many a time meself," he added as he put a flame to the solitary candle. And with this, and having wished me a genial goodnight he left me, whilst I quickly undressed and climbed between the sheets. Weary as I was, however, and toss and turn as I might, so insistently preyed upon were my thoughts by all manner of dark forebodings, that it was well into the small hours before sleep, happily, came, at last, to obliterate them.

Chapter VI

"Mornin', Sir. Shavin' water all ready and pipin' 'ot."

Half awoken by this pronouncement from the depths of a heavy sleep into which I had at last mercifully fallen, I imagined myself, for the moment, to be back in my old cabin on the *Sirius* and that the events of the previous evening, which all at once came back to me, to have been nothing more than the substance of a well-remembered dream.

This illusion was soon to be dispelled however, for as I opened my eyes, there grinning down at me from the end of the bed were the patently solid features of Joseph Leckley.

"Fine mornin' and no sign of the Frenchies yet, Sir," he added cheerfully, as he turned away to pull back the curtains.

"It's . . . er, Joseph Leckley, isn't it?" I said, giving a yawn and at the same time shielding my eyes from the sun's rays, which came slanting towards me through the sash window opposite.

"That's right Sir. But just Joe, if it's all the same to you Sir. My old mother, God rest 'er, she called me Joseph when I was a lad. But I never took to it. Felt I could never live up to a Bible name like that Sir, you see. Joe now, that's a good size different. Nobody expects too much of a Joe, now do they Sir?"

"No, I suppose not," I agreed doubtfully as I sat up to confront him.

"Mother would never 'ave it though," continued Joe as he emptied the water can into the wash-basin. "Furious she was when anyone called me Joe. Not respectful like, she said. A good Bible name like Joseph oughter be treated proper. That's what she always said. Me young brother now, 'e was christened Noah. She reckoned, I suppose, there'd be no monkeyin' about with that."

"It would certainly be difficult," I agreed with a laugh.

"There's nothing else you'll be wantin', is there Sir?" he then asked, as he moved over to face me from the end of the bed.

"No, I don't think so Joe."

"You're sure? Right, Sir, I'll be off then. Oh! P'haps I ought to jus' mention it. But they breakfasts at nine," he then added by way of an offhand afterthought, as he reached the door.

"What time is it now then Joe?" I asked anxiously.

"I can't say as I rightly know, Sir" he replied. In a tone of such bland innocence, however, that I suspected he knew perfectly well, and that it was already past the breakfasting hour he had mentioned. Indeed, when I stretched over to have a look at my watch it was, I discovered, already in fact, a quarter past that hour.

"Oh dear, it's a bit later than I thought, is it Sir? he said, in anticipation and in the same innocent tone as before.

"Yes, I fear it is," I said, leaping from my bed as I spoke.

"I would 'ave called you afore," he said with some contrition now. "But rememberin' that little bother we 'ad last night, I thought you wouldn't want to be disturbed too early like."

"Thank you Joe, it was very considerate of you," I replied, not without a certain irony, for I had more than a shrewd suspicion that it had been a reluctance to leave his own bed, rather than any nice regard for my own well-being, that had prompted his belated appearance.

"Don't mention it, Sir," he said, and with this he skipped out of the room, whilst I, having hurriedly shaved and dressed, went in search of the breakfast room.

"Ah! Come along in and sit down Farrant," Sir George warmly greeted me, as I appeared at the door. "I trust you slept well and found everything to your satisfaction. You won't mind our starting without you, I hope, but I'm afraid we don't stand on much ceremony here," he added, between mouthfuls of toast.

"Yes, thank you Sir. I was very comfortable," I said as I took my place among the assembled company in the vacant chair between Sir George and a fair-complexioned, well-favoured, young girl of about my own age who, I imagined, must be the daughter of the house.

"My father will not be kept a single moment from his meals, you must know," she said, as she turned towards me with an apologetic smile. "It's one of his little foibles which we are all obliged to humour, I'm afraid. I hope you'll excuse us."

"Foibles be damned!" exploded Sir George, before I was able to reply. "I never heard such nonsense. Why, I declare that humanity wouldn't be plagued by half its ills if a strict regard was kept to the punctuality of mealtimes, as I am sure Mr Farrant will agree."

"Whether Mr Farrant agrees with you or not, Father," interrupted his daughter good-humouredly, "I think we ought at least to observe the common courtesies. For he is, as you may recall, as yet unacquainted with either my aunt or Major Fripp, or indeed with myself for that matter."

"Forgive me, my dear fellow, so you ain't," cried Sir George. "Me daughter Catherine. Me wife's sister, Constance Beauchamp, Major Fripp – Mr David Farrant," he then formally pronounced, as he unceremoniously waved a well-laden fork towards each of us in turn. "Well, now that's done with perhaps Mr Farrant may be permitted to have some breakfast," he added impatiently. "I'd recommend the ham myself, that's if you've a liking for it. I have 'em especially cured by a farmer of me acquaintance and you won't come across better, I'll wager."

"The ham will do splendidly," I said.

"Some ham for Mr Farrant, Craddock!" cried Sir George turning to the old butler, who was standing in attendance by the sideboard. "And no skimping mind!"

"My father has just been telling us, Mr Farrant, of your unfortunate escapade," interposed Miss Catherine with concern, as Craddock placed an amply filled plate before me. "I understand you were almost taken by the press-gang down in Gravesend last night. It must have been an awful experience for you."

"Yes, that's quite true Ma'am. I was really very lucky to escape."

"Quite an adventure for you, what?" put in Major Fripp. "Not the sort of thing you're commonly likely to experience in your line of trade, I imagine," he then added with more than a suspicion of a sneer, I thought. He was a smallish, sharp-featured man of thirty or thereabouts, who had about him a pompous, self-important air which did little to recommend him. Although I could not deny he looked resplendent in his scarlet uniform which, I imagined, must be of some regiment of the line.

"Oh! I don't know, Major. We do sometimes have our little excitements. The discovery of some rare folio perhaps; that kind of thing. Though such adventures are, I suppose, rather more of the mind," I replied meekly. For, stung as I had been by his supercilious tone, I was quick to remind myself of the part I was supposed to be assuming, and that I must be careful not to say anything which might arouse suspicion.

"Ho! Ho! That's good! Adventures of the mind, eh? I don't suppose you experience many of those. Do you Major?" chuckled Sir George in good-humoured raillery, giving me as he spoke, a wink of collusion.

"Not that you're likely, I'm afraid Farrant, to find much to excite you among my little collection, for as I said last night, you'll find the bulk of 'em are sermons and religious stuff of that sort, and which I can't say I've ever been very partial to. The one old Crookshank mumbles from the pulpit every Sunday is quite as much as I can stomach!"

"Really, George! I've no patience with you," vigorously interposed Miss Beauchamp, an amply proportioned woman of some fifty years or so, attired in a loose-fitting breakfast gown and mob-cap; and with a complexion perhaps over-generously laden with powder and rouge. "As you will know, Mr Crookshank has a splendid voice, and if you paid more attention to what he was saying instead of having your head stuck into one of those racing books of yours, it really might do you some good!"

"'Pon my soul, Ma'am, I don't know what you're talking about!" retorted Sir George, reddening with confusion.

"My dear George. I'm not quite as blind as you may think," went on Miss

Beauchamp with vigour. "For I am perfectly capable, I can assure you, of distinguishing the *Turf Register* from the *Book of Common Prayer*."

"I am delighted to hear it, Ma'am!" retaliated Sir George, his hackles visibly rising. "For I was under the impression that you had no eyes for anything other than Mr Crookshank."

To which insinuation Miss Beauchamp stonily forbore to reply.

Embarrassed as I was at the time by the acrimonious nature of their exchanges, I was soon to discover that the two of them seldom communicated upon any other than such mutually abrasive terms. Indeed, I quickly came to accept it as a matter of course and, I might add, to derive no small amusement from their dialogue.

"I understand, Mr Farrant, that young Leckley was of some assistance to you in your escape," said Miss Catherine, breaking the awkward silence which had ensued.

"Yes, that's so, Ma'am. In fact I don't know what I should have done without him," I said. "It was really most good of him to have put himself out on my behalf the way he did. I am exceedingly grateful to him."

"Yes, he's a good-hearted lad. There's no denying that," put in Sir George. "And willing enough when he cares to be and . . ."

"Willing! Why he's never done an honest day's work in his life," interrupted Miss Beauchamp vehemently. "You've always been too soft-hearted with him George, that's your trouble. And as a consequence he's grown up to be nothing more than a lazy good-for-nothing, as everyone knows. I don't know what he does with his time unless it's larking about with the servant girls, for he seems to have plenty of occasion for that. I really don't know why you continue to employ him, so little use is he to anyone. Why only yesterday I found him asleep in the gun room when he should have been helping Craddock with the silver. And surely it's high time something was done about that unfortunate girl, and those children he's fathered upon her. It's really quite disgraceful the way he's behaved."

"I can't see that it's any concern of yours, Ma'am, or of any of us for that matter," rejoined Sir George hotly. "He treats her and the children well enough by all accounts, and if he doesn't propose to make an honest woman of her, well that's his affair and no one else's. The young rascal, I should mention, has taken a liking to the niece of a tavern keeper down in Gravesend," he added, with a sly grin, as he turned to me by way of explanation. "The landlord of the 'Three Daws', in fact, where you were last night, so you may well have seen something of the girl?"

"Yes, I believe I did," I said, recalling the serving girl I had seen scurrying about the parlour. And a comely young thing she looked, I remembered thinking.

"Anyway, the young blighter has sired a couple of children by her, without 'benefit of clergy', as they say," added Sir George with a chortle.

"I think it's all perfectly disgraceful," interposed Miss Beauchamp.

"The young scallywag once said, I remember," continued Sir George, ignoring his sister-in-law's interruption, "that marriage was well enough for them as had the stomach for hard tack, but for them that hadn't they'd best keep single. It was an odd way of putting it, but I think I see what he meant."

"He certainly seems to have the best of both worlds, eh what!" commented Major Fripp obviously pleased with his little pleasantry.

"You men really are dreadful," put in Miss Thurlow with good-humoured indignation. "You don't seem to have any regard for the unfortunate girl. Anyway, I'm quite sure Mr Farrant doesn't hold with such sentiments," she added, giving me an arch smile.

"I don't quite know what to say, Ma'am," I replied in some confusion. "Marriage is something that I haven't as yet seriously contemplated."

"Sensible fellow!" exclaimed Sir George emphatically. "Sensible fellow!"

And with this and the latter's seemingly insatiable appetite having at last been satisfied by successive platefuls of ham, grilled kidneys and game pie, we all arose from the breakfast table, whence Sir George and I repaired to the library.

"Well, Farrant, this is our little collection," he said, as we entered.

It was a larger collection than I had imagined it would be, for it was a spacious room, with each and every wall lined with books from floor to ceiling. The only interruptions being a large marble fireplace and two domed alcoves containing classical busts, which faced each other from opposite ends. In the middle of the floor stood a handsome mahogany desk, which was all the furniture there was, save for a couple of easy chairs by the hearth and a pair of library steps.

"I'll do what I can," I said, as I looked around the closely packed shelves. "But I can't promise to accomplish very much."

"Oh! Don't bother yourself about that. Do just as much as you think fit. After all, it's only going to be for appearance's sake, and you needn't worry that anyone'll take much notice, although, as I've said, you may have to watch your step with Dr Argent. He dines here most weeks and it's possible, I suppose, he might show some interest in what you're doing. Now I fear I must be off. I'm due on the bench this morning, and I mustn't keep the scoundrels waiting, I suppose. If there's anything you want, just ask Craddock. But I think you'll find all you need on the desk there. Oh! And I've told young Leckley to give you a hand, so he should be along in a moment."

And with this he hurried away whilst I turned my attention to the books.

Chapter VII

For the remainder of that morning I was content to busy myself in the library. The collection was, as I was soon to discover, much as Sir George had intimated. Bound in a full, rich calf, as the majority of the books were, they looked outwardly an impressive enough array; but as to their subject matter, a drearier assemblage it would have been difficult to conceive, and I could well understand that anyone who was not theologically disposed, would find little there to divert him.

Indeed, it soon became evident that the cataloguing was going to be a pretty dull business, and thankful I was when Joe eventually appeared to assist me. For, apart from the trojan work he performed on the steps, he did much by his idle and continuous chatter to relieve the monotony of the proceedings. So much so that we made, I fear, scant progress. And by the time old Craddock appeared to inform me that luncheon was ready, I doubt whether we had listed as many as twenty books all told. However, it was a beginning, and I had done enough, I supposed, at least for the time being, to satisfy any prying enquiry.

Anyway, having partaken of a pleasant luncheon in the company of Miss Beauchamp and Miss Thurlow, an occasion which, I must confess, was in no small measure enhanced by the opportunity I was afforded of furthering the acquaintance of the latter, I decided that I ought to discover something more of the neighbourhood, and while I was about it, to search out the abode of Captain Wakeley who, at least, would be someone in whom I could safely confide. I was also hopeful that he might well add something to the little Mr Atterbury had been able to impart.

Following a different route from the one I had taken the previous evening, I approached the port this time from a more westerly direction. And in so doing I discovered that a vast chalk-pit had been excavated just inland from the river on that side, although by that time it had clearly become disused, for its base was much overgrown with shrub and clusters of small trees. I have special occasion to mention it as, not many nights hence, I was to find myself fleeing across its depths in mortal peril of my life.

That, however, as I say, was yet to be. My concern for the moment was to search out the abode of Captain Wakeley, and so moving on into Gravesend,

I proceeded to meander in and out among the maze of narrow passageways, of which the riverport appeared to be largely constituted. Until at last, as I turned into a small court situated some way back from the river, I espied what I was seeking. For there, affixed above the entrance of one of the small habitations, was an old ship's figure-head of a dolphin. And, it being unlikely that there would be another dwelling so distinguished, this must, I imagined, be where the captain resided.

To my repeated knocking there was, at first, no reply, and believing that he must, therefore, be out I was just about to depart when, upon chancing to look up, I was puzzled to observe that I was being scanned by a telescope, which projected from a small window just below the roof.

As I continued to stare up at this strange phenomenon the telescope was suddenly withdrawn, to be followed a moment later by the appearance of a head, which brusquely demanded what I wanted.

"I was wondering if by any chance Captain Wakeley might be about," I shouted back.

"I don't know you, do I?" came the suspicious response and with it the realisation that it must, in fact, be the captain himself whom I was addressing.

"My name is Farrant," I cried back. "Mr Atterbury, whom I think you know, suggested that I call upon you."

"You're from Atterbury, you say?" This not without some alarm, I sensed.

"Yes, that's right," I confirmed.

"Wait there a moment and I'll be down," he then said, albeit reluctantly. So saying he disappeared, and a few moments later I could hear him unbolting the door, which he then cautiously opened by no more than was sufficient to allow me to pass through, before hurriedly securing it behind us again.

"You shouldn't come here in daylight, you know. It really is most imprudent," he said reprovingly, as he led me into a tiny room adjoining.

"You're quite sure no one was following you?" he then added, as he darted over to the window, where, having first peered cautiously out, he quickly drew the curtains together.

"No, I don't think so," I said. Such a possibility, I must admit, had not even occurred to me.

"You're not sure then?" he went on nervously.

"Well, no, I can't be absolutely certain, but I think it most unlikely. I didn't arrive down here until last night and I would scarcely imagine that anyone could know what I was about," I replied, with some irritation, for I was beginning to be nettled by his unwelcoming reception.

"Perhaps not, but you can't be too careful, you know. Anyway come along and sit down," he then added more kindly, as he proceeded to put a spill to the fire and set light to a pair of candles on the mantelshelf, which at least did something to relieve the gloom, as well as giving me an opportunity of making an appraisal of the old fellow.

He was of a small, wiry build, and in years approaching seventy, as I estimated. Although, like many who have spent a life at sea, his face was so wrinkled and weatherbeaten as to make him look older, perhaps, than he was. He was dressed, I should add, in his old service uniform, white breeches and naval bluetails, the latter now much faded and with a distinct shine about them, as I noticed.

"You must forgive me if I appear a little unwelcoming," he then said. "But I'm beginning to find this whole business most unnerving, especially after what happened to that other fellow. You've heard about that, of course?" he added, giving me a meaning look.

"Yes, Mr Atterbury did say something," I confirmed.

"I kept warning him that he ought to be more careful. But he didn't take any notice, of course. Still, it's the sort of risk you fellows have to take, I suppose. But then you are young and must be used to it. I'm an old man now, as you can see, and living alone as I do, doesn't make things any easier. To be quite honest with you, I wouldn't have agreed to help if I had known that it was going to lead to this sort of thing."

"But surely you're not in any danger!" I said.

"Not in the way that you are, of course, that's quite true. But the way they set about poor Thornton, I don't imagine any of us are safe. He had been horribly mutilated, you know, when they found him," he added grimly.

"Is that so?" I said, giving an involuntary shudder.

"So, as you can imagine," continued the captain, "I live pretty much on my nerves these days, and don't care to venture out more than I can help, and certainly never after nightfall. You may think it faint-hearted of me, and not what you might have expected from someone who has spent a not wholly undistinguished career in His Majesty's Service, but believe me, when you get to my age you don't much relish having to live in constant fear of one's life, as I do these days."

Now that I am approaching the age he must then have been, I must say that I can, more readily, appreciate the way he felt. At the time, however, with the insensitivity of youth, I had, I'm afraid, little sympathy with his fears which, anyway, were surely much exaggerated, I thought.

"But I mustn't trouble you with my little problems," he went on after a pause, "for you must have plenty of your own to worry about, I imagine, and are doubtless anxious to know what I can do to help, which, I fear, isn't very much. However, before we go into that, some refreshment might be welcome, coffee, perhaps, or something a little stronger."

"Thank you, some coffee would do splendidly," I said. And with this he disappeared to prepare it, so that I was afforded a chance to look about me.

It was a snug enough little room, with good carpets on the floor, and some nice furniture. In particular a brass-cornered service chest which stood against one wall, whilst above it, there hung a portrait of a midshipman which, although now barely recognisable, must, I imagined, be a portrait of the captain himself, painted at the outset of his career. The most singular feature of the room however, was a collection of miniature ships which had been set out upon shelves, the space beneath them being occupied by a workbench of sorts, upon which there stood the half-completed model of a frigate.

I was still absorbed in fascinated scrutiny of the display, when the captain reappeared with the tray of coffee.

"Not bad for an old fossil like me, do you think?" he said, with some pride as he came over to join me.

"They are quite remarkable!" I said. "Did you make them all yourself?"

"Well, yes, gradually that is, over the years," he replied modestly.

"They are all so wonderfully detailed," I added admiringly, as I continued to peer closely at a frigate which was a virtual facsimile of the *Sirius*.

"You know something of naval craft then?" interposed the captain eagerly.

"No, not really," I said. "But no one could surely fail to appreciate their exquisite workmanship," I added with sincerity, as I carefully replaced a ship of the line which I had been examining. I had, for the moment, been tempted to disclose our common allegiance, but decided that it was, perhaps, wiser not to. Although thinking to ingratiate myself, I did later mention that Lord St Vincent was a friend of the family's. And happily so, for as it chanced, the latter had once served under him, an association of which the captain was clearly proud.

"It's really not so difficult as you might imagine," rejoined the captain lightly. "You see, I have scale drawings sent down by an old acquaintance at the Admiralty."

"Nevertheless, it must require a great deal of patience," I put in.

"Yes, I suppose it does," agreed the captain. "But then, I have really little else to occupy my time these days, and at least it provides a welcome distraction from all the worry of this other business," he added, as we returned to the hearth.

"Now, as to that," he continued as he poured out the coffee, surreptitiously lacing his own cup from a bottle as he did so, I noticed. "Atterbury, I imagine, will have told you what little that other fellow had been able to discover, which, I confess, wasn't very much. He told you, of course, that he strongly suspected that the fellow who keeps that inn down by the river was somehow mixed up in it all."

"You mean Nathaniel Cruden at the 'Three Daws'," I interposed. "Yes, I've already seen something of him, when I called in there last night."

"Was that wise?" rejoined the captain in some alarm. "For now that they know that we're on to their game, they will surely have been on the alert – on the look-out for a likely successor to poor Jack Thornton."

“Oh! I don’t think it did any harm,” I put in cheerfully. “He’s bound to see me about the place anyway, and as it happened, my visit may, I think, have done something to reassure him.”

“I suppose you must know best,” commented the captain doubtfully, as he took a gulp at his coffee. “Anyway, you must have seen what sort of a fellow the man is. He’s already got a black enough reputation, that I do know. And it would certainly come as no surprise to hear that he was somehow implicated. However, he’d certainly be no more than a pawn in the conspiracy, for he’s quite illiterate, I understand. There’s a much bigger intelligence behind it all, of course.”

“Thornton had no idea who that might possibly be?” I interjected hopefully. “He had no sort of suspicion of anyone?”

“Not that I know of. That’s what he was aiming to discover of course, and he had some hopes that this innkeeper would provide a lead of some kind. He kept a close watch on the place, I do know that, and also shadowed him on a number of occasions, I believe. But nothing ever came of it, as I know of. Wait, though, yes, there was one occasion, it must have been the night before the poor fellow met his death, I think. He had apparently tracked him as far as the old windmill. You must have noticed it, I expect, up on the hill there. Anyway, nothing came of it, I’m afraid. Still there it is, for what it’s worth. And that, I fear, is about as much as I can add.”

By this time we had finished our coffee, and it being clear that Captain Wakeley had nothing more to tell me, I rose to leave.

“You’ll let me know, of course, as soon as you discover anything of importance,” he said as he accompanied me to the door. “But next time be sure to remember to call after dark now, won’t you?” he then added admonishingly, and with this, and without any further ceremony, he ushered me out into the court.

Chapter VIII

Whatever else I may have derived from my visit, one thing at least was evident, I thought ruefully, as I heard him hurriedly rebolting the door behind me. Any hopes I may have cherished that he would be someone from whom I could draw counsel and confidence were clearly to be disappointed.

If I was to achieve anything, it would have to be entirely by my own devices, it seemed, and what they were going to be, I had for the moment, I must admit, no very exact ideas.

Still, I had to make a start somewhere, I supposed, and with no very clear purpose in mind, I decided that I would pay a further visit to the "Three Daws".

It was, after all, to be the focal point of my investigations, seemingly, and it might therefore be as well, I thought, to get a more precise idea of the inn's location, and at the same time familiarise myself with its general topography.

It was, I discovered, when I came up to it, a rather larger establishment than I had at first imagined.

As I could now see, it had, in fact, as many as three storeys, and was, besides, a building of some considerable depth, extending, as it did, right up to the river's edge.

To one side, and flush with it, was a boat-builder's yard, beneath the rear of which must have stretched the tunnel, through which I and the others had made our escape from the press-gang.

The other side faced on to a landing-stage with steps leading down to the water, and from here admission to the inn could be obtained, I discovered, by way of another, and smaller, parlour than the one I had patronised the evening before.

To complete my survey, I decided that I ought to see something of this other parlour, and so having first made sure that Cruden was not about, I made my way in.

It was a rough, barely furnished little room, with nothing of the snug comfort of the larger parlour; such few solitary customers as there were, no doubt preferring the quieter atmosphere it afforded. In place of a bar there was simply a small serving-hatch for the procurement of liquor, whilst the only other feature deserving mention was a narrow open stairway set into one corner and which, I imagined, must lead to the upper rooms.

Behind the hatchway stood the young girl whom I had noticed the night before, and whom I now knew to be Cruden's niece. Taking more particular notice of her as I now did, there could be no denying that she really was a most attractive young thing. No wonder, I thought, as I made my way over towards her in request of a pint of ale, that Joe should have succumbed to such obvious charms.

She had the same dark complexion and raven black hair as her uncle's. But that was all. Of his coarseness of feature, especially, there was certainly no evidence. Indeed, so dainty and well-favoured was she, that it was difficult to believe that they could have been of the same blood. What a pity it was, I thought, as I sat there with my ale musing over Joe's relationship with the girl, that they and the children could not all be together in some abode of their own; for their present situation could scarcely be an agreeable one, I imagined, especially with someone like Cruden overlording everything.

I was thus continuing to reflect upon their unhappy predicament, when of a sudden there shuffled into the parlour an old pedlar, his body bent almost double by the weight of the leather satchel, which lay strapped across his shoulders.

Brandishing a handful of sheets he proceeded to limp around the parlour, croaking out his plaintive refrain as he did so.

"'Ere yer are. All about Bonaparte's murderin's and killin's. 'Orrible account. Jus' new printed, and only one penny!"

Curious to discover what fresh infamies the pamphleteers had conjured up to vilify the little Corsican, I duly handed over the appropriate coin, and set to perusing the sheet.

Somewhat crumpled, and much faded as it has become after all these years, it is still in my possession, and I have it, in fact, before me as I write.

'Who is Bonaparte?' it is headed and then continues.

'The most heinous monster imaginable. An obscure Corsican who began his murderous career by turning his artillery upon the citizens of Paris, who put helpless innocent and unoffending inhabitants of Alexandria, men, women and children to the sword till slaughter was tired of its work.' It then proceeds to recount a succession of further barbarities concluding with the warning: 'Such is the TYRANT we are called upon to oppose, and such is the FATE which awaits ENGLAND should we suffer him and his degraded slaves to pollute OUR soil.'

It is, I suppose, typical of many such sheets which poured from the presses at that time, each successive effusion having some fresh exposé of Napoleon's barbarous activities. Most of it being the purest invention of course, as eagerly devoured as it was by an ever credulous public.

Anyway, the old pedlar, having completed his round of the parlour, then advanced towards the hatchway.

"Off with you! I want none of your rubbish!" cried the girl disdainfully, making at the same time a shooing motion with her arms.

Undeterred the old man, nevertheless, stubbornly stood his ground.

"I tell you, I want none of yer rubbish," repeated the girl. "I've got better things to spend my money on. So be off with you!"

"Is your master anywheres about Miss? As like I 'ave something that might take 'is fancy," he then said, ignoring the girl's further rebuff, and peering expectantly the while into the recess behind her.

"No 'e's not, and I reckon e'd 'ave 'ad you out into the street long afore this if 'e 'ad bin. So begone with you," she cried with mounting annoyance.

"Not so 'ard Miss. You wouldn't begrudge an old cripple an honest penny now, would you Miss?" whined the old packman appealingly.

"Honest indeed!" exclaimed the girl scornfully, and with this she came from behind the hatchway and started to hustle him towards the door.

The old pedlar still firmly refused to be ejected however, insisting that he must see "'er master." Indeed, so roughly did he resist her, that I was just about to go to the girl's assistance, when Cruden himself suddenly appeared above the hatchway.

"Stay a moment Sal. Maybe 'e's got something I might like to 'ave a look at," I then heard him say.

"Really, Uncle! I don't know what you can be thinking of, wastin' yer money on such stuff and nonsense," said his niece impatiently, as she stood aside to allow the pedlar to shuffle back to the hatchway.

Needless to say, at the sight of Cruden I had hastily concealed myself as best I could by ducking down behind my broadsheet, whilst furtively peering round the edge of it to see what was going one. I observed that the pedlar, having first lain the sheets he had been holding on to the counter, was now searching in the depths of his satchel, whilst Cruden was making what was clearly a pretence at examining those already displayed.

"If you've got anything else to show me, be quick about it for I haven't got all day," he growled irritably at last, as the old man continued his search.

"They be 'ere somewheres, Sir. Don't be afraid, I'll lay me 'ands on 'em in a moment," returned the pedlar.

"Well 'urry up about it then," added Cruden roughly.

"Ah! This'll be 'em. I knew I 'ad 'em safe," cackled the pedlar with a cry of triumph, as he produced what appeared to be a small bundle of sheets fastened together with string.

"There ye are, Sir. These'll be more to yer liking, I'll be thinkin'," he then added, as Cruden, having snatched up the bundle, disappeared into the interior, whilst the old pedlar continued to hover expectantly by the hatch.

That my curiosity, by this time, had been rather more than casually aroused, you can imagine. Not only by the transaction itself, which had plainly been no straightforward one, as was evident from the something special in the nature of the package which had passed between them, but also, for all his attempts to conceal it, by the furtive and distinctly self-conscious manner in which Cruden had conducted himself during the proceedings.

Whatever the nature of their business, I felt quite certain that it was something of which he had good reason to be ashamed.

Just then Cruden re-emerged, and with a gruff "Now be off with yer," he leant over to press some coin or other into the pedlar's hand, and then disappeared again. Whilst the old packman, having first pocketed his fee with a leer of evident satisfaction, hoisted his satchel back on to his shoulders and limped off out into the street.

By now, more than ever convinced that something other than the simple traffic of broadsheets had taken place between them, and in the determination, if I could, to discover what it could possibly have been, I hurried out of the parlour, and set off in pursuit.

It was quite dark by this time, and at first I could neither see nor hear any sign of him and I was beginning to fear that he might have eluded me, when, looking up the High Street which led directly inland from the river, I caught sight of him disappearing into the dusk, and moving at such a pace as to suggest that the limp he had earlier affected was nothing more than a sham to solicit sympathy. Indeed, so fast was he moving, that it was clear he had done with Gravesend for that day, and was making for the open road and the next town.

Keeping, for the while, some few paces behind him, for I had decided that it might be wisest to postpone my approach until we were clear of the port, and beyond the busier thoroughfares, I thus continued to trail him as far as the hillock. There he turned left along the coach road, and judging that the moment was now right, I proceeded to quicken my step and shortly drew up alongside of him.

"All about Napoleon and 'is 'orrible deeds. Slaughterin' of women and children. Just one penny a sheet, Sir," came the familiar refrain, as, stopping in his tracks and reaching for his satchel, he extracted a handful of sheets.

Wishing to ingratiate myself, I made a random selection of three or four of them, and then pressed a shilling into his hands with an indication, as I did so, that he keep the change.

With a grateful "thankee, Sir!" he returned the remainder to his pack, and then made to move on.

"As we appear to be going the same way, perhaps we might keep each other company," I said.

"I 'as no objection, Sir, if you've a mind to," he replied with indifference. "I don't knows where you may be aheaded. It's Rochester I'm makin' for."

"Well, yes, that's my general direction," I said, as we moved off together into the darkness.

For half a mile or so we walked on in silence for, impatient as I was to interrogate him, I did not wish to appear too eager, especially as he himself plainly had no inclination to converse. Indeed, he appeared to be quite oblivious of my presence, as with his bead bent low, he continued to stride along beside me at the steady pace of one long accustomed to a life on the road.

We had, in fact, left the manor gates some way behind us, and were beginning to climb up on to the stretch of road which bordered the marshes, before I ventured, at last, to draw him out.

"You must be finding trade pretty brisk just now, I would imagine?" I suggested tentatively.

To this he made no reply, and thinking he must be hard of hearing, I repeated the question raising my voice a little as I did so.

"Aye, not so bad," he acknowledged laconically at last.

"All this invasion scare can't be doing trade much harm I imagine?" I then added quickly, as he relapsed into his shell again.

"It's certainly 'elped, Sir. Yes, it's certainly 'elped. Wars and such like are allus good for business."

"And Napoleon himself. He must be pretty good for trade too."

"Old Boney? That 'e is, Sir! That 'e is! 'E's a rare one for the 'orrors and no mistake. Just what folks want. Something to curdle their blood a bit, that allus gets 'em buying. Yer right, Old Boney's no enemy o' mine, I can tell 'e," chuckled the old fellow appreciatively.

He seemed to be such a simple old creature, that I was beginning to wonder whether I had not been altogether over-quick in persuading myself that he could, perhaps, be in some way implicated in the treacherous scheme of things. The evidence for any such assumption was, after all, pretty tenuous, resting solely as it did upon the suspiciously underhand nature, or so it had seemed to me, of the transaction which had taken place between himself and Cruden.

I was, nevertheless, determined, if possible, to get to the truth of it one way or the other, and so after a further pause, I continued gently to interrogate him.

"Do you often trade in these parts?" I asked

"More'n I used to," he replied. "I tread this road twice a month regular now!"

"You must find Gravesend a pretty good place to trade, I should think, with all those inns there are there?"

"Aye, not so bad, Sir. Better'n some. The sailors are the ones. If you catch 'em just off the ships that is. Then they're allus free with their money."

"I believe I saw you down by the river front earlier this evening," I then interposed matter-of-factly.

"Could've bin yer did. I was thereabouts."

"You seem to have a good customer in the landlord of the 'Three Daws'," I then said, having decided to take the bull by the horns at last.

"'E 'ad a few a sheets off o'me," he returned guardedly, and there could be no mistaking, I thought, the sudden note of wariness in his voice.

"Is he a regular customer?" I then asked.

"Fairish."

"Something rather special he had off you, wasn't it?" I then added quickly.

To this he made no reply, but instead made a sudden dart forward in an attempt, it seemed, to draw away from me, so that I was obliged to quicken my pace to keep up with him

Although his obvious unwillingness to pursue the subject seemed to vindicate my original suspicions, I did not quite see how I was going to prevail upon him to divulge anything. I had no official status, and so was in no position to threaten him. Anyway what evidence had I that he had committed any misdemeanour? I could, I supposed, have confiscated his pack by force if necessary, on the chance that it might still contain some incriminating material, but as he had already transacted his business with Cruden, such a possibility seemed unlikely.

I was still puzzling the dilemma over in my mind as we continued to stretch out together, when of a sudden, I recalled the avaricious look on his face as he had pocketed Cruden's fee. If anything was likely to loosen his tongue it would be the sight of gold, I decided.

I knew that I had a couple of guineas upon me and so, extracting my purse, I removed one of them, and then proceeded to make a show of holding it close up to him, so that, even in the darkness, there could be no possibility of his mistaking its colour.

Having peered at it for a moment or two, he all at once made an instinctive grab for it.

"Not so fast," I said, at the same time closing my fist round the coin. "First I must know something of that package which you handed over to the landlord of the 'Three Daws'. I should like, for instance, to know what it contained, and from where you obtained it?"

For a while it seemed that he was not to be tempted. However, as I continued to make play with the coin, the allure of it became too much for him.

"There's nothing I can tell 'e, Sir. I knows nothing about it," he pleaded moaningly at last. "They pays me well and I asks no questions. I just delivers the sheets, that's all."

"But surely you must know what the packages contain?" I insisted, holding the coin at some distance from him now.

"No more than that they be sheets as I allus carry. The string round 'em came loose once and I 'ad a look at 'em. But they were no different, I tell 'e, Sir," he replied.

“You mean they were exactly the same as the sheets you normally hawk around?” I said disbelievingly.

“That’s right, Sir. I didn’t study ’em close like, but there was no difference as I could see. Now, I’ve told you all I knows, Sir,” he then added beseechingly, making as he did so a tentative gesture towards the coin.

“Come, my friend. You’re not going to earn the guinea as easily as that,” I replied firmly. “There’s a good deal more I have to know before it’s yours. For one thing, when was it that you first began delivering these packages?”

“I don’t rightly remember, Sir. Could be three months, a bit longer maybe,” he replied reluctantly.

“And how often do you make these visits to the ‘Three Daws’?”

“Could be twice a month, no more’n that, Sir. That’s all I can tell ’e. So you just ’ands over that bit o’gold, and I’ll be gettin’ along,” he croaked.

That the old pedlar knew himself to be engaged in some kind of illicit activity was, of course, by now perfectly plain. But as to whether he had any inkling of the precise nature of what it was, I was now becoming doubtful. In all likelihood, if he was, as I surmised, transmitting secret military information, he was quite unaware of the fact. He was simply the conveyor of the packages, that was all. His promptitude in delivering them being determined by the generous reward, which he knew that he was going to receive.

So be it, I was, nevertheless, anxious to discover, if possible, the source from which he obtained the packages.

“There’s just one thing more,” I said. “When you’ve told me this the guinea’s yours. These packages you deliver, how do you come by them?”

“Someone ’ands ’em to me.”

“Where?” I said.

“Just out of Dover. By the first mile-post on the London Road,” he then blurted out. “’E just ’ands ’em over and says I’m to deliver ’em to the landlord of the ‘Three Daws’ at Gravesend. That’s all I does, Sir, and that’s all I knows. More’n that I can’t tell ’e, and that’s the truth.”

“And when do you meet this person?” I then quickly added.

But this, press him as I might, and with the promise of a further guinea, he adamantly refused to divulge, having the wit to realise, no doubt, that were he to do so, his profitable little undertaking could well be jeopardised. Although he could, of course, had it occurred to him, easily have misled me by mentioning the first hour and day that came to his head. Anyhow, as it now seemed that any further probing was likely to be useless, I handed over the guinea and left him to continue his journey, whilst I, forthwith, turned about and footed my way back to the manor.

Chapter IX

"If I am not mistaken, that, I fear, must be checkmate," pronounced Dr Argent diffidently as, with obvious reluctance, he took up his queen and moved it diagonally across the chequered table.

"Eh! Come now, Doctor, surely not!" expostulated Sir George in disbelief.

It was after dinner that same evening and, the household together with Dr Argent, who was paying his weekly visit to the manor, had retired to the drawing-room where we were, severally, engaged in whiling away the couple of hours or so before bedtime.

Miss Catherine and Major Fripp, to my envy of the latter I might add, sat in close tête-à-tête over a hand of piquet, some little way apart from the rest of us, who were gathered round the hearth, where Miss Beauchamp was hard at work on a tapestry frame, and the doctor and Sir George were, as you will have gathered, playing chess. Whilst I sat close by, my attention about equally divided between their game, and Dampier's *Voyages*, an old favourite of mine, and a copy of which I had discovered in the library.

"Why, look here! I can take it with the castle," cried Sir George triumphantly, as he took hold of the chessman and started to move it across with the intention of replacing his opponent's queen. Upon which the doctor, with an indulgent smile, gently tapped his bishop, which had been uncovered by Sir George's move.

"Dear me! It seems that I must give you best once again, Doctor," sighed Sir George at last, as he continued to stare down at the remains of what had patently been a most one-sided contest.

Mindful of Sir George's warnings respecting the doctor's bookish interests, I must confess that I had experienced some inward qualms, when, upon my belated return to the manor, I had discovered that he was one of the company, who had already assembled round the dinner table. And my misgivings were in no way diminished, to discover that I had been seated next to him.

He was some few years younger than Sir George. In his early forties I would imagine. A powerfully built man of gentlemanly appearance, and of a courteous, if somewhat reserved, manner. He seldom spoke, but when he did his words were carefully chosen, and to the point, I noticed. Even if the curious habit he had every now and then, of emphasising them by a sudden sideways twitch of the head, was a little disconcerting.

Anyway, of his intelligence there could be no doubt. Indeed, attired as he was in sombre black, he had more the look of a scholar, than that of a small town practitioner. At any rate he was, I soon decided, someone with whom I was going to have to tread very warily indeed, if I was to retain any semblance of credibility as to the role of a bibliophile which I was assuming.

My credentials, in fact, had soon been put to the test, for following some general conversation he had, no doubt in deference to myself, raised some obscure bookish topic or other, of which, needless to say, I was in perfect ignorance.

However, by being as vague and non-committal as I was able, I had managed, I think, to bluff it out. It had been an awkward few moments nevertheless, and relieved I was, I can tell you, when Sir George had come to my rescue by deftly turning the conversation to some general speculation upon a rumour which had apparently reached Gravesend earlier that day, of the sighting of some enemy barges off the Sussex coast. A topic which, happily, was pursued for the remainder of the meal.

"You haven't lost again Father, have you?" exclaimed Miss Catherine teasingly from across the room.

"If your father would show a little more respect for his pawns, Miss Catherine, instead of sacrificing them the way he does, he would be more than a match for me, I can assure you," responded the doctor modestly.

"I can scarcely believe that, Doctor!" responded Miss Catherine. "But I do think that he might do rather better if he was to drink a little less port. Don't you think so, Father?" she added feelingly.

"Nonsense child!" retorted Sir George. "A glass of wine could not possibly affect my play one way or the other."

"I dare say one glass might not," intervened Miss Beauchamp, pointedly emphasising the singular. "But the best part of a decanter could not help but do so I would have thought. It's really a miracle to me that your father can play at all, considering the amount he drinks. His brain must be utterly befuddled, as I am sure you would agree Doctor."

"We all like our glass of port Ma'am," replied the doctor tactfully.

"That's as may be," went on Miss Beauchamp in the same quiet reproving tone, as she continued to thrust her needle into her canvas. "But there is moderation in all things. One glass can do little harm, that I will allow. But when it comes literally to sousing oneself in it, you must surely admit Doctor . . ."

"I'll thank you to hold your tongue, Ma'am!" exploded Sir George as, unable to contain himself any longer, he suddenly swung round to face his sister-in-law, his face aglow with anger. "When we want your opinion we'll ask for it. I never knew such a monstrous, interferin', plaguin' old . . ."

“Now there’s no need to be insulting George,” responded Miss Beauchamp, her nostrils visibly tightening. “I was only speaking for your own good. You must surely know – for heaven knows everyone else does – that you drink far too much, and always have done!”

In response to which aspersion Sir George was restrained from giving expression to another broadside of invective by the appearance, at that moment, of Craddock bearing a tray of coffee.

“Perhaps Mr Farrant would like a game with the doctor, Father? For I’m sure he plays,” said Miss Catherine, when the old butler had departed.

“My dear fellow. Of course, it’s quite unpardonable of me. I should have asked you before,” cried Sir George apologetically.

“No, really, thank you,” I hastily excused myself. “I scarcely know the game, I’m afraid.” Which, as it happened, was true. Although even had I been in any way proficient I would certainly have declined the offer, determined as I was, in view of my experience at dinner, to avoid any possible chance of intimate converse with the doctor.

“You don’t? You’re a sensible fellow, for it’s a monstrous provoking game,” replied Sir George. “Oh well, Doctor, I fear that you’ll be obliged to put up with me again. That is, if you would care to.”

“Certainly, if you wish it,” responded the doctor willingly. “But pray do look to your pawns this time. You’re really much too profligate with them, you know.”

“I shall. Don’t you fear, Doctor, I shall,” exclaimed Sir George cheerfully, as he eagerly began to set his pieces out again.

“And for all the port I may have inside me,” he added, looking pointedly across at Miss Beauchamp, “I shall defeat you yet, Doctor.”

“No doubt, Sir. No doubt,” concurred the doctor courteously, as he made the opening move.

Having remained just long enough to observe that Sir George, true to form, had lost little time in squandering the bulk of his pawns, I quietly slipped away to the seclusion of the library where I could the better, I had decided, ponder over the events of the day, and consider how best to act upon them.

Taken all in all, it had been, I felt, as I sat there absently poking the logs in the grate, by no means a discouraging beginning. It was true that Captain Wakeley had been a disappointment, but on the other hand, the encounter with the old pedlar had been a most singular piece of luck.

The temptation was, perhaps, to read into it rather more than was justified, for, as patently shady as his business with Cruden was, I had no real evidence of course, that it had, in fact, anything to do with the espionage activities I had been commissioned to investigate.

And besides, I thought, as I went on to consider the supposition, would it not, on the face of it, be a pretty cumbrous and haphazard method of collecting military information? But then, as I went on to argue the case, such a scheme would, no doubt, have certain merits.

It should, perhaps, be mentioned that at the time of which I am writing, pedlars such as the one I had encountered were a common feature of our highways and byways, as they trod their way along immemorial tracks to the furthest corners of the land. By the very nature of their itinerant trade, a solitary and anonymous fraternity they must always have been, and therefore never likely to have attracted much official notice. Thus, was it not possible, or so I began to persuade myself, that by such an undercover use of these nomads, a whole network could have been organised as a means of conveying intelligence from coastal sources to various focal centres, where the information could be collated and then transmitted to the Continent? Was such a notion really so very far-fetched?

However, whether it was or not, I did not quite see how I was going to capitalise upon it. My concern, after all, was purely a local one, to ferret out as much as I could of the espionage goings on in Gravesend, and in this context such information as I have been able to extract from the pedlar did not seem to have advanced things very much; unless, of course, I could obtain a sight of the sheets which he had handed over to Cruden. But to achieve this I would somehow have to gain admittance to the latter's private quarters at the "Three Daws", and make a search for them. The mere thought of which was, as you may imagine, enough to give me the shudders, even before I went on to consider the immense difficulties such an idea posed. Nevertheless, unappealing as the proposition was, the longer I sat there pondering over it, the more I became persuaded that, whatever the hazards, this was what I must plan to do.

I was still dolefully chewing over the project, with all its daunting implications, when, to my consternation, Dr Argent suddenly appeared at the door, bearing an armful of books.

"You must forgive me for disturbing you like this, Mr Farrant. But I have had these books of Sir George's longer than I care to remember, and when I heard that the library was to be catalogued, it became more imperative than ever that I return them," he said, his head nodding vigorously the while, as he spoke.

"Yes, of course," I said. "But please don't bother to put them back," I interjected hastily, as he advanced towards the shelves. "I can easily see to them myself."

"Oh! It's no trouble, and anyway, I must ensure that they go back to their rightful shelves," he said, as he began to replace them.

"I don't know how much progress you've already made, but you are going to be disappointed, I'm afraid, if you were hoping to make any great discoveries here," he then asserted. "Not that there aren't one or two good things. There's a nice *Faerie Queene* which I certainly covet, and also a first edition of *Comus* somewhere, but it's in very poor condition, I fear."

"Is there? That will certainly be worth seeing!" I exclaimed with feigned interest. For I must admit, to my shame, that at the time I was not even aware that such a work existed.

"Still, with your knowledge and experience," added the doctor deferentially, "you could well hit upon something that I have missed. For although there are one or two fields in which I am particularly interested, in comparison with yourself I must be counted the merest dilettante."

"I fear I must confess that I am pretty new to it all myself," I put in quickly.

"I can hardly believe that, Mr Farrant!" he roundly responded.

And with this, and having replaced the last of the books, he wished me a goodnight and started, to my relief, to make towards the door. He had, however, taken no more than three or four steps, when all at once he hesitated, and to my consternation declared:

"Wait though, there is just one thing upon which I really should like to have your opinion. I'll just see if I can find it." And so saying, he retraced his steps and moving across to one of the shelves, proceeded to extract from it some volume or other.

"It's something I discovered only last week," he exclaimed eagerly, as he bore down upon me with the book. "It had slipped round to the back, and must have remained hidden there for years, I imagine," he added, as, with a sensation almost amounting to panic, I received the book into my hands, fully expecting it to be some ancient and obscure tome with which I would be wholly unfamiliar, only to discover that it was, in fact, Butler's *Hudibras* of which I could at least claim to have heard.

"It's a first edition if I am not mistaken. Although you would scarcely believe it, in such fine condition as it is," he said keenly as he took up the candelabra, and held it over me so that I could examine the volume the better. "But, what do you think?"

In spite of its new appearance, the style of the binding certainly had the look of an earlier age about it, I thought, as I turned the book about in the way that a connoisseur I imagined would have done. So it was unlikely to be a recent edition. But was it, in fact, a first one? Opening it I stared desperately down at the title page to see if I could discover a publication date. Those roman numerals at the bottom, they must indicate it, I decided. As they danced before my eyes in the flickering light of the candles, it wasn't easy to decipher them, but I at last concluded that the date must be 1663. Not that it was much help, since, for all I knew, the work could have been first published much earlier.

"Yes, it's certainly a very fine copy. Quite remarkable!" I said appreciatively, as I let the pages run through my hands, to discover – as I had until then been unaware – that the work had been composed in verse, rather than the prose form I had previously imagined it to have been.

"It's part one, of course, as you can see," observed the doctor. "As you know, the others weren't published until some years later."

"Yes, of course," I said studiously. Although I was, I need hardly tell you, quite ignorant of that fact or, indeed, that the volume I was holding did not comprise the whole work.

"So it must be the rarest of the three, I imagine," went on the doctor. "I haven't come across the other two, so I don't think they can be here. Even so, it's quite a find, don't you think?"

"Yes, I agree. A real collector's piece," I said. "It's a first edition, there can be no doubt," I added with authority, deciding that there was nothing to be gained by prevaricating.

"I thought I couldn't have been mistaken, but it's reassuring to have one's opinion vindicated by someone such as yourself," he said as he retrieved it.

"I have the three parts in a later edition, the one with the Hogarth plates. But that's no great rarity, as you know," he added as he moved away to replace the book.

Casually as he had spoken, and for all that there appeared to be no hint of guile in his voice, had he, I wondered, already begun to suspect that I was an imposter and that his mention of such an edition had been no more than a trap, laid to confirm his suspicions. I had certainly never heard of it. Not that that was any criterion, one way or the other. However, innocently motivated or not, it would be wisest, I decided, to ignore the allusion and so instead replied evasively, "You are something of a collector yourself, I take it then, Doctor?"

"Well, yes, I suppose I am. In a small way, that is," he replied modestly. "My collection is nothing like as extensive as this, of course. A little more selective perhaps. Not that I can claim to possess anything of much rarity. But still, I have one or two things that, I think, might interest you. Perhaps you would care to come over some time while you are here and look them over, for I should certainly value your opinion."

"I should be very pleased to," I said, with a great deal more enthusiasm than I inwardly entertained, I can tell you.

"You would? Well then, we must try and arrange an evening together."

And with this thankfully he departed, leaving me still with the discomforting uncertainty as to whether or not I had managed to deceive him. Whatever the case, there was one thing upon which I was firmly resolved. There could be no question of my fulfilling the invitation he had proposed. That, at all costs, was something that must certainly be avoided.

Chapter X

During the two or three days following my encounter with the pedlar, nothing occurred, as I recall, that warrants much relating.

For the most part they were spent in the library, where, although I managed to make some further, if desultory, progress with the cataloguing, a good deal of the time all that I did, I fear, was to sit in front of the fire gloomily brooding over my unhappy plight, and all the awesome problems which it posed.

Indeed, so despondent did I become, that I came very near, once again, to throwing in my hand. I did, as I remember, actually draft a letter apprising Mr Atterbury of such a decision, and it was only after much heart-searching that I was finally persuaded to tear it up. As abject and discouraged as I was, there was nothing for it, I reluctantly decided, but to press on and, come what may, do the best I could. Although by what means, I am afraid, I had no very tangible ideas.

On successive nights I had ventured down into Gravesend with the notion of keeping a watch upon the "Three Daws", and on one occasion, I did, in fact, shadow Cruden to another quarter of the town. But he had simply passed an hour or so with some cronies at another inn, and then returned to his own.

Nevertheless, it had at least established that he was in the habit of leaving his inn of an evening, and for a period which would allow me sufficient time, perhaps, to explore his private quarters and hopefully obtain sight of those sheets, which he had had from the pedlar.

For want of any better scheme, it thus seemed that I would just have to continue my nightly vigils of the inn, and if and when I saw him leave, forthwith take my chance.

Such then had been my intended plan when, as it happened, a much more favourable opportunity seemed likely to present itself.

Cruden, as you may remember, had some local reputation as a pugilist, and when Joe happened to mention that he was shortly – a couple of days hence, in fact – to contest a match in the ring, it at once occurred to me that such an event, guaranteeing Cruden's absence from the inn for a longish period, as it must, would afford me just the chance I was seeking.

As propitious an opportunity as it promised to be, it nonetheless still posed certain hazards. For one thing, there was the question of my gaining surreptitious admission to those upper rooms of the inn. That there was a flight of steps up from the side parlour I already knew, but whither they led, I had no idea. By some discreet probing, however, I managed to discover from Joe that they would, indeed, provide the access I needed.

Another thing which I was able to learn from Joe, was that Cruden had recently turned one of the attic rooms into a sort of private den, where he had apparently, of late, been in the habit of spending a good deal of his time. From which, it seemed reasonable to deduce that this was the room I should make for. Thus, all considered, the undertaking, anyway on the face of it, appeared to present no undue risk.

The fight, I gathered, was to take place somewhere on the marshes, was to be one of thirty rounds, and would commence at nine in the morning; it being the custom, as I was informed by Joe, for Cruden, together with his entourage, to be conveyed to the scene of the fight by boat, the party embarking from the landing-stage adjoining the "Three Daws", and thence continuing down river.

It would thus, I thought, be simply a matter of my lurking about the vicinity of the inn until they were safely away, and then effecting my entry.

Such then was my plan, and it was in a mood of quiet confidence that I lay in my bed that morning awaiting Joe's arrival with my shaving water.

My scheme was soon, however, to receive an unwelcome check. Indeed, as soon as Joe appeared, so down in the mouth did he seem, that I suspected, knowing how eagerly he was looking forward to the fight, that something must have gone amiss. What it was, I was soon to discover when he glumly proceeded to inform me that a rumour had got about that the authorities were intending to stop the match as soon as the two contestants had entered the ring.

As you may remember, such fights were at the time illegal, and although a blind eye was commonly turned, the local law officers did, now and again, take it into their heads to interfere.

Anyway, whether the rumour had substance or not, here was a complication that I must admit I had not envisaged, and one that clearly put a rather different complexion upon it all.

For were the fight not to take place, an unpalatable element of risk would be introduced, inasmuch that Cruden might elect to return to the inn forthwith, and thereby surprise me before I had had sufficient time to make my search. As pusillanimous of me as it may appear, this was a chance that I was certainly loath to take and, after much soul-searching, I decided that I would first ensure that the fight was on, watch the first round or two to see how things were shaping, and then foot it back to Gravesend as speedily as I could.

Cruden, it appeared, was a firm favourite to win. Indeed, Joe was quite adamant that the fight would not last more than a few rounds. In which case, however, another bruiser would apparently be on hand to guarantee that the crowd would have their money's worth; so I need not worry, it seemed – should Cruden, as was expected, quickly prevail – that the proceedings would be curtailed.

My only fear was that Cruden himself might be summarily vanquished, for such an eventuality might, I supposed, lead to his early return. Even so, by watching the first round or so I would, I imagined, be able to gauge how the contest was likely to go and act accordingly.

Thus it was that I found myself a little later that morning, in the company of Sir George and Joe Leckley, as we set off in the family gig down the manor drive, and out on to the high road towards the marshes.

It was, I remember, another fine day with a cloudless blue sky overhead.

The weather, indeed, could not have been better for such an event and I only wished, as I sat perched high up there on the back of the gig, that I could have shared some of the light-hearted enthusiasm for the outing, which my two companions so evidently displayed.

Instead my mood, I fear, could scarcely have been a more contrary one, as I anxiously brooded upon the project which lay ahead of me.

For one thing, I was already beginning to doubt the wisdom of my alteration of plan, especially as Sir George had firmly pooh-poohed the notion that the fight might be stopped. After all, he was, as he said, a Justice of the Peace himself and if anyone should know, he surely would.

There was, furthermore, something else which was beginning to add to my uneasiness, for it soon became apparent, as we continued upon our way that the location of the fight was destined to be at a distance considerably further from Gravesend than I had imagined, and that, as a consequence, I was going to be faced with a much longer walk back to the "Three Daws" than I had bargained for.

Still, it was too late to worry about that. I could but trust either that Cruden would achieve a quick victory and be committed to another bout, or that the fight would go to something like its full extent.

Anyway, filling me with disquiet, as such uncertainties were, my attention was shortly to be diverted to my more immediate safety for, now that we had reached the broader stretch of road above the marshes, Joe had begun to drive with such vigorous application that it was requiring all my presence of mind, not to say body, to preserve anything like a secure hold upon my seat.

"Steady, Joe! Steady! You'll have us over if you're not careful!" exclaimed Sir George in alarm, as the near wheel skimmed the edge of the ditch. "Why must you always drive at this madcap pace?"

"It's Bess, Sir. There's no 'olding 'er this morning," responded Joe blandly. "I can't think what could have got into 'er. Unless it's them oats I gave 'er afore we left."

Notwithstanding this admission, he then proceeded to give her such a hearty crack across the rump, as to cause the mare to bound forward with even greater expedition.

"Confound it, Joe! Hold her, I say. If you carry on like that you'll have her bolting next, you young idiot!" bellowed Sir George as the off wheel landed in a rut, and we came within an ace of toppling over, and must have done, had it not been for the weight of Sir George ballasting the near side.

His remonstrations, were, however, but vain cries in the wind, as, to the accompaniment of pleading groans from Sir George, as well as angry shouts of other drivers whose vehicles we continued to sweep by in close and terrifying proximity, we proceeded at a rate so furious, that I could only imagine, as I clung desperately with both hands to the rail behind me, that the horse must, indeed, now have bolted. That we were, anyway, foredoomed to some dreadful disaster, seemed certain. For with the traffic in front of us becoming denser, it seemed impossible that there would be a way through, and there certainly would not have been, had not some warning of our precipitate advance preceded us; thus allowing the stream of pedestrians and carriages ahead of us, to draw hurriedly aside to give us passage.

In my midshipman days I had experienced many a fearful moment aloft the rigging in a high sea, but they were, I can assure you, as nothing compared to the torment I suffered on the back of that gig, as we pursued our headlong career with the dreadful certainty, or so it seemed, that we were all shortly destined to be catapulted into the ditch or, if not, between the wheels of some other carriage.

Not that such a view appeared to be reflected in the demeanour of our intrepid Jehu, who not only remained perfectly composed the while, but was, I suspected, relishing every moment of it as, now up on his feet like some charioteer in the arena, he somehow succeeded in steering a way through, albeit with, I swear, no more than inches to spare.

Meanwhile, as we hurtled round a bend it seemed that even Joe's expertise could not possibly save us. For there, lumbering towards us, and in full possession of the road, or so it appeared, was an immense stage wagon. With a collision surely inevitable, I had already made as if to jump when, with a deft flick of the reins, Joe swung the gig sharply to one side, and to the echoes of a deep groan of despair from Sir George, we shot past through a space which, by all reasonable calculation, had been unnegotiable, at least not without some awful catastrophe.

With this, thankfully, the mare appeared to have shot her bolt. Anyway, our speed now gradually slackened until eventually Joe was able to ease her back to a gentle jog trot.

"Heaven forbid that I ever experience anything like that again!" moaned Sir George when he had at last recovered his composure. Adding as he rounded upon Joe, "And how you didn't come to break all our heads, you young lunatic, I shall never know. Anyway, there's one thing I'll swear to.

You'll never handle the reins again, that's if I know anything about it! I'll be damned if you do! And it's no use you adopting that air of offended innocence. If you hadn't driven her like some mad thing as you always do, she would never have bolted off like that. And well you know it!" continued Sir George passionately.

"It wasn't my fault, Sir. It was Bess. Something must 'ave got into 'er," pleaded Joe.

"Nonsense, Joe! She's always as quiet as a lamb when anyone else drives her," retorted Sir George.

"Then it must 'ave bin them oats I gave 'er, that's what must 'ave done it, and made 'er go off like that!" persisted Joe.

"Oats be damned!" exploded Sir George. "It's your infernal mania for speed, that's what it was and it's no use your trying to pretend otherwise, so don't let's have any more of your lame excuses. . . . Dear me! Farrant, I had quite forgot for the moment that you were with us," he added, as he twisted round to address me. "And I must say it's a wonder you still are. I really must apologise for this young imbecile here. God knows I had a fearful enough time of it keeping my seat here in front, so I can imagine what you must have suffered perched up there behind. Anyway, I trust you weren't too much knocked about?"

"No, not really," I said, albeit untruthfully, for there seemed to be no part of me that hadn't suffered from the tumbling I had received. "Although I must admit," I added with a laugh, "that it was an experience I wouldn't care to repeat too often."

"That I'll wager you wouldn't!" exclaimed Sir George, feelingly. "It's nothing short of a miracle we didn't have all our necks broken. And it's no thanks to you, my young friend," he added severely, turning upon Joe again. Which was, perhaps, a little unjust, I thought. For although there could be no denying that he had, in the first place, offered every encouragement to the horse to bolt, his subsequent handling of the situation had been a truly remarkable feat of equitation. Anyway, as the pair of them continued to wrangle, Sir George in admonishing tones and Joe the while doing his best to disclaim all responsibility, we had soon left the high road behind us, and having turned down a narrow side lane, we had come upon a narrow stone causeway, that crossed the marsh at this point, and upon which there stretched away in front of us a closely packed stream of carriages and pedestrians.

"Confound it! If they don't get a move on we shan't be there before the fight begins," exclaimed Sir George with sudden impatience. "I can't think what they can be about up there in front."

"'Fraid we shall 'ave to keep our place, Sir. It'd be a bit risky trying to overtake this lot. But I could 'ave a go if you like," added Joe teasingly, giving Sir George a sly look as he spoke.

"Don't you dare! You young rascal. We've had quite enough of your hare-brained antics for one day," returned Sir George in good-humoured alarm at such a proposal.

"Of course, you've already seen something of Cruden, haven't you, Farrant?" he then added, as we started to move ahead again.

"Yes, that's right, I have," I said. "And I must say that from what I saw of him, he certainly looks the part."

"You're right. He's not a pretty sight, is he? Mind you, I don't know what sort of a shape he's in just now, but if he's in any kind of trim, this fellow he's fighting will have to be a lot better than the novice they say he is, if he's going to remain on his feet for long. From all accounts he's a good mover and can take a fair bit of punishment and, by George, he'll need to once Cruden starts to lay about him. Not that there's anything at all pretty about the way Cruden fights, but if he does manage to land a punch, his opponent will certainly know about it, I can tell you. He broke the jaw of the last chap he fought, you know, and they say it was half an hour or more before they could bring him round again."

"Is that so?" I replied with a shudder.

By this time we had advanced well into the depths of the marsh, its bleak expanse putting me in mind of my Norfolk homeland with its lush, miry turf and its intersecting network of narrow, reed-filled dykes. A few head of sheep were grazing in the drier parts where the ground was raised a little above the general level, but there was nothing else to relieve the bleak monotony of the locality. Although, away on the horizon, I could dimly make out the solitary abode of the strange Mr Fenton, of whom Joe had spoken.

"Not a particularly cheerful spot, is it?" remarked Sir George, as if reading my thoughts. "On a day like this it doesn't look so desolate, I suppose. But when the mist comes down it can be really treacherous, especially after heavy rain. I have too much respect for me gout these days to venture down here too often, but when I was a younger man it provided me with many a good day's sport. You'd be surprised at the quantity of wildfowl there is, and I've even bagged a hare or two when the weather's dry."

"I can well believe it," I said. For I had already caught the plaintive whistle of a redshank, and, as he spoke a flight of shovellers passed overhead.

"It seems an odd sort of place for a prizefight though," I added.

"Well, yes, I suppose it does," agreed Sir George. "But the old battery over there ahead of us, as you'll see when we get there, provides an excellent arena, and its remoteness at least has the advantage that we are less likely to have any interference from the law."

Just then we turned aside from the causeway, and on to an area of stone-bedded ground where, having drawn up among the other vehicles already gathered there, we dismounted from the gig to continue on foot the three or four hundred yards we still had to cover to reach our destination.

"Now, Joe, you'll see that Bess behaves herself while we are away, won't you, for we don't want her bolting off again, do we?" said Sir George archly, as the two of us prepared to move away.

"Do you mean, Sir, that I am to stay here with Bess and miss the fight?" responded Joe with a look of crestfallen dismay.

"I'm afraid so, Joe. With the way Bess has been behaving, and none of your doing, as you insist, we can't take any chances now, can we?" affirmed Sir George blandly as we both started to move away. So much affected had I been by Joe's forlorn look of disappointment, that I felt compelled to intervene and was, in fact, about to do so when Sir George said with a chuckle, "I'll wager you never saw anything so glum in all your life! But I couldn't resist having a little game with the young rascal after that fright he gave us. He just lives for these fights, you know, and he'd never forgive me if he was to miss one." And so saying, he turned and shouted back, "All right Joe, if you can get someone to look after Bess you can see the fight. But be sure that you are back here promptly when it's all over, mind."

"That I will, Sir," responded Joe joyfully, and with this Sir George and I, having regained the causeway, joined the hurrying throng converging upon the battery, where a large crowd, as I could see, was already gathered upon the surrounding ramparts.

As we were crossing the drawbridge which guarded the entrance to the arena there went up a great cheer, which, as I quickly realised, was in deference to my companion who, with a broad grin of embarrassment, waved his hat back in acknowledgement.

"They always greet me like this," he said shyly. "But I'm sure it's only because of the lenient way I treat 'em when they come up before me on the bench, the blackguards!" he added, as he proceeded to lead the way to a section of the rampart which had been cordoned off, and where some benches had been provided for the benefit of himself and one or two other local dignitaries.

As Sir George had intimated, the old battery could scarcely have been bettered for such a contest, affording, as it did, a splendid amphitheatre with its spacious arena and its encircling ramparts which, together with the sea-wall on the river side, afforded excellent vantage positions for the spectators. A square of ground in the centre had been roped off to form a ring, and beyond this there was another outer ring for the accommodation of the officials and the whip handlers, the latter's purpose, so Sir George informed me, being to discourage any undue encroachment by the crowd.

To my surprise, for it now wanted no more than a few minutes to the time of the commencement of the fight, I could see no sign of Cruden, whereas his opponent, together with his attendant seconds, were already patiently waiting in one corner of the ring.

He looked a good deal younger than Cruden, being no more than twenty years or so, I would have thought, and although well-muscled enough, and with an ample girth of shoulder, plainly nothing like as powerfully built. Nevertheless, as he then commenced to prance and shadow-box about the turf, he certainly promised to be much the nimbler on his feet, I thought.

Anyway, with his challenger having come up to scratch, all eyes were now turned expectantly towards the sea-wall for Cruden to appear.

"If the fellow doesn't get here soon, he's going to forfeit the match, I'll be damned if he isn't," growled Sir George as he anxiously fingered his watch. "It's always been his way to cut it devilish fine. Suits his damned arrogance, I suppose, to keep us all on tenterhooks. But this time it looks as if he really may have overstepped the mark. I'll be damned if it don't! He's only got another three minutes, that's all, and they won't hear of any excuses, you can be sure of that. And with all the money he must be carrying, not to mention fifty guineas of me own, I certainly wouldn't like to answer for the consequences if he does forfeit the match. There won't be a timber of the 'Three Daws' standing. I'll be hanged if there will," he added in a tone which implied such a reprisal would be no more than just retribution. And from the angry murmurings which had begun to echo among the crowd there might well be, I thought, some substance in his prediction. Scarcely, however, had Sir George spoken, than a great cheer rose from the direction of the river and a few moments later, a section of the crowd on the sea-wall began to fall aside.

"By Jove, I believe he's just made it," cried Sir George with evident relief, as Cruden all at once emerged through the gap that had been formed. With his massive frame already bare to the waist, he stood for a moment or two with arms aloft, as he acknowledged the roars of the crowd, and then, having been joined by a bevy of attendants from behind, who then proceeded to encircle him like pilot fish about a shark, he strode majestically down the incline and over to the ringside.

So close run a thing was it, in fact, that no sooner was he over the ropes, than the timekeeper sounded the bell. A coin was then tossed for choice of corner, and the outer ring, having been cleared, the two contestants moved to the centre of the arena to take up their stance.

With Cruden, in contrast to the pale yellow colours favoured by his opponent, clothed in hose of the deepest black, which gave him, I thought – and perhaps not inaptly – the appearance of a medieval executioner, the two men, having glared for a while in defiance at each other, began tentatively to spar.

So apparent was the disparity in their respective physiques, for almost puny did the Hampshire man appear now that he could be measured beside Cruden, that I could not but wonder at his temerity in embarking upon the match. That he was, however, as I had suspected, much the livelier on his feet, was soon apparent, as they continued to circle about, each cautiously probing the defences of the other. Cruden, indeed, seemed scarcely to shift his ground, as he stood there, rock-like, in the centre of the ring, whilst his opponent, keeping just out of arm's length, continued to dance and weave around him.

Such was the pattern of the first round, with no blow of consequence being struck, although the Hampshire man had clearly had the better of things, scoring with several darting jabs to the body which Cruden had scarcely bothered to counter, his only acknowledgement being a smirk of disdainful indifference. The second round proceeded in much the same way, with Cruden patently biding his time, as his opponent, the while, still warily kept his distance. Indeed, so disinclined did they seem to come to grips, that the crowd soon began to express its impatience, with a mounting crescendo of jeers and catcalls as the two fighters continued lamely to confront one another with a display of little more than token sparring.

The third round had scarcely begun, however, when, of a sudden, the fight was on. It was the Hampshire man who made the move, as having feinted with his left, he then slipped under his adversary's guard and administered the full force of his right to the face. Obviously hurt, for I could see him wince, Cruden at once retaliated, as, with eyes blazing and arms swinging wildly, he lumbered after his nimbly retreating opponent.

Had any of his punches achieved their target the fight must have ended there and then, for the whole weight of his massive shoulders was behind each one of them. But agile as a cat, his opponent had calmly ridden the onslaught, and slipped away unharmed.

Incensed by the rebuff, and spurred on by the roars of his supporters, Cruden pounded on in pursuit.

This time, however, not only did his blows miss their mark, but they were countered by a left hook to the jaw which sent him back upon his heels, as well it might, for it was a punch that must have felled most men to the ground. Then before Cruden could recover, his opponent had sprung in again and unleashed a volley of blows which sent Cruden staggering to the ropes, his defences in helpless disarray. With punch after punch thudding successively into his head and body, it seemed that he must go down, and would have done, I am sure, had he not been saved by the bell.

"Well, Cruden will have to do a lot better than that if he's going to get the whiphand of this fellow!" exclaimed Sir George glumly, as the fighters retreated to their corners. "This fellow can box, there's no question of that, and he's plainly the fitter of the two by a long chalk. I've never seen Cruden in such dreadful trim. He's always been a devil for the liquor, of course, but he keeps off it as a rule before a fight, or so I've always understood. But from the look of him today, I must say there's precious little evidence of it. He must be carrying at least a stone overweight, by the look of him."

As Sir George had implied, Cruden appeared to be anything but hard-trained. For all his powerful physique, there was a flabbiness about him which contrasted markedly with the fine-drawn body of the other man which, so one-sided had the fight been, scarcely appeared to have been marked as yet. Whereas, Cruden, with one eye already closed, his lips all puffed and bruised and blood still trickling from one nostril, looked a veritable shambles as he sat there, slumped in his corner whilst his seconds feverishly strove to remedy the damage.

"I fear that unless Cruden can manage to land a big one soon, the fight's as good as over," commented Sir George gloomily, as the two men squared up to each other for the commencement of the next round. For all his obvious ascendancy it was apparent, however, that the Hampshire man was now in no hurry to settle the issue, having decided, no doubt, that the match was already as good as his, and that he might as well bide his time and give the crowd something of a run for their money. Anyway, for the whole of that round and the succeeding one, he did little more than play with his opponent, as he continued to harass and tease Cruden with an exhibition of skilful ringcraft which, although in no sense punitive, at least served to underline his opponent's singular lack of the same. In fact, so ungainly and seemingly spiritless were the local champion's attempts to make a fight of it, that his supporters soon began to express their displeasure in terms so abusive as to suggest that Cruden was now clearly suspected of throwing the fight. A suspicion to which Sir George, I might add, was quick to give expression, as the bell sounded for the end of the fifth round.

"Cruden's putting up no sort of a fight at all!" he exploded angrily. "There can be no doubt of it. He's stacked his money on the other man to get the better odds. It's as plain as a pikestaff, the damned scoundrel! He'll never fight again if I know anything about it. That's quite certain!" he added emphatically. Not that there was, as far as I could see, anything to warrant Sir George's accusation. For, clumsy as Cruden's performance had been, there had, as far as I could see, been no evidence that he was being actuated by any such perfidious motive.

Anyway, by the alacrity with which the Hampshire man sped out of his corner at the commencement of the next round, it was evident that he was now determined to put an end to the fight forthwith.

Indeed, Cruden had barely risen from his stool, before his opponent was upside of him and had knocked him back on to the ropes with a resounding upper-cut to the jaw.

"What's the game, Nat? This isn't a picnic yer know!" shouted a wag in ridicule, as Cruden, half-buckling under the blow, was obliged to cling to his opponent to prevent himself from going down.

No sooner were they separated, however, than the Hampshire man had sprung in again, striking with left and right to the body and head. Great thudding blows that had Cruden reeling back on to the ropes again. To stifle the onslaught he now resorted to wrestling, and by grappling his opponent around the waist, managed somehow to manoeuvre him to the centre of the ring. The respite was nevertheless short lived, for as they were ordered to break, the Hampshire man – now throwing all caution to the winds – proceeded, with remorseless application, to crash one fist after the other into his opponent's virtually unprotected body. With blood pouring from his mouth and nose, both eyes reduced to the merest slits, and his face battered and bruised almost beyond recognition – like some great man-o'-war with topsails and gallants adrift but with colours still bravely flying – Cruden still, miraculously, did not founder. For all my abhorrence of the man, I could not but admire the grim courage of it all. Indeed, even the crowd – among which even the most prejudiced must by now have realised that their champion was fighting straight – had been awed by the valiant spectacle into a respectful silence, so that with the contest approaching its apparent conclusion, an unearthly hush had all at once descended upon the arena. The only sound to break the stillness being the pad of the men's feet, the dull thud of fist against flesh, and, now and again, the distant cry of some marshland bird.

Then, of a sudden all was pandemonium. Exactly how it happened, I am not sure; for, sickened by the sheer brutality of it, I had, for the moment, averted my gaze. However, from the account I was to have later that evening from Sir George, it seemed that the Hampshire man, impatient no doubt to end the fight, had for once missed his mark. Whether he had stumbled, or whether Cruden had somehow slipped the punch, Sir George was not certain. Anyway, his opponent, it seemed, had overbalanced, and falling forward as he did so, his jaw had been met by the right fist of Cruden with the full impact of his remaining strength behind it. Albeit, all that I saw as I returned my gaze to the ring, were the knees of the Hampshire man buckling under him, as he sank senseless to the ground.

The count clearly was nothing more than a formality, as, with arms raised, Cruden stood there athwart his opponent's prostrate and motionless body, triumphantly acknowledging the tumultuous applause.

Anyhow, this was the moment I had been awaiting, and so having mumbled some excuse to Sir George – of which he was patently oblivious, for he was on his feet cheering as wildly as the rest – I slipped quietly away through the crowd and started off hotfoot along the sea-wall and back towards Gravesend and the "Three Daws".

Chapter XI

I had, I estimated, some three miles to cover, and spurred on as I was by the knowledge that I had no time to lose, I need hardly tell you I was quickly into my stride, and soon moving at a fair rate of knots.

Although the fight had ended in a way that had been anticipated, there was surely little likelihood – after the battering he had received – that Cruden would have any stomach for a further encounter, and consequently every chance that he, and his entourage, would be returning to the "Three Daws" somewhat earlier than I had bargained for.

Nevertheless, with the cheers of his exultant supporters still echoing behind me, there was at least some consolation in the thought that such a victory was unlikely to be celebrated without a good deal of ceremony of one kind or another. And, from what I knew of Cruden, he was certainly not one to be laggard in exacting as much vainglorious adulation as he could from such an occasion.

Even so, in the realisation that every second saved could well be vital, I had soon broken into a run, and with the tumult behind me rapidly dwindling to a distant murmur, it was not long before I had arrived at the point where Joe and I had disembarked after our escape from the press-gang.

Here the sea-wall came to an end as it sloped downwards to a path which skirted the river bank for some way further before turning inwards to join the roadway which I knew would lead me to the "Three Daws".

Dropping my pace almost to a saunter now, for I had no wish to attract attention to myself by any appearance of unseemly haste, I thus made my way up to the front of the old inn.

As one might have expected, all seemed to be reassuringly quiet. The main parlour I could see, as I furtively glanced through a window, boasted no more than three or four customers. Whilst the smaller one overlooking the quay, appeared, to my relief, as I moved on round to it, to be quite empty.

So, without more ado, I cautiously lifted the latch and went in. Then, having hesitated for a moment or two by the door to ensure that no one had heard me, I tiptoed over to the stairway and made my way up, to find myself as I reached the top, at the head of a passageway, which led off at right-angles to the interior.

Able to breathe more easily now, I thus duly set off in search for a further flight which would take me to the topmost floor and that attic room which, as you may remember, was my objective.

It soon became apparent, however, that this was not going to be the simple matter I had imagined, for as I continued to explore my way about, I was to discover that the place was a veritable maze of dark, narrow passages, and short stairways which twisted and turned about in such a complex and rambling fashion that I soon became utterly confused.

Such rooms as I hopefully peered into I found to be mere cubby holes furnished with nothing more than the crudest of shakedowns which served, I imagined, to provide accommodation for casual seamen and the like.

Eventually making my way to the rear of the inn, I did, with some heightening of expectation, come upon a larger room overlooking the river, and which, if only by the size of the bed, must I decided be where Cruden slept. Not that there was much there to raise my hopes and, having hurriedly rummaged through a chest of drawers and an old sea chest which had, no doubt, been discarded by some former tenant of the inn, I withdrew.

Beginning by this time to lose heart as well as becoming the while ever more fearful of Cruden's premature return, I decided that, frustrating as it was, any further time spent in the search would be foolhardy; and so turning about, I began to retrace my steps back to the parlour.

As I did so I must have lost my bearings again, and taken a wrong turning. Anyway, it chanced that I found myself at the head of a dim passageway that I had not, as I remembered, previously encountered.

Anxious as I was to get away, it would, nevertheless, be weak-spirited of me, I decided, to leave this last stone, as it were, unturned, and so I hurriedly set off down it to see whither it might lead.

At first it did not seem to promise much. However, upon reaching its far end I was to discover that from one side there ascended a narrow flight of steps.

Realising that this could well be what I had been searching for, I quickly made my way up to find myself, beyond the door at the top, in a small wedge-shaped, windowless garret of a room with a low sloping ceiling into which had been set a skylight to provide what little illumination there was. A small oak bureau bearing a single brass candlestick stood against one wall, and this, apart from a couple of chairs, was all that the room contained. There was, I must also mention – such providential use was I to make of it upon a future occasion – an adjoining room of similar proportions which, as far as I could see, as I peered into its dim interior, contained nothing more than a collection of empty bottles.

But, it was the bureau, as you can imagine, to which my attention was drawn and so moving over to it, I hurriedly proceeded to search through it. All the drawers were quite empty, however, save for the top right one which was securely fastened.

Feverishly applying the point of a pocket knife, which I had been careful to bring with me, I managed, however, to slip the lock and a moment later I was staring down at a heap of printed matter similar to the kind I had purchased from the old pedlar.

Scarcely able to contain my excitement, and quite forgetful, for the while, of any other consideration, I removed three of four of the topmost sheets and laid them side-by-side on top of the bureau and commenced to examine them. To my mortification however, as closely as I scrutinised them, no suspicious marks or alterations of any kind could I detect. They appeared, indeed, to be in exactly the same state as they must have left the press. As it chanced, among the sheets was a duplicate of the one vilifying Napoleon, which I had purchased from the pedlar, and which, as luck would have it, I still had about me, so I was able to make a comparison. Here again, however, as minutely as I proceeded to compare them, I was unable to discover any difference whatsoever.

For all the evidence to the contrary, could it be that my surmise had been quite unfounded, and that Cruden's interest in the sheets was, after all, a perfectly innocent one, concerned purely and simply with the inherent subject matter? On the face of it, it certainly seemed so.

With a heavy sense of disappointment I carefully collected the sheets into the order in which I had found them, and was about to replace them, when I suddenly espied a small magnifying glass lying in the far depths of the drawer.

Realising its possible significance, I quickly took hold if it and excitedly started to re-examine the duplicate of my own sheet. At first I could see nothing extraneous to the letters. However, upon holding the glass a little further away so as to increase the magnification, there was, all at once, revealed a series of minute but clearly defined indentations as might have been made with the point of a needle and which occurred in varying combinations over certain of the letters. And, what was more, a magnified scrutiny of my own sheet failed to reveal any such marks.

That the microscopic imprints represented some code or other, I was in no doubt, and, quite unheeding, in the excitement of my discovery, the risk I was running in further delaying my departure, I hurriedly commenced, with the point of my knife, to transcribe the dots above the relevant letters upon my own sheet. I was thus busily absorbed and had, I suppose, copied a couple of lines or so when, to my horror, I was all at once alerted by the sound of a stealthy footstep on the stairs below me.

For a moment or two, so petrified was I, that I just stood there with my knife still poised over the print, before – as the steps continued to approach – I was able to regain some presence of mind and, having thrust the sheets back into the drawer and resecured the lock, desperately cast around for some possible refuge.

My first impulse was to make for the adjoining room, but before I could do so, a hand was already upon the latch, and the sole recourse left to me was to flatten myself against the wall beside the door, and thus avail myself of the temporary concealment which the opening of it would afford me before, hopefully, making my escape. Even now as I pen these words, I can vividly recall the agony of suspense I endured as, rigid to the wall and with my knife clutched ready in my hand, I watched the door gradually inch open to reveal, as there then crept furtively into the room, a small boy of some five or six years!

So far removed was he from what I had so dreadfully envisaged that I could scarcely suppress a laugh of relief as, quite unaware of my presence, for his back was towards me, he hesitated for a moment with his ear cocked, as if listening for someone.

Having done so, he then gave a mischievous giggle and, moving over to the bureau, started to insinuate himself backwards into the depths of its recess.

He was, in fact, on the point of disappearing and I was beginning to be hopeful that I might be able to tiptoe away unobserved when he chanced to look up.

"Why, hallo! That's a good hiding-place you've got, I'm sure no one would ever think of looking for you there," I said gently, as he continued to stare up at me with a look of the most fearful alarm.

My words, as quietly spoken as they were, plainly did little to reassure him however, for as I moved away from the wall he hurriedly scrambled to his feet and all the while eyeing me with the utmost horror, began to sidle round towards the door.

"Come now, there's nothing to be afraid of," I said in an attempt to allay his fears, whilst taking care meanwhile to cut off his retreat, for the last thing I wanted was that he should hurry off and raise the alarm.

"Really, there's no need to be frightened. I'm not going to hurt you," I persisted soothingly as, with the same fixed stare of horror, he continued to back away from me.

Somewhat puzzled by his behaviour, for I had always imagined my appearance to be rather benign than otherwise, I then said, "Perhaps you could tell me your name, for I should like to be friends."

For a moment or two he did not reply, but then, giving a deep gulp, he said in a voice scarcely above a whisper:

"Andrew. Andrew Leckley."

From my first sight of him, such a close facial resemblance to Joe did he have, that I had, in fact, been in no doubt of the relationship.

"And how old are you, Andrew?" I then quickly added.

"Six," he replied with more boldness now, and then added proudly, "and a half."

"Only six! Why, I could have sworn you were quite eight at least," I said in feigned surprise, for having plainly inherited his father's slightness of build he was, as it happened, rather small for his age.

My attempt at flattery appeared to do little to placate him however, for although his dread of me appeared somewhat to have abated, he still continued to eye me with a look of considerable awe.

Puzzled by this, I was about to say something in a further attempt to calm his fears, when he suddenly blurted out, "Are you Old Boney?"

"Old Boney! Good heavens, what an idea!" I responded with a laugh. "Whatever could have made you think that? Why he's quite a little man and wears that funny cocked hat. Don't you remember? And besides, he'd speak French, now wouldn't he?"

He appeared to appreciate the logic of this, for altogether more at ease now, he then said, "Uncle Nat told me that Old Boney would get me if I ever came up 'ere. 'E said 'e would cut me into little pieces. Do you think 'e would?"

"Oh! I don't think he's quite as bad as that!" I replied. "He's very wicked of course, and they say he does some terrible things but I'm sure he wouldn't do anything to hurt someone like you. But perhaps it was rather naughty of you to come up here if your uncle had told you not to."

"Yes, I suppose it was," the boy replied, albeit with little conviction.

"Who were you hiding from?" I then asked anxiously.

"From Emmie. She's my sister," he replied. And then added with the disdain of an elder brother, "She's only four."

"Is she likely to look for you up here?" I then said with some concern. For, having allayed her brother's fears, I certainly did not wish for another such confrontation. Especially as I was to discover, by a quick glance at my watch, that a good hour or more had already elapsed since the fight had ended and, quiet as everything still appeared to be, it could surely not be long now, I thought with an upsurge of alarm, before Cruden and his company of jubilant supporters would be returning.

"She'd be much too frightened," retorted the boy scornfully. "She'd never come up 'ere." Just then, however, there came from the passage below, the sound of a little girl's voice impatiently calling out, "Andrew, where are you?"

"'Ere she comes now," whispered the boy as, plainly taking no chances with his sister's want of audacity, he darted back to the bureau.

"Can you keep a secret, Andrew?" I said as he began to disappear into the recess. "Will you promise not to tell anyone that you've seen me if I promise not to tell your uncle that you've been up here?"

"All right," agreed the boy cheerfully.

"You won't forget now, will you?" I then added earnestly.

"No, I won't. And you won't tell Emmie where I'm 'iding, will yer?"

"No, I promise," I reassured him, and so saying, I hurried off through the door and down the steps.

I had reached the bottom one, I remember, where I was hesitating to see if I could hear anything of the little girl when, to my alarm, a great cheer echoed up from the river close by.

With all thoughts of the little girl on the instant dispelled, and with the sole aim now of getting clear of the inn with all possible haste, I darted off up the corridor, almost tumbling over the child, I remember, as I swept round the corner at the far end, and then sped on through the maze of passageways until I, thankfully, found myself once again at the head of the steps leading down to the side parlour.

As I did so, from the landing-stage just below me, there resounded another great burst of cheering. In acclamation, I could have no doubt, of Cruden's coming ashore.

Anyway, I should be able to get safely away without being seen, I thought, as I bounded on down the steps. But then, as I emerged into the parlour, with whom should I come face to face, as luck would have it, but one of Cruden's cronies whom I remembered seeing at the inn during my first visit, and who would have been sure to have noticed me then.

It was for no more than a brief moment that our eyes met. Nevertheless there could, I fear, be no mistaking the look of malevolent suspicion he gave me, as I swept past him, and sped on out through the cheering mob.

Chapter XII

With my thoughts overshadowed by the hapless encounter with that familiar of Cruden's, it was, I fear, in spite of what I had managed to achieve, with no light-hearted step that I made my way back to the manor.

A most unsavoury-looking character this fellow was, I should mention, with a face like a ferret's, and a cast in one eye which served only to enhance his general air of malevolence. He was, I was later to learn from Joe, one Reuben Snade, although more popularly know as The Crab, a nickname deriving from the peculiar swaying motion of his walk, resulting from a shortening of one of his legs.

That he was a particular crony of Cruden's, I was fully aware, for he had been one of his seconds as well as bottle holder at the fight.

I could thus be left in little doubt that he would not be slow in acquainting Cruden of his suspicions of me, and that, as a consequence, I was in future going to have to tread very warily indeed.

That such a prediction was unhappily only too well founded, you shall shortly hear. As soon, in fact, as that very night, when something occurred which, in the event, was to leave me in no doubt whatever that I was already a marked man.

I had once again spent the best part of the day in the library, where, in the intervals between cataloguing, I had studiously applied my mind to the sheet upon which I had transcribed the coded dots, to see if I could make any sense of them.

Needless to say my endeavours were quite fruitless, for, apart from having no knowledge of such esoteric matters, there was also, I fear, precious little to work on for, owing to the boy's untimely interruption, I had, as I have said, been unable to transmit more than the first line or two.

Nevertheless, meagre as the sample was, an expert in such matters would, I had no doubt, be able to decipher something from it. And so, having waited until it was dark in accordance with the Captain's strict injunction, I set off down to Gravesend with the sheet.

His reception of me, I might mention, was no more cordial than before and, indeed, so plainly agitated was he by my coming, that having handed over the sheet, I stayed no longer than was necessary to give him some account of how I had obtained it and what it was about, and then made my way back to the manor where – after spending a mortifying evening of it in envious observance of Miss Catherine and Major Fripp in close tête-à-tête over their customary after-dinner game of piquet – I duly retired to my room.

Sleep, however, was slow in coming. Try as I might, I just could not divest my thoughts of all the grim forebodings which would persist in crowding in upon them.

For a good hour or more I had lain there vainly tossing and turning about in my attempts to induce the necessary repose when, all of a sudden, I was alerted by the sound of a tap at my door.

I was given no time to reply, or even to conjecture whom it might be, for upon the next instant, there burst into my room the becapped and nightgowned apparition of Miss Beauchamp bearing a candle tray!

"Oh! Mr Farrant, they've come. They're here. The French have landed!" she cried out frantically as she advanced upon my bed.

"Oh, dear! What's going to become of us all! We shall all be murdered in our beds. I know we shall!" And, with this lugubrious prophecy, she gave a great wail of despair, and collapsed on the bed beside me!

"There now! You really must try and calm yourself," I said soothingly when I had recovered from the surprise of her startling intrusion. "And tell me what it is that makes you think that the French have landed."

"I'm quite sure of it. I know they have. For I've just seen the lights. Oh dear! And the awful things they do. It's all too terrible even to think about!" she cried, between heaving sobs.

Just then the door behind her gave a sudden creak, at the sound of which she swung round with such a look of ill-boding, as if expecting, I am quite certain, to see Old Boney himself standing there and ready to pounce, that I had the greatest difficulty in suppressing a laugh.

"Come now, Miss Beauchamp. You really must compose yourself," I said with some impatience now, "and tell me, what it is that makes you so sure that the invasion has begun. And anyway, if it had, we can't be in any immediate danger, now can we? Why, we must be fifty miles or more from the coast, and even if they have managed to land, it would take them a day or two at least before they could reach this far, now, wouldn't it?"

That there was, in fact, no foundation for her belief I was, anyway by now, pretty sure, since my bedroom looked out upon the hillock, and I could certainly see no glare in the night sky, which there would have been, had the beacons been lit.

"Oh dear! I suppose it is silly of me to be so frightened. And what must you think of me, coming in and disturbing you like this, Mr Farrant?" she said, as she made some attempt to control herself.

"But they've landed, I'm sure they have. For when I awoke just now, I happened to look out across towards the windmill. Like yours, my room faces that way, and I can see it quite clearly, and there was this light which kept flickering on and off and . . ."

"But it couldn't have been the beacons. They're not burning, as you can see," I interrupted her, pointing towards the window.

"No, no. It wasn't the beacons. They haven't been lit yet, but it won't be long, I'm sure. Oh! Mr Farrant. Whatever's going to become of us all? When you think what they did to their poor King and Queen, and all their nobility! We are all going to be guillotined – Sir George and the rest of us, I know we are!" At this she broke down again, and began to heave and sway about with such violence, that I was obliged to relieve her of her candle tray which, in her agitation, she was swinging about so violently, that I was becoming anxious for the safety of my bed curtains. For, whatever the chances of a conflagration on the hillock, I certainly had no wish for one here in my own room!

"Come, now. You really can't believe that!" I said firmly. "Why, the revolution was over long ago. Nothing like that's going to happen, I can assure you," I added, drawing the counterpane up and around her shoulders; for she was plainly now beginning to shiver as much from cold as from fright.

"Now, these lights you say you saw. Couldn't it just have been the moonlight? Or perhaps you just dreamt it all. Now, couldn't that have been it? Anyway, as you can see, it's still as dark as ever outside. If the invasion had come, the beacons would have been set alight by now, and the sky would all be aglow, wouldn't it?"

"But it wasn't a dream. I was as wide awake as could be, and it wasn't the moon, I am sure," persisted Miss Beauchamp. "The light kept going on and off, and it was coming from the top of the windmill, like as if they were signalling across the river to the other side, I'm sure of it."

"But even if you did see these lights, I'm sure that they could have nothing to do with an invasion. Besides the church bells would surely be ringing by this time," I then added – reminded, as I was all at once, that they were to sound the alarm in the event of such an emergency.

"You can't hear them, now can you?"

"No, that's true," she admitted as she turned her head to listen. "Oh dear! Those lights I saw didn't mean anything after all, you think?"

"I'm quite sure they didn't," I put in firmly.

"What a silly goose you must think me, working myself into such a silly state, and waking you up like this. I really don't know what to say," she then said, her former alarm giving way to embarrassment, as the delicacy of her situation all at once occurred to her.

"Come now, you haven't been foolish at all," I said, patting her hand consolingly. "Anyone would have been alarmed. I would have been myself. I know I should, it was perfectly natural. Especially with all these invasion scares we've been having."

"It's kind of you to say so, Mr Farrant, but I can see now that I've just been a fanciful, foolish, old woman. What you must think of me, I really can't imagine!"

“There’s nothing to be ashamed of,” I said. “Indeed, I think you acted most sensibly.”

“You won’t say anything to the others, will you?”

“No, no, of course not,” I reassured her.

“But, there, I’ve already made quite enough nuisance of myself as it is, disturbing you all for nothing like this.” And without more ado, she coyly disengaged herself from the counterpane, retrieved her candle tray, and hurried awkwardly from the room.

As the door closed behind her, I snuggled down between the sheets again, and tried once more to compose myself. But it was all to no purpose. Hard as I tried to resettle my thoughts, they would keep reverting to those flashes of light from the windmill, which Miss Beauchamp was so insistent she had seen. That she could well have imagined it all – for she was clearly a most impressionable old thing – was very possible, of course. Nevertheless, I could not but help being reminded of what Captain Wakeley had told me of Thornton’s belief that the old windmill was somehow implicated in the conspiracy. Such being the case, was it not incumbent upon me to set forth and investigate? Little appeal as such a proposal had, and loath as I was to relinquish the warm comfort of my bed, I eventually decided that I was in duty bound to do so. So, having reluctantly dragged myself into my clothes, I crept stealthily from my room, down the stairway, and out into the night.

And a bleak, inclement one it was, I remember, as I sped off down the driveway with the trees in the park plunging and swaying in a fierce, howling wind, and great black clouds, heavy with the promise of rain, scudding across the sky above.

The moon was high and full though, so I was soon afforded, as I moved on up the high road, a clear view of the windmill perched up there on the hillock, as well as of the river below me. I was thus well placed to detect any possible signalling from either quarter. Not that I was sanguine of seeing anything of the kind, for, even if Miss Beauchamp had not imagined the lights, the chances were that it would all have been over by this time. Indeed, the nearer I approached the hillock, the more did I persuade myself that it was nothing more than a wild-goose chase that I was upon, and I was already beginning to debate in my mind whether it was, after all, worth pursuing, when, of a sudden, I saw a light flash three times in quick succession from a ship at anchor in mid-river, and then upon turning my gaze towards the windmill, there came, after a brief interval, a series of answering flashes.

That there was something afoot there could now be no question, and so quickening my step, I proceeded to hurry on towards the hillock.

The entrance to the windmill which was by way of an ascending flight of steps, on the side facing away from the river, and my aim being to take up an observation post as close to them as possible, I decided that my best approach would be from the direction of the rearward slope, especially as I would be able to obtain some cover from one of the beacons which had been sited close to that side of the mill. So, proceeding leftwards along a path which circuited the base of the hillock, I then started off upon the ascent.

As luck would have it, the moon just then was eclipsed by a heavy bank of cloud, so that all was, for the moment, quite dark. Nevertheless I was careful to keep close to the ground, crawling for the most part on my hands and knees. Thus no easy progress did I make of it, especially as I was now being buffeted by the full force of the wind, as it continued to howl and swirl about me.

However, by slow degrees, and all the while keeping a weather eye upon the steps of the windmill above me in case anyone should emerge, I gradually eased my way up towards the beacon.

For the moment all appeared quite desolate. The two beacon men would, I imagined, be safely ensconced within the shelter of their hut, which I could see on the far side of the mill, and there was not much likelihood, I reassured myself, of their venturing forth upon such a night, at least, not without good cause. Anyway, having selected a suitable vantage point well within the shadow of the beacon, I stretched myself flat to the ground and commenced my vigil. And an uncomfortable one I was soon finding it, lying out there on the hard turf, and all the while in the grip of the piercing north-easterly, which continued to whistle and whine through the furze beside me. Indeed, so painfully cold did I soon become, that, after several minutes of fruitless watching I had decided that I could bear it no longer, and that there was nothing for it but to return to the comfort of my bed, when there came the sound of a door creaking open, and a moment later I saw someone emerge on to the top of the steps.

At first, against the dark background of the mill, I could distinguish nothing more than an indistinct shape; but then, as he turned from securing the door and stood at his full height, I knew at once that it was Nathaniel Cruden for, even in the poor light, there could be no mistaking those massive proportions.

For a while he remained standing there, looking furtively around, and in so doing seemed at one point to gaze so fixedly down to where I was lying, that for one awful moment as he then began to descend, I was sure that he must have espied me.

To my relief however, as he reached the ground, he made instead over towards the beacon men's hut, and then, while still some distance from it, he paused and I heard him give a low whistle. I had not long to puzzle over the purpose of this, before I saw someone emerge from the shadows, and, dim a view as I had of him, I knew almost at once from the peculiar manner of his gait as he sidled over to join Cruden, that it was, in fact, Crab Snade who, I could only imagine, must be one of the beacon men, which indeed was the case, as Joe was later to confirm.

Anyway, they had been standing there for some while conversing together, and I was becoming sorely tempted – so painfully afflicting was the cold – to creep away and proceed back to the manor, when, to my horror, they started as if upon a sudden impulse, or so it seemed, to hurry over towards where I was lying!

That they must somehow have spotted me seemed certain, and I had, in fact, already braced myself to make a run for it, when they suddenly altered course and made instead for the other side of the beacon.

So quickly had it all happened, and so petrified was I, that it was some moments before I was able to collect my wits sufficiently to realise that it had begun to rain heavily, and that this it was that had prompted their move.

Nevertheless, I now dared scarcely to breathe, let alone move, for they were now no more than the length of a bowsprit from me, albeit that we were separated by a projecting spur of the beacon.

So close were they, in truth, that I could hear the low murmur of their voices, or rather, Crab Snade's who chanced, at that moment, to be speaking. Not that I was able to make any sense of what he was saying against the noise of the wind.

After a while however, Cruden suddenly broke in, and such was the deep pitch of his voice that, not only did his words come over all too clearly, but were so unequivocal in their implication as to freeze the very blood within me.

"You're quite sure it was 'im? That fellow who was in the 'Daws' the other evenin', and is stayin' up at the manor sortin' Sir George's books or somethin'? Leastways that's what Joe told me 'e was doin'."

That the reference was to myself, and that Crab Snade must have been informing Cruden of the suspicious circumstances of our untimely encounter, I could be in no doubt.

Anyway, Crab Snade must have made an affirmatory reply, for Cruden then went on: "So, they're still snoopin' about, are they? If you ask me the game's gettin' too 'ot for comfort, and if we're not careful, it's goin' to be the noose for the lot of us." Here, he paused for a moment, and then with a grim emphasis added, "Well, 'e's got to be got rid of that's certain, and it 'ad better be done quick afore 'e's rumbled too much. One thing 'e looked easy enough game, so yer shouldn't 'ave much trouble with 'im; but make sure yer leave no traces this time, Crab. Don't leave the body lyin' about as yer did afore. Bury it away somewhere secret like so as nobody'll know what 'ad 'appened to 'im, and see that yer make a clean job of it. We don't want no bunglin', mind!"

What my feelings were as I lay there eavesdropping upon the very contriving of my own destruction – in the dread realisation that were they to shift their position by but a few feet, their design could be so easily achieved then and there – I need hardly describe.

Mercifully, however, the shower soon passed, and to my heartfelt relief they then moved away to go their separate ways. Although, so shattered and dispirited was I by what I had overhead, that it was minutes, I remember, before I was at last able to bestir myself, and set off wearily back to my bed; where, thankfully, sleep soon interposed to drown all desolate thoughts of what the morrow might bring.

Chapter XIII

With the happenings of the night still lying heavily upon me, I had, as you may imagine, little stomach for my breakfast the next morning. Nor was I in any sort of a mood, I fear, to join the general excitement occasioned by yet another rumour of a French landing which, like all its predecessors, I need hardly say, proved to be quite as unfounded.

So, as soon as I was decently able, I slipped away to the seclusion of the library, where I could be alone with my thoughts, and ruefully ponder the awesome plight which, in the light of my now being so unequivocally exposed, I unhappily found myself.

Hazardous enough as had been my situation before, it had now become so imperilled, that I could not see how I was going to be able to make any sort of a move without my being under constant dread that Crab Snade might be lurking somewhere in the shadows. Albeit that there was some small advantage, I supposed, in my having been so clearly forewarned of their intentions. Not that I could see that my prospects were really any the less bleak, for all that!

It was of course true that, with the evidence of the coded sheets, a charge of high treason could now, I imagine, be preferred against Cruden. However, as much of a relief to me as his incarceration would be, if such a course were pursued, any chance I might have of his leading me to the arch-conspirator of the organisation – which was, after all, the chief object of my mission – would thereby be lost.

Anyway, I had little opportunity to brood further upon the seeming hopelessness of it all, for just then Joe appeared, to assist me with the cataloguing. A task in which, I might mention, we were already making some considerable headway, and one which in the event – albeit an unlikely one – of my being there to complete it, could well furnish a, by no means valueless, record of the library's contents. Or so I was beginning to flatter myself.

Howsoever that might be, Joe's arrival was, as always, most welcome. His cheerful disposition, as well as the droll nature of his incessant chatter, being such that it was impossible to remain dejected in his company for long, so that all black thoughts were, anyway for the while, soon dispelled.

In my guise as a cataloguer of books, he looked upon me, I think, as something akin to a fellow servant, and as a consequence treated me with a degree of familiarity which, apart from affording me much amusement, was instrumental to my learning a good deal of what was going on in Gravesend and, more particularly, something of the way of life at the "Three Daws", as well as of the manor and its occupants.

Of his devotion to Sir George I have already given some indication, and that such feelings were reciprocated, there has, I am sure, been ample evidence. That he was equally devoted to Miss Catherine was also quite evident. Their bond of mutual affection having, I gathered, been forged very early in life. Being much of an age, they had grown up at the manor together, and from the way Joe had spoken, it was plain that, in spite of their difference in station, nothing had been done to discourage their childhood intimacy.

That I was all eagerness to hear as much as he could tell me of Miss Catherine, must here be owned; for truth to tell, from the moment of our first meeting, there had arisen within me certain heart stirrings which – deeply significant and of far-reaching consequence, as they were to be to myself – would nevertheless make tedious reading to dilate upon, so I will, anyway for the moment, say no more.

Of the high regard in which Sir George was held in the neighbourhood, there could also be no disputing. From Joe's account, he was clearly as much loved by his tenants, as he was liked and respected by the people of Gravesend in general; to whom he stood in the position of both squire and magistrate. In which latter capacity, he had, I gathered, a reputation for administering justice with both compassion and leniency.

Something of which I was also to learn, was the way in which the family's fortunes had sadly declined. Sir George's old father, Sir Horace, had apparently been a notorious profligate and, by the reckless squandering of his very considerable inheritance, had whittled away the estates to a mere fraction of what they had once been.

Unhappily, Sir George, in his turn, had done nothing, it seemed, to rectify matters; and by a partiality for the gaming-tables had compromised much of what was left, and would in Joe's opinion, "have done the lot" had not the timely intervention of a profitable marriage, and the responsibilities of a family, prevailed upon him to forswear the allurements of London, and settle down to the more prosaic life of Gravesend.

That he was still, nevertheless, fond of a wager, I could tell by the eagerness with which I had noticed him devour the sporting papers. Something he was obliged to do with the utmost circumspection, I gathered from Joe when Lady Thurlow happened to be about.

She, at least from his account, appeared to be a veritable virago in fact, of whom everyone, including Sir George himself, went in considerable awe.

It was thus not surprising, especially from what I knew of Joe's casual ways, that he regarded her enforced absence as a heaven-sent deliverance.

Not that he was alone in his opinion, for it was, I gathered, one which was generally shared below stairs, where great had been the dismay upon it being rumoured that Sir George had some hope, at last, of arranging his wife's repatriation. That the report had, in truth, some foundation I knew, for he had announced as much to the rest of us only the day before. If without, I sensed, quite the enthusiasm a devoted husband might have been expected to evince.

It was Dr Argent, however, of whom I was particularly anxious to learn something more; especially as Sir George, in spite of their long acquaintance, had been able to impart singularly little. It was apparently some seven years or so since he had first settled in Gravesend where, although he had succeeded to no established practice, had soon acquired a considerable following. Sir George had been one of his earliest patients, and a particularly grateful one, owing to the relief he had obtained from some herbal mixture or other that the doctor had prescribed for his gout, an affliction to which he had long since been a martyr. Thus had their friendship begun, and led subsequently to Sir George's open invitation to the doctor to dine at the manor whenever he was free to do so.

In spite of their long acquaintance, however, so discreet had the doctor always been concerning himself and his affairs, that Sir George knew nothing of his antecedents or, indeed, really much else about him. That he was a bachelor and lived, save for one manservant, alone in an unpretentious house situated a little way out of Gravesend was, in fact, about all that I could discover. To this, Joe, as I have said, was able to add really very little. Although he did speak darkly of whispers current down in Gravesend of weird goings on in the secrecy of the doctor's house, experiments on animals, dead bodies and the like.

He had apparently been sent there once to collect some medicine, and had been admitted to what sounded like a laboratory, where there were "a lot of glass things abubblin' and smokin'." But he hadn't apparently seen any dead bodies. "Not that there mayn't 'ave bin," he added darkly. "I jus' didn't care to stop and look around. As soon as I'd picked up the physic, I scuttled off quick, I can tell yer!"

It was, of course, Joe's close association with the "Three Daws" in which his greatest value to me lay, especially as he never needed any encouragement to talk about Cruden or the day-to-day goings on at the inn.

That Cruden was not a native of Gravesend was one thing I was able to discover. He had, in fact, been born and bred in Cornwall, where, in his earlier days, he had achieved some local renown as a wrestler. This had prompted him to graduate to the boxing-ring and it had been the attraction of the fatter rewards to be gained nearer London, which had induced him to leave his native county.

For a year or two he had worked as a bargeman, at the end of which time he had, by his pugilistic prowess, accumulated sufficient prize-money to enable him to purchase the freehold of the "Three Daws".

Shortly afterwards his wife had died, and his niece, Sally, who, as it chanced, had just then been orphaned by the successive deaths of both her parents from the smallpox, had been prevailed upon to leave Cornwall and join him in the management of the inn, with such happy consequences for Joe as have already been related.

That he considered the inn to be no proper sort of abode for Sally and the children, I had been left in no doubt, however. For, although Joe did all he could to help when he was able to escape his manorial duties, it was obvious that the girl was treated as little more than a drudge, being so hard put upon by her uncle, that she had little time to spare to be with Joe and the children. In addition, there were times, notably when he was flush with drink, when Cruden had made their lives intolerable. Indeed, upon more than one occasion, so violent had he become that they had been obliged to flee the inn for fear of what he might do to them.

Thus, all in all, it would have been surprising if Joe had retained any sort of regard for the man. On the contrary, that he held him in considerable abhorrence had, in fact, soon become quite obvious.

Indeed, so confident was I of his loathing of Cruden, that there began to be planted in my mind the seeds of a notion, ill fated as it was to be, I fear, to take Joe into my confidence and seek his collaboration.

In this, however, I am anticipating a little, for it was not, as I remember, until some day or so later – and after much soul searching – that I did eventually bring myself to approach him. Anyway, that morning our relationship was still an uncomplicated one, as yet undeepened by the dangers which we were shortly to share.

"There may be a quantity o' learnin' along o' these books," said Joe, suddenly interrupting my thoughts, "but from the amount o' dust that's lyin' atop of 'em, I wouldn't be thinkin' that there was many about 'ere as was eager for it. Why, you could plant a row of taters along o' these."

"I imagine you might well," I replied with a laugh, as he blew a great cloud of dust from the pile he was handing down.

"I 'spect you've read most of 'em though, 'aven't yer Sir? Spendin' all yer time in libraries and the like."

"No, I'm afraid I can't say that I have," I said. "And from what I have seen of them so far, I don't think that I'd really have much wish to. I don't imagine you get much time for reading yourself, do you Joe?"

"'Fraid I don't, Sir. Books and me, as yer might say, are not much acquainted. The plain fact is, Sir, I can't read. I've often thought about 'avin' a go, but I never seem to 'ave got round to it. Sally always spells out anythin' that I want to know. She's a rare scholard. Even got the children alearnin' of their letters, A, B, C, and that."

"Did you never get to school then, Joe?" I asked.

"Well, you might say as I got there sometimes, but no more often than I could 'elp. The old woman that 'ad charge of us 'ad too ready an 'and with the birch for my likin', and I wasn't exactly one of 'er favrites as yer might say," responded Joe feelingly.

"But didn't you tell me your mother was a great reader? How was it she never instructed you?"

"She did sometimes 'ave a go Sir, but I never seemed to get the 'ang of it. P'raps it was the sort of books she 'ad, the Bible, prayer books and the like, which put me off. All evenin' she'd 'ave us children sittin' round 'er listenin' to 'er readin' of 'em and scarcely understandin' a word; leastways, I didn't. I went and 'id 'er Bible once, but it was no good, for she found it quick enough. Said as God 'ad told 'er where it was. And I reckon 'e 'ad, for I'd 'idden it where you wouldn't 'ave easily 'it upon it."

"You really must have been an incorrigible little boy, Joe!" I laughed. "But your father now, shouldn't he have taken you in hand?"

"I'm afraid 'e couldn't Sir. I wasn't long born when 'e died, you see. 'E fell off a shrimp boat and was drowned. I 'ave 'eard tell 'e meant to, and when I thinks o' mother, I sometimes thinks there mayn't 'ave been some truth on it."

As he was speaking he had happened to place beside me a set of volumes, which, by their new appearance, promised, unlike the vast majority of the books there, to be a fairly recent addition to the library. They comprised, I discovered, as I placed them on the desk, *Hasted's History and Topographical Survey of Kent* and, as a glance at the title page of the first volume confirmed, the work was, in fact, a fairly recent publication. Anyway, I had entered the relevant particulars into a catalogue, and was collecting them up for Joe to replace, when I noticed that there was a marking slip projecting from between the pages of one of them.

Idly curious to see what had been of such interest to the reader, I laid the volume open, to discover that the chapter which had been thus earmarked, was the one dealing with the coastal area of the county.

With my curiosity by this time somewhat more aroused, I was proceeding to turn over some of the adjoining pages when my gaze was met by a folded piece of paper which had lain concealed there. As I unfolded the sheet, I was to discover, with a quickening of interest, that across it had been drawn a series of irregular lines, above which, and at irregular intervals, had been inscribed groups of geometrical symbols, triangles and circles in varying combinations; whilst below the lines, and in close proximity to the other symbols, had been penned, again variously, the Greek characters alpha, beta and delta.

So totally absorbed did I become in my puzzled scrutiny of all this, that I had, for the moment, become quite oblivious of Joe; who meanwhile had been standing patiently beside me with a further pile of books.

"I am sorry to have kept you waiting, Joe," I said, as I was all at once reminded of his presence.

"That's all right, Sir, it's no trouble. I'll just put 'em down 'ere on the desk and collect some more," he answered cheerfully.

"I really think we've done enough for one morning, don't you think so Joe? Anyway, it must be nearly time for luncheon. You run along and I'll put these books back myself," I said, anxious as I was to be alone with my discovery.

When he had left I eagerly set to re-examining the sheet. The delineations had all been done with considerable care, as was plain from the neat way in which they had been executed. But what they, and the symbols, could have been meant to signify, I was at a loss to conceive; until it suddenly dawned upon me that the irregular lines might well represent certain sections of the Kentish coastline, and, if this was so, couldn't the symbols perhaps be a means of indicating the dispositions of our anti-invasion forces in those areas? Did such an explanation, I thought, really seem so fanciful? Whatever the case, I could think of no other which was any the more likely, and whether my assumption was correct or not, there at least seemed to be no doubt that someone – and from the fresh appearance of the sheet it must have been fairly recently – had had occasion to take rather more than a casual interest in the topography of one of the likely areas of a French invasion.

That he could simply have been some amateur strategist or other – his choice of Greek symbols indicating, perhaps, a classical turn of mind – was very possible, I had to admit.

Nevertheless, as I then set about making a careful transcript, my thoughts began to postulate all manner of startling and sinister surmises.

Chapter XIV

It must have been during the afternoon of that same day, if my memory serves me right, that a fever, which was to keep me to my bed for the next couple of days or so, first laid its hold upon me. I was sitting quietly in the library, with my thoughts full of my morning's discovery and all its possible implications when, of a sudden, the bookshelves began, or so it seemed, to sway and heave around me.

I was, at first, inclined to attribute it to the heat of the room, which, as a consequence of the huge log fire which was kept burning there night and day, tended to become oppressive.

However, no sooner had the fit passed, than I began to shiver and shake, and to be seized by a heavy sense of malaise. Indeed it soon became quite clear that some kind of chill, occasioned, no doubt, by the drenching I had received on the hillock, was overtaking me.

As the afternoon wore on my plight grew steadily worse. My limbs began to ache intolerably, my throat felt as if it was on fire, and whenever I stood up, I was overcome by a helpless dizziness.

By dinner time, so thoroughly miserable did I feel that, having made my excuses to Sir George and Miss Catherine, I snatched up a candle and stole wearily to my bed, trusting that a good night's sleep would see an end to it. But alas, it was not to be. Far from achieving any repose I lay there for most of the night in a sort of feverish delirium. Such fitful sleep as I did manage to summon, being visited by a phantasmagoria of the weirdest dreams imaginable.

One moment, I remember, I was climbing, or rather floating, towards the old windmill which, as I came up to it, suddenly resolved itself into the quarter-deck of the *Sirius* where I was being hoisted to the yardarm by a triumphant Major Fripp. The next moment, I and Sir George, together with Miss Beauchamp, who had charge of the reins, were aloft the gig as we were being pursued across the marshes by a horde of French soldiery. And then again, in another nightmarish fantasy, which I have especial reason to remember – for by some strange chance it anticipated, anyway in broad outline, something I was actually to experience – I was in desperate and leaden-footed flight from Cruden, through the rambling passages of the "Three Daws". A nightmare which, I might mention, even now still occasionally comes to terrify me out of my sleep.

Anyway, as the night advanced, my fever became so hectic, and I began to suffer, besides, such excruciating pains in my head and limbs, that as I continued to lie there in the dark morbidly speculating upon the nature of my disorder, I was reminded of a strange contagion with which a number of seamen aboard the *Sirius* had been stricken a few weeks before. The malady had, as I recalled, quite mystified Captain Yelland, as well as the old loblolly man, who had declared that he had seen nothing like it in all his long years at sea.

The poor fellows, as they had lain tossing and groaning in their hammocks, had, at first, complained of much the same symptoms as I appeared to have; whilst their bodies had, in due course, turned a bright yellow. And further, as I remembered with a shudder, two or three of them had eventually succumbed to the affliction!

Filled with alarm by this gruesome recollection, I lay there, I remember, in considerable dread for dawn to break, ever more convinced, as the minutes slowly passed, that my skin would reveal the ominous discoloration. Happily, however, anyway as yet, my fears were to be proved groundless when it became clear, by the first light, that, apart from a certain flushness about the face, my skin was still its usual hue.

A relief to me as this was, I nevertheless still felt utterly wretched, and when Joe arrived to call me I was unable to raise anything more than a perfunctory grunt in reply to his cheerful greeting of "Good-mornin', Sir. No sign of the Frenchies yet. Can't think what can be keepin' 'em with all 'em boats lyin' there ready, and the tides right an' all. Still, it won't be long now, Sir, I'll reckon," he added, with evident relish, as he poured out the shaving water.

"No, I imagine it won't, Joe," I managed to retort, with, I am afraid, little enthusiasm. Indeed, the way I was feeling just then, I don't think I would have much cared if he had informed me that the French were storming the manor itself.

"They say as Old Boney 'as 'is armies all ready and lined up in the boats just waitin' for 'is order to shove off. It's just the weather that's not to his likin' that's keepin' 'im, I suppose," continued Joe, as he turned towards the bed. "That's all it must be. 'E'll be 'ere soon enough – Why! Are you all right, Sir?" he then suddenly broke off to exclaim, as he approached my bed.

"No, I'm afraid I'm not feeling too well, Joe. It must be some kind of chill, I imagine."

"You certainly don't look too good, Sir. You'd best stay where you are. I'll bring yer breakfast up. Don't yer worry."

"No thank you, Joe. It's very kind of you. But I don't think I could eat anything," I said, my stomach giving a sudden heave at the very thought of food.

"I 'ope it's nothing too serious, Sir," Joe then added lugubriously, as he bent over to have a closer look at me. "There's bin some funny complaints goin' about these parts of late. Some poor folks as I've 'eard 'ave bin taken off scarce afore the doctor could get to 'em. As right as rain one day and afeedin' the worms the next, as yer might say."

"Oh! I don't think it can be anything as bad as that," I replied, with an attempt at a laugh. Not that I altogether relished his macabre allusion.

"I wouldn't be too sure, Sir. You look awful sick to me. It couldn't be that marsh ague p'raps now, could it? I've seen 'em like this, all 'ot and red on the face and shiverin' and shakin' in their beds," he then added, hastily moving back a pace or two as he did so, his face a mixture of wonderment and alarm, as he continued to gaze down at me from a safer distance.

"If you go on like this, Joe, you'll have me believing that there really is something seriously amiss with me," I grunted with some irritation, for his grim forebodings were certainly doing nothing to allay my own direful apprehensions.

"Oh! I'm sure you've no need to worry, Sir. I've known of quite a few as 'ave got over it," my Job's comforter then went on to add. "Still, Sir, I think I ought to go and fetch Sir George to come and 'ave a look at yer. I should just catch 'im afore he starts 'is breakfast." And before I could stop him, he was out through the door and hurrying off down the passage, leaving me to speculate upon his gruesome prognostications, as I waited for Sir George to arrive, which he shortly did.

"Joe tells me that you're not feeling too well, Farrant. Some sort of fever is it?" he cried in a tone of reassuring cheerfulness, as he came over to peer down at me.

"There's a devilish lot of it about. I had a dose of it meself a while back. It makes you feel wretched, I know. Sweated like a pig, I remember. Felt as if me limbs were being racked. Didn't last more than a couple of days though. After that, was as right as rain again. Anyway, this'll soon put you to rights. There's nothing like it, in spite of what that old quack Argent says. It's the best medicine there is. Three or four bottles and you'll soon be on your feet again." And so saying he proceeded to fill a glass from a decanter which he had brought with him, and which contained, I could only imagine, some pet medicinal concoction. Having filled the glass to the brim, he then leant over and held it to my lips. Apprehensive as to what it might be, I was careful at first, to take no more than a tentative sip; only to discover that it tasted remarkably like port wine, and having, at Sir George's insistence, gulped down the remainder, I could be in little doubt that this, in fact, was what it was!

"There, that'll soon make you feel better. There's no physic like it," he declared. "I'd as soon have a bottle or two of good vintage port by me at such times, than Argent's whole dispensary of tricks put together. Damn me if I wouldn't!" Even had I a mind to, I was given small chance to challenge this therapeutic pronouncement, for he already had a further glass poured out and would not be satisfied until I had drained it.

"Now, just let that soak into your veins and I'll warrant you'll soon be feeling yourself again. I'll leave the decanter so that you can help yourself, and I'll see to it that another one's brought up later."

"It's very kind of you, Sir George, but I'm sure this one will be more than sufficient," I said, eyeing the decanter, which was a sizeable one, and must have contained a good bottle and a half.

"Nonsense me boy! You just empty that one down, and another like it, and I'll wager you'll be as right as a trivet by tomorrow; if there's anything else you want, just pull the bellrope, and Craddock will come and see to it."

And with this he left me, to hurry off to his breakfast.

As the morning progressed I had to admit, as Sir George had promised, that I did soon begin to feel very much better. The pains about my limbs had disappeared, my fever appeared to have abated, and, all in all, it really did seem that my earlier fears concerning the seriousness of my affliction were unfounded.

Although how much of my improvement could be attributed to Sir George's panacea, rather than to the natural course of the malady, it was difficult to say.

Whatever the case, come the afternoon, I had drained not only the original decanter, but also a good part of its replacement with which old Craddock had duly appeared; and it was debatable whether I was not, by that time, more drunk than ailing!

Thus I continued to lie there fitfully dozing and tippling the hours away; the only interruption to my solitude being periodic visits from Joe, who came, or so he said, "to see if I might be wantin' somethin'." But in reality, I shrewdly guessed to discover whether I had begun to exhibit any further symptoms of the marsh ague which, largely from hearsay I suspected, as well as a fanciful imagination, he had endowed with the most bizarre assortment of symptoms imaginable.

Anyway, as the hours passed, and my malady persisted upon its prosaic course, Joe's evident disappointment that his forebodings were not being fulfilled began so to affect me that, eventually, I decided that I must do something to rectify my shortcomings, and make some attempt when he next appeared, to simulate some of the features which he had so graphically described. It was a childish caprice, of course, and one largely inspired, I had no doubt, by the quantity of port wine which I had drunk! Whatever its inspiration it was a prank which, as you shall see, I was heartily to regret; destined as it was to rebound in no small discomfiture, upon myself.

Howsoever, when next I heard Joe's step approaching, I was all set for a well-rehearsed performance, and when he came in, instead of the rational patient he had formerly encountered, there was I in an apparent state of complete mental and physical disorder, displaying all the weirdest contortions of body and gibberings of speech that my fancy could devise!

For a minute or more he just stood there transfixed as he gazed down upon me with a look of such wondrous amazement, that I had the greatest difficulty in keeping a straight face. Indeed, I was just about to dissolve into helpless laughter, when, all at once, his look of spellbound fascination gave way to one of alarm and, before I could stop him, he had darted off through the door and was away up the corridor. His urgent intention being, as I could only ruefully imagine, to acquaint some member of the household or other with the news of the dire turn which, as he could only have supposed, my condition had taken.

This was something I had certainly not bargained for, and as I lay there upbraiding myself for indulging in such a senseless prank, I anxiously speculated upon whom it might be that Joe would summon.

Sir George, as I knew, was out exercising with the yeomanry; whilst Miss Beauchamp, as was her custom of an afternoon, would be resting in her room, where doubtless, Joe would be chary of disturbing her. The most likely recipient of Joe's alarming intelligence must therefore, I imagined, be Miss Catherine; a visit from whom in less embarrassing circumstances I would, as you will have gathered, have looked forward to with eager expectation.

Instead it was, I fear, with no little disquiet that I awaited her arrival. For what would she think of me, I reflected, when I came to explain that Joe had simply been the victim of a childish leg-pull and that she had been deceived into nothing more than a fool's errand.

However, as the minutes passed and no one appeared, I began to feel easier in my mind. I must, I thought, either have mistaken Joe's intention, or Miss Catherine having, perhaps, been unavailable, there had been no one from whom he could suitably seek advice.

So having poured myself another glass of port, I proceeded to settle back in the confident expectation that Joe would shortly return by himself; and finding me to be perfectly rational once again, the whole ridiculous episode would be done with.

Anyway, in this reassuring belief I must have dozed off again, only to be suddenly awoken by the sound of voices approaching along the corridor outside.

My immediate reflection was that it must be Joe, together with Sir George, and I was still in the throes of debating within myself whether I should hold my peace or make a clean breast of my tomfoolery when, to my consternation, instead of Sir George, there appeared the burly figure of Dr Argent with Joe close at his heels! This certainly was a dénouement that I had not anticipated. It having, foolishly perhaps, never occurred to me that Joe would go to any such lengths as this!

Indeed, so taken aback was I that I was at a complete loss as to how I should respond. Loath as I would have been to embarrass Joe, had it have been Sir George I would, I think, have made a full confession.

Dr Argent, however, was quite another matter, he being, I imagined, scarcely the sort of person who would relish such levity, even at the best of times, let alone when it had been the cause of such a trespass upon his valuable time.

Nevertheless, there can be no doubt that I should, of course, even if only to spare him further trouble, have owned up to what I had been about. But somehow such an admission, with all its attendant embarrassment and humiliation, was something I could not bring myself to face, and so coward that I was, I decided to keep my peace and say nothing.

"I am sorry, Mr Farrant, to hear that you are not well. Leckley here appears to be most concerned about you and was insistent that I came over at once," he said solemnly, as he approached my bed.

"It's very good of you to come, Doctor. But I am sure there was no need to have bothered you. It's some sort of chill that's all," I replied hastily.

"Very likely, very likely. But from what Leckley here tells me, you must, I think, have had a convulsion of some kind," he declared gravely as he seated himself on the bed beside me.

"Oh! I don't think I could have had anything like that. I might have been a bit delirious and had some sort of nightmare; but that's all it was, I am quite sure," I hastily replied, as he continued to look searchingly down at me in a cold, clinical appraisal, whilst giving every now and then that sudden sideways twitch of the head which, as I have mentioned, was such a peculiar mannerism of his.

"I fear that it seemed to be rather more than that. Isn't that so?" asserted the doctor turning to Joe for confirmation.

"No, it wasn't just a nightmare you can be certain o' that, Sir," affirmed Joe emphatically. "'E wasn't asleep you see, Sir. 'Is eyes were wide open, all starin' like. And as I said, there was this gurglin' in 'is throat, and 'is mouth was all afrothin' and 'is whole body was twistin' about somethin' terrible."

As much ingenuity as I may have put into my performance, Joe's description was, nevertheless, I felt, a good deal exaggerated.

"Have you ever had anything like it before? A fit of that kind, I mean?" went on the doctor earnestly.

"No, no, never," I quickly reassured him.

"You are quite certain?" he then insisted.

"Yes, absolutely," I replied with vehemence. "In fact, I've always been very healthy. I'm sure it was nothing like a fit, as Joe seems to have imagined. Anyway, I'm already feeling very much better so I don't think there's any need to take up any more of your valuable time Doctor. I can only apologise for having troubled you like this, especially as you must have got other . . ."

"It's no trouble, I can assure you," interrupted the doctor. "These fevers can be most deceptive. They tend, I fear, to fluctuate a good deal so that any sense of well-being is liable to be short-lived, the bouts returning with even greater severity than before." With this he then started to question me about my symptoms which, such as they were, I then went on to recount.

He nodded gravely when I had finished, and then proceeded to examine me. He felt my pulse, looked down my throat with the aid of a candle, thumped me about the chest, and, in fact, went pretty well all over me, the whole being performed without a word of comment, and with such a grim air of solemnity, that something of my old fears regarding the seriousness of my complaint began to return.

When he had finished with me he said nothing for a while but just sat there as if in deep deliberation whilst I anxiously awaited his verdict.

"Your condition, I'm afraid, Mr Farrant, is rather more serious that I had at first thought," he pronounced at last. "No, no, you mustn't alarm yourself," he then added hastily, doubtless observing my look of dismay. "You're in no real danger, I'm sure." For all the reassurance of his qualification there was, however, I sensed, no great ring of conviction about it.

"However, it appears," he went on darkly, "that your blood must have been poisoned by some infection or other and, as a consequence, has become seriously overheated, and this, it must have been, that caused the convulsion which Leckley observed. No harm, perhaps, has been done as yet, but should you suffer another such fit, it could well be most injurious. Therefore, I am sure that the wisest course would be to relieve you of some of this overheated blood."

"You mean that I shall have to be bled!" I exclaimed in some alarm.

"Oh! It's really nothing very terrible," rejoined the doctor cheerfully. "Just a few ounces, that's all. It's quite a painless procedure, and when it's over you'll feel all the better for it, I can promise you."

My ill-considered jest had certainly come home to roost in no mean fashion, I thought ruefully, as the doctor began to search into his bag for the necessary implements. Was it even now too late, I thought, as I espied the scalpel, to make a clean breast of it all! However much embarrassment such a confession would occasion me, might it not be preferable to losing a quantity of one's life-blood so needlessly?

In fact, I did, I think, begin to murmur something or other to that effect, but so little heed did he appear to give to what I was trying to say, that I soon desisted.

Anyway, by this time, the preparations for the letting were almost complete, and realising that further resistance would be fruitless, I decided that there was nothing for it, but to resign myself to the sanguinary procedure with as good a grace as possible.

And so, with Joe standing close by me in readiness with the bowl, the capacity of which, I must own, had already filled me with no small alarm, the doctor took a firm grip of my wrist with his left hand, and then seizing hold of the scalpel, held it poised over the bend of my right elbow.

"Just keep quite still, Mr Farrant. The pain will only be momentary I can assure you," he said, as, with averted eyes, I tensed myself for the knife.

Indeed, as he had avowed, so little did I feel that I could scarcely believe that he had made the incision until, upon turning my head, I saw the crimson jet spurting into the bowl.

Uncanny an experience as it was, thus passively to witness the very essence of one's being draining away unchecked, I was, nevertheless, content at first to observe the phenomenon quite calmly, if not with a certain fascination.

But then, as the flow was permitted to continue, and the quantity of blood I had already lost seemed to have well exceeded the few ounces the doctor had mentioned, a creeping sense of unease began to take hold of me.

I had no real knowledge of the amount of blood one's body contained or, indeed, the fraction of it that could be safely withdrawn. Nevertheless, from my perhaps prejudiced viewpoint, it soon seemed, as I continued to observe the receptacle being inexorably accommodated, that I must surely be near to losing as much as I could comfortably spare. Try and console myself, as I did, with the reflection that such misgivings must be the common experience of anyone undergoing such an operation for the first time, and that, besides, Dr Argent, by repute a most competent physician, must know what he was about, as the exodus was permitted to continue my sense of mild unease soon began to be replaced by one of considerable anxiety.

In search of reassurance, I scanned the doctor's face for some sign of encouragement, or at least some indication that he was near to being satisfied. To my consternation, with his head nodding almost continuously now, his expression looked to be more grimly purposeful than ever; whilst the hold he had of my wrist seemed, if anything, to have tightened.

Unable to contain my anxiety any longer, I at last felt constrained to murmur, albeit matter-of-factly, for I was still chary of betraying my disquiet, a query as to whether he might be nearly finished.

It is very possible, of course, with his attention so fully engrossed in the operation, that he did not hear me. Anyway, he certainly gave no indication that he had done so, his impassive demeanour exhibiting not the slightest flicker of acknowledgement of my apprehension, unless it be, perhaps, of some further hardening of the grip he had upon me.

It was this, his seemingly callous indifference to my, surely not unreasonable plea for reassurance, which, I think, first began to arouse within me, intimations of such a sinister nature as suddenly to turn what blood I had left cold within me.

By a mind in its sober course, a conception so fantastic would, I am sure, have been summarily dismissed, and that it was not so, can only be attributed, I imagine, to the intoxicating influence both of my fever and the quantity of wine I had drunk.

Howsoever, the terrifying notion was not only entertained, but by quick degrees soon became a ghastly obsession. I was, I was quite convinced, being bled to death!

To this day I still shudder at the recollection of that awful moment, as this terrible belief took hold of me, whilst my life's blood continued to flow inexorably from me.

To add to the horror of it all, my room, together with its homely furniture, seemed of a sudden to have undergone a sinister transformation; in the midst of which Dr Argent and Joe appeared to have become participants in the enactment of some primitive rite, of which I was the victim and my bed the sacrificial altar.

To find words adequately to describe my feelings, as I lay there in the throes of this horrible conception is, I fear, beyond me. A sickening terror was, I suppose, the paramount emotion; a terror made the more profound by my apparent helplessness. For coincidental with the onset of my fearful delusion, a stupefying paralysis had taken hold of my limbs, so that my body had become, as it were, petrified.

For how long I lay there in the grip of this frightful fantasy, it is difficult to say. In point of measured time its duration, I have little doubt, was scarcely more than a minute; but to myself, as experienced, it seemed an eternity.

It must be questionable, indeed, whether I was by this time fully conscious, for I must admit that my memory of it has more the quality of a nightmare than of an actual happening, and what I do in fact recall, must be very largely subjective.

However, my recollection that I did, in fact, manage at last to shake off my inertia, and make a frantic attempt to release my arm from the doctor's remorseless grip is, I am sure, a substantial one; as in my memory of the futility of it, for struggle as I did, so effective a restraint did he have upon me with his other free arm, that I was quite powerless to break his hold, and soon fell back exhausted with the attempt.

Bereft of any capability of further resistance, and in the conviction that all was inevitably up with me, my earlier sense of terror seemed, strangely as I remember, to have subsided. Indeed, it was with a feeling of something approaching serenity, as I recollect, that I awaited what I imagined to be my imminent dissolution. I had earlier been aware of an insistent drumming about my head which had reached such a pitch, that the whole room had seemed to reverberate with it. But this had quite gone, and in its place a cold numbness had begun to steal upwards through my limbs, and into my trunk; until eventually my mind seemed to have become a thing so apart, that all sense of physical being was quite lost to me.

In fact, so complete was this sense of dissociation, that I seemed to have floated quite away from my corporeal self, and to be suspended upon a horizontal plane some few feet above where I actually lay. As I have said, any emotion of terror had, by this time, quite left me. On the contrary, it was, as I recall, with a feeling of complete unconcern; indeed, one of complacency, that I was continuing from my, as it were, ethereal viewpoint, to observe the exsanguination of my body that was taking place beneath me; when, all of a sudden, there came a resounding crash as of something exploding on the floor below me.

With the shock of it, and on the instant, I was one with my body again. The former trance-like state had quite evaporated, and simultaneously there came the realisation that, although the stream of blood was still issuing from it, my arm was perfectly free.

Hurriedly snatching off the tourniquet, I quickly withdrew my arm beneath the safety of the sheets, and began feverishly to compress the bleeding point with the sleeve of my nightshirt. So overcome with relief was I, that it was some moments before it occurred to me to wonder what could have become of the doctor and Joe, who appeared to have vanished.

At first I could only imagine, unaccountable as it was – for the doctor's bag still lay there on the bed beside me – that they must already have left, until upon hearing a groan, I looked down to discover Joe lying there prostrate on the floor, with the doctor bending over him.

How they had come to be there I had little time to conjecture, for I must, just then, have dozed off, and, when I next awoke, it was morning, with the rooks cawing in the elms outside.

As I lay there still only half awake, and something of the previous day's happening began to filter through to me, my first belief was that it had all been nothing more than a fearful dream; and it was only when I became conscious of the dull pain in my arm, and felt over the point where the incision had been made, was I persuaded that it had, essentially at least, actually taken place.

My memory of it all was none the less very confused, and how much of what I did hazily recall was more delusional than otherwise, I could by no means be sure. Although my recollection of there having been something decidedly shameful about my behaviour was, I feared, only too substantial.

Anyway, startled as I was to discover how much paler I appeared to be, I felt, apart from a certain languor, almost myself again. The fever seemed quite to have passed; my mind was clear, that aching about my limbs had disappeared, and all in all it really did seem, as Dr Argent had promised, that the blood letting had benefited me.

As I have said, I was still perplexed as to how much of what I remembered of the operation had actually happened, and how much was the purest fantasy. Particularly puzzling was that final, albeit shadowy vision I retained, of Joe lying there outstretched upon the floor, with Dr Argent kneeling beside him. Had I, I wondered, just imagined it all, or could it really have happened?

Whatever the explanation, the puzzle was soon likely to be resolved, for, just then, Joe himself appeared bearing a breakfast tray.

That he was not his usual jaunty self I could tell at once. Indeed, his customarily cheerful greeting of "Mornin' Sir," was uttered in so dispirited a tone as to be almost inaudible, and the hangdog manner in which he then proceeded to approach my bed could not have been more out of character.

"I don't know as whether boiled eggs is what yer might fancy, Sir? They're 'avin' kidneys downstairs, but I didn't think you'd be wantin' them, not being well like," he said apathetically, as he thrust the tray down beside me.

"No, I don't think I should," I said. "The eggs will do very well thank you. You don't seem to be quite your usual cheerful self, Joe. Is there anything wrong?" I then added anxiously as, his face a picture of dejection, he continued to stand there beside my bed.

"No, nothing Sir. I'm quite all right," he replied in the same sullen tone.

"It was very good of you to have gone to all that trouble in fetching the doctor," I then said, breaking the awkward silence that had then ensued. "That bleeding he gave me really does seem to have done me some good."

"It was no trouble, Sir," responded Joe laconically.

"I'm afraid I don't remember very much about it, but I don't think I behaved very well, when the doctor was with me, did I Joe?" I then ventured shamefacedly. For it had all at once occurred to me that his strange demeanour was, perhaps, just a way of expressing his disapproval of my unmanly conduct.

"Oh! You couldn't 'elp it, Sir. The way you were in that fever an' all, it wasn't surprisin'. It takes yer like that," responded Joe quickly, and in a tone of such reassurance that I knew at once that this could not be the explanation.

"I must say it gives you a weird feeling seeing your blood flowing away like that. I really thought he was never going to stop. You've never had anything like it done to you, I suppose, have you Joe?" I then said.

"No, Sir, I can't say as I 'ave, and I wouldn't care to neither. I'd be thinkin' all the while he might be takin' a drop too much, and I can't see as 'ow it could be put back again," responded Joe with something of his usual good humour.

"No, I don't imagine it could," I said, and then added tentatively, "the sight of all that blood didn't upset you then, Joe?"

As soon as I had put the question, I knew at once by his embarrassed look that my recollection of his prostrate form had, in fact, been no fanciful one, and that this, doubtless, was the reason for his discomfiture.

"You couldn't 'ave seen what 'appened then, Sir?" said Joe in bashful surprise.

"Why, how do you mean, Joe?" I said, thinking it best to feign complete ignorance.

"Well, the truth is, Sir," went on Joe awkwardly, "it did give me a turn. I don't know 'ow it was, but seeing' yer blood spurtin' into that bowl, and you goin' as white as a badger, fair made my stomach turn. Anyways, I must 'ave fainted off like, 'cos the next thing I knows I'm lyin' there all stretched out with yer blood all over me, and the doctor slappin' me face. And none too pleased he was about it neither. Not that I can blame 'im."

"Oh dear, I am sorry Joe. I had no idea anything like that had happened. I trust you didn't hurt yourself though?"

"It made me feel all queer like for a bit, and I 'as a lump on the back of me 'ead. No more 'arm that that, Sir. But there was a 'orrible mess, I can tell yer," added Joe sheepishly.

"It's nothing to be ashamed of Joe. It could have happened to anyone. Anyway, between the two of us, it seems that the doctor must have had quite a time of it!" I remarked laughingly.

"Yes, I reckon 'e did, Sir," agreed Joe giving a broad grin at last. "Any'ow, you seem to be a good bit better, Sir."

"Yes, thank you, Joe. I'm really feeling almost myself again."

"Well, if there's nothing more you'll be wantin' Sir, I'd best be off. For Sir George wants 'is boots cleaned afore 'e goes out, and I 'aven't started on 'em yet." And with his self-assurance plainly restored, he skipped out of the room, whilst I, hungrily, turned my attention to the boiled eggs and toast.

Chapter XV

As quick a recovery as I appeared to have made from the more immediate effects of my indisposition, I was soon to discover that it had, in truth, left me much debilitated. The slightest exertion demanded no mean effort, and whenever I had occasion to rise from my bed, I would sway about most disconcertingly.

For the most part, my limpness was, no doubt, attributable to my illness, although I was inclined to suspect that the quantity of blood I had lost was also, in some measure, responsible.

I was obliged therefore to keep to my bed for a further two or three days, before much semblance of strength returned to me. An imposition which was, I might add, not altogether unwelcome, honourably releasing me as it did meanwhile, from any active pursuance of my mission.

During this time both Sir George and Miss Catherine were, I should mention, kindness itself, and could not have done more to smooth the way of my recovery. Indeed, so greatly did I relish the frequent small attentions with which the latter found occasion to indulge me, that I only wished that my recovery could have been the slower.

Miss Beauchamp was, as well, scarcely less attentive, taking it upon herself to sit with me for a good hour or more each day, while she worked away at her embroidery. Although, I must admit, that much as I was touched by her kind solicitude, I did, I am afraid, find her visits a little wearisome; captive audience as I was, for the unburdening, in an almost ceaseless monologue, of the poor dear's seemingly unending catalogue of woes.

Paramount among these, as you may imagine, was her consuming dread of the impending invasion, and all the fearful happenings which she was quite certain were to follow upon it. Nothing that the pamphleteers had been able to conjure up being half as horrific as some of the atrocities she grimly prophesied for us. Indeed, so wildly preposterous were some of her forebodings, that I had the greatest difficulty, at times, in keeping a straight face.

As fanciful as I may have considered Miss Beauchamp's doom-laden predictions to be, I was, however, certainly anything but sanguine regarding my own fate which, as I lay there convalescing, I had perforce ample opportunity, dolefully, to reflect upon.

With my recovery proceeding all too rapidly, it was plain that within a day or so, I was likely to be well enough to resume my responsibilities; not, as I have said, that I could really see how I was going to set about doing so, at least not without exposing myself to the most fearful jeopardy.

At any rate by the morning of the fourth day of my indisposition, so much myself did I appear to be again, that I decided I could not, at least with an easy conscience, keep to my bed any longer; and so, after a leisurely breakfast, I reluctantly dressed, and made my way down to the library.

I was still a little unsure on my legs, but otherwise I had little to complain of and so, after spending the best part of the day with the books, I decided, when dusk arrived, that I would pay a further call upon Captain Wakeley to discover whether he had, perchance, received any communication from Mr Atterbury.

His reception of me, I need hardly say, was as timorous as ever, and having unceremoniously ushered me into his sanctum, he, without more ado, thrust into my hands a missive which he had, I gathered, received from Mr Atterbury only that morning.

Without any word of encouragement, or even the briefest commendation of what I had already achieved, which, I must admit, rather piqued me, it simply stated that the coded matter I had submitted was insufficient for a deciphering to be made, and would I therefore obtain further samples and despatch them forthwith; his letter concluding with an imperative to the effect that the matter was to be treated with the utmost urgency.

Put into no amiable humour by the unpalatable implications of this directive, I had little wish to prolong my stay as, indeed, clearly had the captain; so I soon made my departure and returned to the manor, with as heavy a heart as you can imagine as I contemplated all the perils incumbent upon the behest which Mr Atterbury had laid upon me.

That it was anything but an inviting one, I need scarcely say. Indeed, the mere thought even of making another surreptitious incursion to that attic room, was enough to send the shudders through me. I was at first, I must admit, powerfully tempted to shirk the whole issue. I would simply, I decided, let Mr Atterbury know that I had done what I could, but that it had, in the event, been impossible to fulfil his request. He, after all, would be none the wiser. But it was no good. Tempted as I was to funk it, the insistent voice of conscience would keep on intruding itself, until I was finally persuaded that, come what may, I must, at least, make the attempt.

Thus resolved, there was now the question of how I was going to set about it. And no easy one to decide was it. For, looked at from even the most sanguine of viewpoints, it was clearly going to be a most hazardous business.

For one thing, there was little likelihood, of course, that I was going to be afforded the kind of golden opportunity which I had previously enjoyed, and for another, with my activities now so fully exposed, Cruden and the others would be alert to my every move.

During the remainder of that evening and, indeed, well into the night, I continued restlessly to brood over all the daunting uncertainties which such an undertaking posed; especially as, with Mr Atterbury's insistence upon the urgency of the task, there could be no question of my biding my time.

Anyway, there seemed plainly to be no choice open to me, but to keep a continuous watch upon the inn and seize my chance if, and when, a favourable opportunity presented itself. Such then was my intended plan when I repaired to the library after breakfast the following morning, and I was, in fact, already trying to steel myself to set off for Gravesend, when I was reminded of my earlier notion of perhaps seeking Joe's co-operation. There could be no doubt, I argued, that in view of his close association with the "Three Daws", his assistance would be an invaluable advantage. I was aware, of course, that there would be a risk in making such an approach as, for all his apparent abomination of Cruden, I had no guarantee that he would not, in fact, choose to break the confidence. Still, this was a chance I would have to take, I decided, as, after some further heart searching, I eventually persuaded myself that, all things considered, I had really little to lose. And so, when he duly appeared a few minutes later, I proceeded, diffidently, to propose what I had in mind.

As to my doubts regarding his willingness to be of assistance to me, these were soon dispelled. For, having first evinced no small wonder and surprise upon my divulging what my true purpose in Gravesend was, he soon made it quite clear, as I went on to disclose something of the perfidious nature of Cruden's activities, that he would be game for anything.

Indeed, so demonstrably eager was he to do all in his power to help, that my only fear was that I might have difficulty in curbing his enthusiasm. Anyway, regarding the problem which I then put to him, namely of my gaining privy access to Cruden's sanctum, this, he was quite confident, would afford no great risk. In fact, that very evening apparently, a most favourable opportunity would arise, since Cruden had already informed him that he was going out, and had, in fact, requested Joe to be sure to make himself available to serve in the side parlour, as he was likely to be away for some time. Joe could not be certain at exactly what time Cruden would be leaving, but from his experience of similar excursions, it should be somewhere around eight o'clock and, or so Joe reassured me, I could count upon his being away for a good hour or more, which would certainly allow me, I imagined, more than adequate time for my purpose, especially as I now knew my way about the inn.

It really did seem, anyway upon the face of it, a most favourable opportunity, and all we had now to consider were the finer details of the plan's execution. For one thing, we had to decide upon a scheme whereby I would know when Cruden had, in fact, safely departed. My first idea, that I would simply loiter in the vicinity and wait for him to emerge, we dismissed as being too chancy, as, with three possible exits, I might well, in the dark, fail to spot him.

After examining various alternatives, we decided that our best plan would be for me to ensconce myself, some little while before eight o'clock, in the front parlour window of the "Pope's Head" tavern, which stood on the other side of the street a little way up from the "Three Daws", but which, nevertheless, would, so Joe assured me, provide an excellent vantage point from which I could keep a watch upon the side entrance of the latter. Our scheme being, that as soon as Cruden had left Joe would appear and then, as a signal that the coast was clear, ostentatiously wring out a cloth.

It having also been arranged that he would leave a lighted candle outside the attic room, our plan appeared to be complete, and as far as I could see, free of any undue risk. The only thing which really worried me was the possibility that Cruden might chance to return prematurely. If, perish the thought, such an eventuality should occur, it was decided that Joe would sound the alarm by loudly breaking forth into the whistled strains of Lillibullero which, he assured me, he was, in fact, in the habit of doing every now and then; so it would occasion no surprise or alarm save, I need hardly add, to myself of course!

All was thus settled between us, and on the face of it I had to admit that the plan did appear to be reasonably foolproof. Although I was not, perhaps, quite as confident as Joe, who plainly had no misgivings whatsoever, and cheerfully dismissed any reservations of my own, that I happened to interpose.

Indeed, as the afternoon wore on, and the time for my departure approached, I must confess that such confidence with which I had earlier been inspired by Joe, had largely disappeared; and it required no small effort of will, as well as several glasses of Sir George's excellent port wine, before I could bring myself to leave the security of the manor, and set out into the darkness for the riverside, foolishly neglecting, so befuddled by the port was I by then, to pocket my pistol. An omission which, as you will learn, I was most sorely to regret.

It was a cloudless and moonlit night, for which I was thankful. Nevertheless, I was in no humour to dawdle, and was careful as well to keep away from the hedgerows, constantly mindful as I was of the possibility of Crab Snade's shadowing menace.

In fact, at such a pace did I go that I reached the river front rather earlier than I had intended. So that when, after collecting a tankard of ale, I had stationed myself by the front parlour window of the "Pope's Head" I had, I discovered, rather more than half an hour to wait before Joe could be expected to appear. And a tense half hour it was, I remember, as with my gaze anxiously fixed upon the entrance of the "Three Daws", I sat there waiting for Joe to emerge with his signal.

Indeed, as eight o'clock approached, so beside myself with trepidation was I, that had it not been for the thought of what Joe would think of me, I would, I am sure, have abandoned the whole venture there and then, and returned to the manor. In any case, I was soon beginning to cherish the possibility of an honourable reprieve for, as the appointed hour arrived and there was still no sign of Joe, it seemed that Cruden may have decided, after all, not to go out.

No sooner had my hopes started to rise, however, than there was Joe with his dishcloth which, to my consternation, he then proceeded frantically to wave about more in the manner of a flag of truce before an advancing army, rather than giving it the casual wringing which, I had fondly imagined, we had agreed upon.

Still, it was no moment to worry about that, for time was clearly of the essence, and so, albeit with a heavy reluctance, I hurried over to the side parlour of the "Three Daws" where, having first peered in through a window to make sure that Crab Snade was not about, I then ventured in, and with a reassuring wink from Joe, furtively made my way across to the stairway.

So dark was it when I reached the top, that in spite of my earlier exploration, I feared that I would have difficulty in finding my way. But I need not have worried, for after making one or two wrong turnings as I groped my way along, I soon came to the stairway leading to Cruden's attic retreat.

There, thankfully, on the top step stood the lighted candle which Joe had dutifully left for me, and taking hold of it, I hurried on in, being careful as I did so, to leave the door well ajar, to ensure that I would not fail to hear Joe's whistled alarm in the event, heaven forbid, of Cruden's early return.

Everything, I discovered, was much as I had last seen it save, I noticed, for the addition of a copy of Lloyd's shipping list, which lay open on top of the desk.

Being anxious, as you can imagine, to be done with the task as quickly as possible, I at once set about tackling the appropriate drawer. This time, happily, the lock gave without any trouble and, to my relief, there lay the sheets as I had left them.

Having hurriedly searched out the sheet from which I had previously copied, I placed it beside my own sheet and feverishly began, by the aid this time, of a more powerful glass, which I had procured from the manor library, to transfer the code from where I had left off.

Unfortunately, such a feeble and wayward light did the candle afford, that, even with the advantage of the greater magnification which this other glass provided, it was soon clear that I was going to have no easy time of it distinguishing the dots, especially as I had to be mindful, all the while, of the scrupulous accuracy of the transcription.

Indeed, so strenuously was I obliged to concentrate, and so wholly absorbed in the task did I become, that I was soon quite lost to all sense of time and place. So much so, in fact, that, when after copying off the best part of one side of the sheet, I happened to glance at my watch, to discover to my alarm that I had already been up there a good hour or more, and that it must, therefore, of course, be somewhat longer than that since Cruden had left the inn.

Anyway, it was high time, I decided, that I made a move, especially as what I had already managed to transcribe must now surely be sufficient, I imagined, for a deciphering to be made. So, having replaced the sheet and re-secured the lock, I snuffed out the candle which I was careful to retain, together with its tray, and then made at once for the stairway.

I had, I think, reached about the third step down when, to my horror, there, all at once, came echoing up from below the unmistakable strains of Lillibullero!

Chapter XVI

Whether it was the note of urgency which I had detected in Joe's whistling, or whether it was just the mortal fear with which Cruden naturally inspired me, I cannot say. Anyway, I bounded down those stairs like a jackhare with the beagles after him. So precipitately in fact, that I missed the last step, I remember, and overbalancing, struck my head against the wall of the passageway opposite.

This, fortunately, seemed to shake some sense into me, making me realise that if I continued at such a headlong pace the resounding clatter of my feet on the bare floorboards would be the surest way of calling attention to my presence; and so, taking hold upon myself, I thence proceeded altogether more circumspectly.

It was just as well that I did, for I had reached no further than the turning into the next passageway, when I was stopped dead in my tracks by the low murmur of voices approaching from somewhere in the darkness below me.

Not daring to move, and with breath held tight, I stood anxiously listening as the sounds drew nearer, my fervent prayer being that they would simply prove to be a couple of lodgers returning for an early night, and thus destined for the bunk rooms further along.

For a while the voices did, indeed, appear to grow fainter, and I was encouraged to believe, with some easing of suspense, that my assumption had been correct. Unhappily, however, it was no more than an illusion, occasioned, perhaps, by some structural anomaly of the inn, for no sooner had I started to move stealthily forward again, than, of a sudden, the sound of their voices became much clearer, and with a start of horror, I was able to distinguish in the deep tones of one of them, the voice of Cruden!

For a moment or two, so stunned was I, that I just stood there in a sort of paralysis of fear, unable to move and quite incapable of any kind of decisive thought. When I eventually did rouse myself to the full peril of my situation my first impulse was to hurry on and attempt to brush past them, in the hope that Cruden would not recognise me.

But somehow the chance was more than I could bring myself to take, and I decided, more sensibly, or so it seemed, that my best ruse would be to retrace my steps, and seek refuge in the nearest of the two rooms, which, as I had noticed, opened on to the passageway behind me. There I would remain until they had safely passed on, and up to the attic room, whither, it now seemed likely, they must be making.

That I had not a moment to lose was all too apparent, for they were by now, as I could tell by the sound of them, no more than the length of the next corridor from me.

Furtively as I was able, for I was fearful lest they might yet hear me, I turned and made for the door of the first room, only to discover to my dismay that it was locked!

With a sickening sense of foreboding, I moved on to the next one. To my horror, it likewise was firmly secured!

I had now, it seemed, no choice but to make a run for it. Indeed, I had already half turned, when I was all at once reminded of that cubby room adjacent to Cruden's den. It was no time for deliberation. Indeed, if I had hesitated, they must have spotted me for I had barely reached the bottom of the stairs, when I heard them enter the corridor behind me.

Anyway, taking care to keep to a tiptoe, and with my heart leaping to my mouth with every creak of the boards, up them I scurried, and only just in the nick of time was I, for no sooner had I taken refuge among the bottles than I could hear them on the stairway below.

I was still fearful, nevertheless, that they might, by chance, have heard me, and it was thus in no little anguish of suspense that I remained crouched there in the darkness, as they continued to make their way up.

That any such fears were happily unfounded was soon apparent, however, for I could tell by the manner in which Cruden was speaking as they entered, that I was safe, at least for the present.

Now that I was able to relax a little, I had to consider what best I should do. That there was another door set into the opposite wall from where I crouched, I knew. But whither this might lead I had, of course, no idea; besides, I could scarcely hope to reach it, especially in the dark, without giving rise to some sound or other.

Plainly my wisest course was to remain where I was until they had left, and then make my escape. Meanwhile, by keeping my ears skinned, there was a chance that I might, perhaps, overhear something of value, as well as discover who Cruden's companion might be.

For, although I could distinguish something of the sense of what Cruden was saying, so quietly pitched was the other's voice, that, anyway, as yet, it had been quite impossible to glean any sort of a clue as to his possible identity.

That whomsoever he might be, Cruden stood in some awe of him was, however, clear, as I could tell by the deferential way in which he addressed him. Also, from what I had already managed to overhear, there could be no doubt that the purpose of their meeting was a conspirational one, and indeed, appeared to be concerned with the coded sheets from which I had just been copying, since, as soon as they had settled themselves down, I had heard the click of a drawer being unlocked, followed by the faint rustling of the sheets as they were lifted.

"These are what I got this time," I then heard Cruden say, to which the other muttered something in return, which I could not catch.

For several minutes further nothing was said, and I could only imagine that his companion was looking the sheets over, and also, perhaps, for I could not, of course, be sure of this, deciphering the code, or some part of it.

At last, however, he appeared to be done with them, for I could hear the sounds of a bottle and glasses being produced, and then, as the latter were being filled, I heard Cruden say, "'E sails with the tide tomorrow. If the wind's right that is. She's a well-sheeted brig, they say, so it shouldn't take 'er long to get across. And don't you worry, I'll see to it that 'e gets the package in good time enough."

All this time, as you can imagine, I had remained perfectly transfixed with my ear pressed hard against the woodwork in an endeavour, not only to catch what they were saying, but also, and this was my prime aim, as I have said, to obtain some idea whom the other, and mysterious, personage might be.

If only, I thought, I could catch a sight of him, even if it was only the merest glimpse. I had already, I should mention, examined the boards close by me for any possible chink between them, but to no avail, and there being no other recourse at hand that I could see, it really did seem, tantalising as it was, that a mystery he would have to remain.

It was then that I was seized with a sudden notion. Might not the latch of the door, I wondered, just possibly afford me the peephole that I needed?

To get myself into the required position meant, of course, that I would be obliged to move across a foot or so, and then kneel down; and with the slightest sound certain to give me away, it was no manoeuvre to be undertaken lightly.

Still, with such a prize at stake, it was a risk surely worth the taking, I decided. So I duly began, with the utmost deliberation, and with no small trepidation, to ease myself across.

At first all seemed to be going well, for I had got as far as dropping down on to one knee without making any semblance of a sound, and I was, in fact, just about to accommodate my eye to the latch, when of a sudden, my other leg gave a convulsive jerk backwards and, to my horror, struck against, and overturned one of the bottles!

For a second or two, I remember, I just froze to where I had knelt, before I was able to bestir myself, and make a dash for the further door, barely reaching it before Cruden burst in behind me. Whither I might be heading I had, of course, no idea. Nor was I, for the moment, much concerned, my sole aim being to preserve and increase, if possible, the few yards' start I had of him. That I should be able to do so I was fairly confident, for my pursuer, as I knew from what I had seen of him in the ring, was certainly no nimble mover.

My one dread, as I plunged headlong down a flight of steps and into the passageway below, was that I might become trapped in some blind corner or other, for not only was it impossible, in the darkness, to see anything much ahead of me, but I was also uncertain, for the moment, in which part of the inn I was, or even of the direction in which I was making.

With the sound of Cruden's footfalls still thundering in my wake I had no choice, anyway, but to hurtle onwards, and trust to providence that I was taking the right turnings, and would soon come upon some familiar landmark which would guide me to the side parlour, and then to the safety of the streets.

It was then that the fates deserted me. I had reached the floor above the public rooms, and had turned into a passageway which I fondly imagined to be the one leading to the stairway to the parlour below, only to discover, to my dismay, that although steps there were at the end of it, they descended instead to the basement kitchen!

With Cruden still hot in pursuit, it was clearly too late to turn about, and there being no other exit from the kitchen that I knew of, apart from the door to the cellars, my one chance, I decided, was to conceal myself somewhere, in the hope that I might, perhaps, while he was searching me out, be able to elude him and double back up the steps.

To my consternation however, as I plunged into the kitchen there suddenly emerged, from the depths of an armchair by the hearth, an old servant woman who, alarmed by my headlong appearance, proceeded to let forth a great shriek.

With any attempt at concealment now patently useless, there was, I quickly decided, only one thing for it now, to proceed on down to the cellars, and only trust that I could somehow manage to get into that escape tunnel, and thus safely away to the further quayside. In a flash I was through the door and down the cellar steps, whence I then struck out frantically for the far corner where, to the best of my memory, the entrance to the tunnel was located. But without Joe to guide me this time, a desperate scrambling business it was, with everything as black as pitch, and barrels scattered haphazardly about my path. I had, I think, just about reached the far wall, when I heard the cellar door being stealthily opened, and then, with a cold thrill of horror, the click of a key turning in the lock!

As I relive those terrifying moments, I can feel once again the sickening scrape of my nails, as my fingers clawed at the stonework in a feverish search for the break in plaster which would indicate the crucial slab.

Fortunately Cruden must, I think, have been unaware of my knowledge of the tunnel, and thus have imagined he now had me safely trapped.

Anyhow, he appeared to be content, for the moment, to bide his time, being wary, no doubt, of making a move before first listening for some sign of my whereabouts. Had he not done so, all would, I am sure, have been up with me. As it was, it was a desperately close-run thing, for I was still tearing away at the stonework when he must have caught some sound of what I was about, and all at once came leaping over. He could in fact, have been no more than a few yards from me when, mercifully, I must have hit upon the relevant square of stone, for of a sudden, a section of the wall gave way to my pressure, and not a moment too soon, for as I dived through, and heaved the stone back into place again, I must, I think, from the oath he let forth, have caught his arm as he made a last desperate attempt to grab me.

With my escape seemingly secure, for he surely had little chance of overtaking me now, or so I imagined, I thus proceeded to scramble off into the void. I had not progressed very far up the tunnel however, when my sense of relief began to be tinged with a certain uneasiness. At first I tried to console myself that my memory must be playing me false, and that it was all just my imagination. However, the further I went, the more did the alarming conviction take hold of me that the dimensions of the tunnel I was now in, were quite different from those of the one I had formerly traversed with Joe and the others, since, whereas before we had been obliged to crawl, I had now scarcely to bend my knees!

There could be no doubt of it and a ghastly realisation it was, that I must, in the panic and confusion of my escape from Cruden's grasp, have set off down some other underground passageway altogether!

I was now faced with a truly awesome quandary.

If I retraced my steps, I might well run into Cruden, for although I could hear no sound of him, as yet, was it not possible I thought, with a shudder, that he had tumbled to my predicament, and was stealthily following on after me!

On the other hand, I had no idea, of course, whither this other tunnel might lead, if indeed it led anywhere. For my great dread now as I sped on, was that it would simply come to a dead end!

Even so, the less perilous alternative, I decided, was to continue onwards, and only trust that I would eventually surface somewhere.

Spurred on by this hope, as well as, I might add, the insistent fear that Cruden might yet be shadowing me, I thus continued frantically to grope and stumble my way forward into the darkness. At first I made good progress enough, but after a while the desperate exertion of it all began to tell upon me. Indeed, so fatigued did I become, that my pace was soon reduced to little more than a crawl, whilst even to breathe I was finding a labour, so dank and airless was the pervading atmosphere.

In an attempt to obtain some sort of relief, I thought to discard my greatcoat. This seemed to help for a while, but I had not progressed much further, when my legs began to buckle under me again, and the heavy sense of oppression returned to my chest.

On hands and knees now, and so choked for air that I was obliged to lie quite still every so often to recover my breath, I desperately clawed my way on.

Of Cruden, anyway as yet, I had thankfully heard no sound, and if he was, indeed, still in pursuit, I had at least the consolation of knowing that he would not be finding the going any easier than I was. Not, I think, that I was capable at the time of any such calculating thought, so exclusively preoccupied had I become by then with my one objective: to escape from the narrow confines, and impenetrable blackness of the infernal, and seemingly endless, tunnel.

How far, in fact, it extended, I later had occasion to estimate, and it certainly could not have been, I think, much short of a quarter of a mile.

Anyhow I must, I suppose, have covered something like that distance and was pretty near the end of my tether, when the dimensions of the tunnel began to broaden, and simultaneously, and to my even greater relief, the atmosphere seemed to be freshening. Enabled now to breathe more freely, and also encouraged by the hope that this must surely indicate the approach of the tunnel's end, I eagerly pressed on.

I had not gone much further, when the darkness as well appeared to lighten a little and soon I was to distinguish something of the tunnel's shadowy contours, and then as I rounded a bend, I could all at once perceive the dim outlines of its mouth, looming up some thirty yards or so ahead of me. With my imminent deliverance now seemingly assured, I need hardly describe the exultant upsurge of relief I experienced as, quickening my step, I hurried on towards it.

Unhappily, however, my exhilaration was destined to be short-lived. For to my dismay, when I eventually breasted the mouth, far from finding myself on open ground, as I had fondly expected, I discovered that I had, instead, emerged into some kind of subterranean vault, and that the break in the darkness, which had so raised my hopes, had simply been occasioned by a shaft of moonlight, which shone through an aperture set high up in the centre of its concave roof.

To add to my mortification there was, as far as I could see, save for the passage by which I had come, no other way out!

Chapter XVII

So overcome with desolation was I, that for several moments I just stood there at the entrance, looking blankly around me. The chamber, as well as I could dimly observe, was, I suppose, about the size of a captain's cabin, if somewhat taller, its walls sloping inwards to a dome-shaped ceiling, which, at its highest point, where the aperture was, must have been some twelve feet or so from the ground.

Scattered about the floor were a number of kegs. Contraband brandy they must have contained, I imagine, being stored safely away from the prying eyes of the excise men.

Apart from these, the chamber was quite empty, and that there was no other way out a hurried exploration, unhappily, soon confirmed. I thus had no choice, it seemed, but to return by the way I had come.

But what if Cruden – for the possibility still haunted me – should be aware of my predicament, and was coming hotfoot after me? If such was the case, he must know that I was securely trapped, and also that he could scarcely have wished for a more favourable locale in which to dispose of me.

Even so, and whether my fears had any foundation or not, my best plan, I decided, was to bide my time. For whereas a confrontation in the tunnel would certainly offer me no sort of hope, by remaining where I was, I might, I thought, have some chance of outmanoeuvring him.

For want of anything with which to defend myself, I proceeded frantically to search around for some possible weapon or other, but there was clearly none.

I then had the wild idea, I remember, of stunning him with one of the kegs, as he emerged from the tunnel. However, I had only to try the weight of it, to realise the utter hopelessness of such a ruse.

There was, it seemed, nothing for it but to conceal myself as best I could, and if and when he should appear, attempt to outwit him, and by so doing make my escape.

The problem was, however, that although the vault, save for a space just beneath the opening, was in deep shadow enough, there was nowhere that offered any real concealment.

I was still at a loss what best to do when I was seized with a sudden inspiration. Might it not be possible, I thought, to pile up some of the kegs in such a way as to provide the cover I needed? It was a desperate enough scheme, especially as it could well be thwarted at any moment by Cruden's arrival.

Still, it was worth a try, I decided, and after all I had little to lose.

To obtain as much room for manoeuvre as possible, the centre of the vault was plainly the most favourable site for such a construction and here, fortunately, there already stood several kegs.

These I hurriedly approximated, and having rolled across two or three others to widen the base, I frenziedly set about erecting the next tier.

This was a much more laborious business of course. However, after a struggle, I managed, with much hoisting and heaving, to achieve it.

All this time I had, as you may imagine, been keeping an anxious ear cocked towards the tunnel. Everything though was still as quiet as the grave, and as I started upon the next layer, it really did begin to seem, for a good five minutes must have elapsed since my arrival at the vault, that Cruden must, in fact, have imagined that I had got safely away. Although it was also, of course, possible, I argued that he could, all this while, simply have been lurking somewhere along the course of the tunnel in readiness to ambush me upon my return, in which case he could well soon become impatient and come on after me!

Spurred on by such a thought, I therefore continued furiously to grapple with the kegs; and an exhausting task I was finding it, for they were no mean weight, as I have said.

Nevertheless, after much heaving, and a good deal of leverage, I had, at last, succeeded in constructing a refuge which should, I deemed, be sizeable enough for my purpose, when, of a sudden the thought struck me that if only I could manage to manipulate one further keg into place to form, as it were, the apex of a pyramid, it might, I estimated, just about bring me within arm's reach of the opening through which, granted a secure enough hold, I might thus escape.

That the task was a daunting one, I was under no illusion, especially as my strength had already been largely spent. Still, it was, at least, worth the attempt, I decided.

In the event, such a fearful struggle did I have of it, that, more than once, I came close to admitting defeat, I remember, before I managed at last, with one final heave, to hoist the keg securely into place.

No sooner had I done so, however, than all about me began to sway, and my stomach so to heave, that all I could do was to slump helplessly astride the keg, with my head between my knees.

I was still sitting there desperately trying to will some sort of vitality back into myself when, of a sudden, and to my horror, my attention was arrested by a faint sound, as of a tentative footstep, arising from the depths of the tunnel. Still powerless to move, I sat there riveted to the keg, listening, in an agony of dread, for a repetition of the sound. For some moments all was deathly quiet again, and I was thinking, to console myself, that it might after all have been caused by nothing more, perhaps, than the scuffling of a rat (of which species there had been ample evidence, I would add) when, all at once, the sound came again, and this time so distinctly as to leave me in no doubt that someone was furtively approaching.

Still too enfeebled for any hope of a leap to the opening, my only recourse now, I decided, was, come what may, to seek refuge behind the kegs where, in an agony of suspense, I proceeded to crouch, as, with my eyes fixed, through a chink between them, upon the mouth of the tunnel, I heard the steps, by a slow and stealthy progression, draw nearer.

Then, for a while, he must have hesitated, listening no doubt for some evidence of my presence. Although, still invisible as he was, so close to the mouth must he have been that I could already just catch the soft murmur of his breathing. The cold and deadly terror of those few moments of suspense, as I continued to crouch there staring into the blackness, still shudders through me as I write. Indeed, it was with a sense almost of relief, as I recall, when, from beyond the shadows, Cruden's massive bulk began, eventually, to take shape, as he cautiously sidled towards the mouth.

As he did so a sudden shaft of moonlight happened to slant through the aperture overhead and, with a thrill of horror, I saw something momentarily glint in the grasp of his right hand. For an instant or two he remained standing there, and as he looked up towards the mound of kegs I saw a great scowl cross his face in the suspicion, no doubt, that he had, after all, been baulked of his prey.

Indeed, the half-hope was already beginning to build within me that he had, in fact, become resigned to my escape when, all at once, he started to move stealthily over towards the kegs.

I must have been perfectly invisible to him, and he could therefore, I am sure, have been acting upon nothing but suspicion, as was indeed apparent by the manner in which, having approached to within a yard or two of the kegs, he then stopped to peer searchingly among them.

Whether he did, in fact, finally catch a glimpse of me, I don't know. Anyway, of a sudden he made as if to move to the left. It must, however, have been no more than a feint, and like a fool I fell for it. Even then all might have been well, had I not, in my panic to escape as he rounded upon me, managed somehow to stumble over a projecting keg.

As it was, my next memory is of my lying there semi-prostrate, and of Cruden, with a horrible leer of triumph, hurtling himself upon me. What saved me, I am not quite sure. Partly it must have been, I think, his over-eagerness, for, with a little more deliberation, and by first pinning me down he must, I am certain, have made sure of me.

However as he plunged his knife to my chest, I must somehow have diverted his aim, for instead of its lethal objective, the blade caught the left side of my neck.

At the same time I had contrived to kick out with my right leg, catching him full in the stomach, which not only caused him to overbalance, but must, I think, also have winded him.

Before he could recover, I had just sufficient time to twist out of range, and then, with no other thought but to keep out of reach of the blade, I managed to scramble up on to the kegs, happily receiving no further damage than a rip to one of my stockings, as he vainly lashed out at my retreating thighs.

Perched on the topmost keg I was now comparatively safe, anyway for the moment, since it was impossible for him to get in any effective thrust without coming up after me, and were he to do so, he would plainly afford me an opportunity of jumping down and making for the tunnel.

That Cruden had equally sized up the situation was apparent, for he had meanwhile darted back to the other side of the kegs, thus placing himself between them and the tunnel's mouth.

Puzzled, no doubt, as to how he was to set about finishing me off, for a good minute or more he just stood there eyeing me with the malignant intensity of a cat surveying a cornered mouse, whilst every now and then making a pretended move in an endeavour to induce me to jump.

An additional concern to me, meanwhile, was the wound in my neck which, although at the moment of its infliction I had scarcely noticed, I now realised was no mean one, and was still bleeding so copiously, as to present an altogether fresh danger.

Whether, in the dim light, Cruden was aware of this, I don't know. Although he may well have been, for I was, all the while, vigorously compressing my stock against the gash, in an attempt to stem the flow.

Anyway, all at once, and upon a sudden impulse as it seemed, he clenched the knife between his teeth, and then started to move over towards the kegs. In the belief that he had, at last, decided to chance it and to come up after me, I started to poise myself for the jump. However, it soon became clear, as he then proceeded to grasp hold of one of the kegs in the second tier, that he had quite another plan in mind. He was going to attempt to bring me down by dislodging the very foundations of my perch!

Such a possibility had not, I must admit, occurred to me. Albeit, as he took the strain of it, little did I imagine, even allowing for the exceptional strength of the man, that he could, with my super-added weight, hope to succeed.

By this time the bleeding from my wound had thankfully almost subsided, and with Cruden making no sort of an impression upon the kegs, my hopes of survival began to rise a little. For the more he exhausted himself in the effort, the greater would be my chance, I thought, when the critical moment came, of eluding him.

That my leap, when I made it, would have to be carefully timed, I knew; for there was little margin for error, and, strenuously occupied as he was, Cruden was, nevertheless, still continuing to watch me like a hawk.

Frustrated in his endeavours, he happened just then, however, to switch his attention to the next keg along, and in so doing moved a little aside from a direct line to the tunnel.

Sensing that this could well provide me with the opportunity I had been awaiting, I thus began, unobtrusively, to prepare myself for the leap.

I was, in fact, I think, already poised to do so, when I felt the kegs beneath me give a sudden jerk. Then to a great roar of triumph from Cruden, the whole edifice began to shudder, and before I was able to steady myself, I was sent helplessly sprawling.

With no secure foothold now from which to launch myself, and in the awful realisation that it would require but another heave or two to bring the entire superstructure tumbling down beneath me, it seemed that everything must surely be up with me.

It was then, whilst I was still trying to regain some sort of a footing, that I chanced, upon looking up, to catch a glimpse of something which I had not previously spotted.

There, suspended in a gentle curve from the roof of the vault, and a yard or so from the opening, was the root of a tree, from which the surrounding earth had fallen away.

It was a desperate do-or-die chance, for I was by no means sure that I could reach it, and even if I did, whether it would support me.

It was, however, no moment for nice considerations and so securing the best purchase I was able, I flung myself up towards it.

A devilishly close-run thing it was too, for, as the fingertips of my right hand closed over it, I could hear the crash of the kegs, as the whole mass disintegrated beneath me.

As the root took my weight, I felt it sag a little bringing a great shower of earth and stones about my head; but then, mercifully, it took the strain, and with my experience aloft the rigging standing me in good stead, I started frantically to swing myself across towards the opening.

Cruden, as I could see from the corner of my eye, had meanwhile scrambled up upon the fallen kegs, and was making frantic attempts to grab hold of my legs.

With a securer foothold he might well have succeeded, but before he could reach me I had swung out of range, and already had one hand firmly grasping the edge of the opening.

My only fear now was that he would let fling his knife, and with the target I must have presented, a very real danger it was.

Indeed, had his aim been but a fraction the better, he might still have done for me, so perilously close must the blade have been as it skimmed past me before sailing harmlessly on into the bushes beyond, whilst I heaved myself through into the open and out of, at least, immediate danger.

Chapter XVIII

So exhausted was I by the desperate gymnastics of that final scramble to safety, that no sooner had I dragged myself away from the opening, than my legs buckled from under me, and all I could do was slump down against the trunk of a nearby tree. The very tree, in fact, it must have been to which I was so much indebted for my timely deliverance.

That I was still alive I could scarcely believe, so hopeless had my plight seemed but a few brief seconds before. Indeed, had I been an inch the shorter, or had the root hung down by that much less, I would, I realised with a shudder, now be lying there lifeless in the vault below.

As it was, the knife wound I had received must have been perilously close to finishing me off, for the gash was a fairly deep one, and could not have missed my jugular vein by much more than a hair's breadth. Not that I hadn't bled freely enough nevertheless, as I could tell by the saturated state of my clothes.

As to where I might be, I had, as yet, scarcely given a thought, so bemused with relief was I by the miraculous nature of my escape, and it was only upon catching some sound of Cruden in the vault below, that I was prompted to bestir myself and, rising wearily to my feet, take stock of my surroundings.

The moon, as I have said, was nearly at the full, so everything was clear enough. Even so, it was in no little bewilderment that I looked about me, for I had emerged, it seemed, into the depths of an immense square-shaped pit, measuring in diameter, I supposed, some three hundred yards or more and bordered on all sides by steep cliffs.

For a minute or more I stood there utterly mystified, before it suddenly dawned upon me that I must have surfaced into the old disused chalk quarry which, as I have already, I think, mentioned, bounded the port for some little way inland from the river on that side.

Anyway, it was no moment for dallying, for I still had some lingering fear that Cruden might somehow manage to come up after me. So having elected the northern side of the pit as the one affording the nearest approach to the manor, I duly made off with all speed in that direction. As I came up to it, I discovered, to my consternation, that the cliff face was quite as precipitous as it had appeared from a distance, and that as far as I could see, there was no visible means of ascent!

With mounting alarm, mindful as I was of Cruden's ability to construct the mound of kegs more swiftly than I had been able to, I hurriedly made over to the nearest of the two corners, where I imagined a stepway to the top was most likely to be located. But all hope of any ascent, at least from that corner, was soon to be dashed. The cliff was plainly quite as sheer there as the rest of its face.

In some panic now, I quickly turned about, and set off for the other corner. The approach here I found, when I eventually drew up to it, to be obscured by thick undergrowth which, albeit less profusely, appeared to extend to some half-way up the cliff. But whether, above that point, there was likely to be any kind of foothold, it was impossible to be sure.

However, it was no moment for hesitation, and so having plunged through the intervening undergrowth, I at once set about the ascent.

To my relief, as I reached the bare chalk, I discovered that it had, in fact, been indented at intervals with some kind of crude stepway.

Nevertheless, I soon found it no easy climb, for such footholds as there were had been much broken away, and the chalk was so friable that more than once I was obliged to hang on for dear life, to prevent myself from falling, before I was finally able to heave myself up on to the grass verge at the top.

A relief as it was to be out of the chalk-pit, I was still mindful of Cruden, and so pausing only to take stock of my whereabouts, which was easy enough now, as I could see the river stretched out below me as well as the windmill on its hillock against the skyline to my left, I hastened towards a trackway which I could see beyond a gated gap in a hedge some yards distant. I had not taken many steps, however, when I was overtaken once again by a fearful languidness; so much so that I was scarcely able to put one foot before the other. Although I managed somehow to struggle as far as the gate, and must indeed have got beyond it, when everything about me started to whirl around and, before I could stop myself, the ground had come up to meet me, as I pitched forward senseless to the turf.

For how long I lay there I do not know. Anyway, when I did eventually regain consciousness, it was some moments, I remember, as I stared vacantly up at the stars in the heavens above me, before I realised where I was and what had befallen me.

Alerted by the sudden recollection, and the dire peril to which I could still be exposed, I at once made shift to get up. I had, however, barely raised my shoulders when, to my horror, I felt a restraining hand grip me from behind!

So petrified was I, that for an instant or two, I just lay there powerless to move, before I instinctively twisted my body aside in an attempt to escape the knife, which I was quite sure was about to be plunged into me.

Instead there came a voice. "You must forgive me if I have disturbed you unnecessarily, but I really don't think that you ought to be lying out here like this, and without a coat too!"

I knew at once that it could not be Cruden, for both the accent as well as the manner of address, had been of the gentlest.

"Dear me! I see now that you have suffered an injury," he then added having doubtless observed the gash in my neck.

"No, no, I wouldn't try to move," he went on as I attempted to rise. "We'll get some of this into you first." And so saying, he produced a brandy flask and held it to my lips.

It was only then, as he brought his head down close to mine that I was able to observe, and not without, I fear, giving an involuntary shudder that his face was horribly disfigured, and all at once I was reminded, as I did so, of what Joe had related of the elderly recluse who resided in the depths of the marshes, and never ventured out, save under cover of darkness. He it must be, I imagined, who was my good Samaritan.

Comforting as it was to have the old gentleman with me, I was, nevertheless, all the while still haunted by the fear that Cruden might yet be on the prowl. For if he were, by chance, to discover us, I had little doubt that he would have any sort of hesitation in dispatching the pair of us.

That I should, of course, have apprised my companion of the danger there can be no denying. My reason for not doing so, I must confess, being my selfish and, I am quite sure, unwarrantable fear that he might, as a consequence, desert me. Anyway, with the brandy beginning to course through my veins, I had started to revive a little, and although still pretty weak, so desperate was I to be up and away, that I now made some attempt to get to my feet.

It was to no avail, however, for no sooner had I raised my head than the giddiness returned.

"You know, I really think that it would be wisest if I tried to obtain some assistance," he said anxiously, as I fell back helplessly into his arms.

"There's a farm close by, and I have no doubt that they would have some sort of conveyance to get you home."

"No! No! I'm sure that won't be necessary. I shall be all right in a moment," I insisted, taking a grip of his arm as I spoke, in the fear that he might leave me.

"But I shall be gone only a few minutes. You'll be quite safe here, surely, until I get back," he answered.

"Whatever you do, please don't leave me!" I cried out in frantic appeal.

"Well, just as you wish," he consented with some impatience. "I don't know how far it is you have to go, but I really don't see how we're going to get you home the way you are, for you're plainly in no shape to walk."

"Oh! It's only as far as the manor," I quickly interjected. "I'm staying with the Thurlows."

"But that's still a goodish distance. A couple of miles at least, I would imagine. So don't you think it would really be best if I . . ."

As he was speaking there came the sound of a footfall approaching along the road, and in the instinctive belief that it must surely be Cruden, I all at once seized hold of the old man, and with my hand over his mouth to prevent him from crying out, I somehow managed to summon the strength to drag him unceremoniously after me to the shadow of the hedge, where we lay huddled together, as meanwhile some nocturnal wayfarer or other, strolled harmlessly by.

What manner of excuse I made for my behaviour, I fear I cannot recall. Anyway, as we crawled back into the open again, I can only imagine that he could, by now, be holding no other belief than that it was a candidate for Bedlam he had upon his hands.

That he must, indeed, have begun to entertain some such suspicion, I could tell, for after regaining his composure, his manner towards me was altogether more wary, I noticed, and such remarks as he did let fall were plainly uttered with the intention of humouring me.

Nevertheless, whatever else the rough and tumble may have achieved, it must, anyway, have persuaded him that I was unsafe to be left alone, for, thankfully, no further mention was made of his going off to seek a conveyance.

As it was, some small degree of vitality was beginning to return to me, so that I was soon able to sit up without swooning. Then, after a further interval, I managed, eventually, to get to my feet and with his arm supporting mine, we succeeded, at length, in stumbling off together into the darkness.

At first it was pretty halting progress that we made. However, as my sense of well-being continued to return, I was soon able to relinquish his hold of me, and stride out more freely, and in so doing, although I did, I must confess, still experience one or two anxious moments when some other wayfarer happened to approach, I gradually shed my obsessive dread of Cruden, and the possibility of his coming upon us.

With my thoughts thus less distracted, I was now enabled, as we trudged along together, to observe my elderly benefactor more closely.

His facial disfigurement was, as I have said, truly horrifying. Indeed, so severely had he been mauled, that the individual features had been almost obliterated, giving them much the appearance of those I had once observed in a well-drowned corpse; save that, in addition, one of his eyes had been so displaced that it peered rather from the side of his head than the front. He had also, as I noticed, suffered an injury to his left arm, which hung down limply to his side, as he walked.

All in all I could not but sympathise with his reluctance to appear before the public gaze. His demeanour, however, as I have intimated, was as gentle as his aspect was repellent, and of his kindly disposition I certainly could not have had more ample evidence.

By this time we were well upon our way to the manor, and being quite myself again and not wishing to trouble him further, I made leave to suggest that I was now well able to carry on alone.

This, however, he would not hear of, insisting that he would not be happy until he had seen me safely as far at least as the manor gates.

"I must say it's very good of you to put yourself out like this on my behalf. I am afraid I've been an awful nuisance to you," I then said.

"Please don't speak of it. I am only too glad to have been of assistance," he replied. And there could be no doubting his sincerity.

"But aren't I taking you out of your way?" I interjected.

"Dear me, no! You really mustn't let that worry you. Whither I walk is perfectly immaterial to me. I really only do it for the exercise, I can assure you. Indeed, I am only too glad of your company."

Having continued in silence for some way further he then suddenly interposed:

"If I am not mistaken, you must surely be the young gentleman Sir George was telling me about, who has come down from London to catalogue his library?"

"Yes, that's right," I affirmed.

"Perhaps we should introduce ourselves," he then added. "My name is Fenton, James Fenton." And as I declared my own name, he reached across and shook me warmly by the hand.

"Sir George and I are old friends, I must tell you," he went on. "He has always been kindness itself, and most generous in the way he has let me have the free run of his library. Dear me, which reminds me, I have several volumes of his at the moment which I must be sure to return before you leave."

"Oh! I am sure that there's no need to put you to that trouble. No doubt I could come over sometime and take down the necessary details of the books you have," I said unthinkingly, and devoutly wishing, as soon as I had spoken, that I could have eaten my words, for I had already suffered enough embarrassment at the hands of Dr Argent, without wishing to expose myself to another such awkward experience. Not to mention the even less inviting prospect of a lone excursion to the depths of the marshes, which, as I was now reminded, a visit to his abode would, of necessity, entail.

"That would be very kind of you," he responded with alacrity. "Perhaps we could make an evening of it. One meets so few people down here in Gravesend with any pretensions to scholarly leanings that to entertain someone such as yourself would be a singular pleasure. Antiquities, I suppose, are what chiefly interest me, but I do have one or two volumes that you might care or have a look at, and upon which I would certainly value your opinion."

"I should be only too pleased to," I said with, I fear, little enthusiasm. By this time we had reached the turning up to the manor gates, and with our parting imminent, I was cherishing the hope that he would not press his invitation further. Indeed, to forestall his doing so, I was just about to interject some irrelevant comment or other when he said:

"Maybe you could come over one evening later this week. Would Thursday, perhaps, be convenient?"

I could, I suppose, have conjured up some excuse or other, and had I but known of the mortal peril to which I was, in the event, going to expose myself, certainly no consideration would have induced me to have done otherwise.

However, so demonstrably eager was he for me to accept, and so much indebted to him was I for all his kind attention, that I could not find it in me to demur.

"You'll come to dinner, of course," he then added. "Shall we say six o'clock? If that would be convenient to you, of course. I live a bit off the beaten track, I'm afraid. Away out in the marshes. But it's the only house thereabouts, and it stands out clearly enough, so if you leave well before dusk you'll have no trouble in finding us. Well, that's settled. I shall look forward to seeing you on Thursday then."

With this, and my having reassured him, upon his kindly enquiry, that I was feeling quite myself again, we parted company. He to continue his nocturnal ramble, whilst I wearily set off up the driveway to the safe haven of the manor.

Chapter XIX

Luckily, for I had no wish to alarm the rest of the household, I was able to get into the manor by a side door, and creep up to my room unobserved. Something for which I was even more thankful, when I came to view myself in the cheval-glass, and discover what a truly deplorable state I was in, with my clothes all asmear with chalk and blood, my breeches ripped down the length of one thigh, and the knife wound agape in my neck. When I had cleaned away the surrounding blood, even this did not look too bad however. And so really, all things considered, there could be no denying that I had come out of the misadventure pretty lightly.

What the morrow might bring was quite another matter. Still, for the moment, I was in no mind to worry about that, and so, having shaken off my bedraggled clothes, I climbed wearily into bed and, scarcely had my head sunk upon the pillow, than I was asleep.

When I awoke the next morning, and came to view the previous evening's events with a clearer mind, I was able to appreciate that the venture had, in fact, been rather more rewarding than I had imagined.

Most frustrating as it was, of course, to have been unable to obtain any sort of clue as to the identity of Cruden's accomplice, I had, at least, this time surely, been able to procure a sufficient quantity of the code for a deciphering to be made.

There had also been, as I was now reminded when I came to think over what I had managed to overhear of their exchanges, that mention of the captain of some ship or other now lying off Gravesend, who was to be entrusted with the delivery of a package to somewhere on the Continent. Holland, wasn't it, if I remembered rightly? This was certainly something that could well be worth following up, I thought. Although the name of the ship had not been mentioned, it should not be too difficult, I imagined, by discreet enquiry, to make a likely shot as to which vessel it was; and having done so, then set about ensuring that the package was intercepted. But how could this best be achieved in the time that we had at our disposal? For the ship, apparently, was due to sail with the tide that very evening. The simplest solution would, I supposed, be to leave the matter in the hands of the local excise people, which, at least, would have the advantage of relieving me of any further responsibility.

Upon maturer consideration, it occurred to me, however, that such a recourse could have its drawbacks, as there was every chance that Cruden would get wind of such an official intervention, and were he to do so, of his then devising some alternative means for conveying the information across the Channel.

For, as I viewed the problem, it was vital not only to gain possession of the package, but also to achieve this without Cruden suspecting that anything had gone amiss with their plans. The question was; how could this be accomplished?

Turn the problem this way and that, as I did, there really did not seem to be any solution to it, and I had, in fact, virtually decided that for all its disadvantages, my original notion was the only feasible one; when there flashed into my mind a scheme which, bizarre as it was, would, if it could be successfully carried through, have every chance, I believed, of fulfilling the requirements I have mentioned.

Sketched briefly, my plan was this. Captain Wakeley posing as the commander of the naval frigate, which still lay, fortunately, anchored upriver, together with myself in the guise of his clerk, would, under some official pretext or other, get aboard the vessel and then, having obtained the privacy of his cabin, prevail upon the master, by force if necessary, to surrender the package!

That the scheme was shot through with all manner of imponderables, I need hardly say. Not the least of which was the willingness of Captain Wakeley to participate; and from what I knew of him, I was, as you may imagine, by no means sanguine that he could be persuaded to do so.

Anyway, before confronting him with my proposal, I had first, of course, to identify the ship. Not, with the information I already had, that this should pose any great difficulty, I imagined, especially as Joe seemed to be alive to everything that was going on along the river.

As it happened, he had omitted to call me that morning; and when he failed as well to join me later in the library, I began to be seriously concerned that, having perhaps tumbled to our collusion, Cruden may have done him some harm. So anxious on his behalf was I, that I was, indeed, just about to leave the library to discover from the other servants whether anything had been seen of him that morning, when, to my relief, his head appeared around the corner of the door.

"Ah! There you are, Sir," he greeted me in his usual cheerful way. "Sorry I wasn't along with the shavin' water, but it 'appened I slept at the 'Daws' last night and some'ow I didn't seem to wake up as soon as I ought to 'ave."

"Never mind, Joe, it was of no account," I said, much too delighted to find him safe and sound, to be in any humour to scold him.

"You got away all right then, Sir?" he then remarked as he took up a pile of books, and made over to the shelves with them.

“I was in a fair old quake, I can tell yer, when Nat came back early, like ’e did, and you still up there an’ all. I set to whistlin’ as soon as I could. So you ’eard me all right then?”

“Yes, Joe, perfectly. You couldn’t have done better,” I said.

“I thought ’e was bound to ’ave nabbed yer. ’Specially when I ’eard all that rumpus goin’ on,” added Joe, as he handed me a further pile to catalogue.

“I don’t mind admitting that I had one or two anxious moments myself, Joe,” I replied. “Anyway, I trust he didn’t suspect you of having any part in it?” I added with concern.

“I can’t see ’ow as ’e could ’ave, Sir. Though he must ’ave ’eard me whistlin’ of course. But ’e’s used to that.”

“I suppose you didn’t happen to see who it was that was with him by any chance?” I asked in eager expectation.

“No, I’m ’fraid I didn’t, Sir. There was someone with ’im, I knew, ’cos I ’eard Nat talking to ’im, but who it was I can’t say. I did ask Sal but she couldn’t tell neither.”

“A pity, Joe. But it can’t be helped,” I said, doing my best to hide my disappointment.

“You ’ad a bit of trouble getting away then, did you, Sir?”

“Yes I’m afraid I did, Joe,” I said. And as he was obviously agog to hear all about it, I then proceeded to relate what had happened.

“Lor’, you certainly did ’ave a time of it, Sir!” exclaimed Joe when I had finished. “Did ’e cut yer badly?”

“Well no, not really,” I reassured him. However, he would not be satisfied until I had pulled down my neckcloth, to let him have a look at the gash.

“It looks awful deep to me, Sir. Don’t you think you ought to let the doctor see it?”

“Oh! It’s really nothing, Joe,” I replied. “It’ll soon be healed, don’t you worry.”

“Any’ow, you got what you went up there for?” he said, when he had finally done scrutinising the wound. Assuring him that I had, I then went on to relate what I had managed to overhear, and of my scheme to frustrate their plans.

Joe, of course, was all enthusiasm for it, and, what was more, he had little doubt which was the vessel we were after. A certain Dutch brigantine, the *Amsterdam*, he was quite sure was the one. In fact, its crew, he informed me, were regular customers of the “Three Daws” and, what was more, he knew the master to be a particular crony of Cruden’s, and had, indeed, seen the two of them with their heads together in a corner of the parlour only the day before.

The evidence, therefore, seemed as near conclusive as could be. So now all we had to do was to prevail upon Captain Wakeley to play his part, and this, as I have said, was something of which I was by no means hopeful, when I set off later that morning for his lodgings.

His reception of me was even more churlish than ever, which was not encouraging. However, having upbraided me once again for arriving during the hours of daylight, he did, if begrudgingly, at least consent to admit me.

"You've got something urgent to report then?" he said impatiently as he ushered me into his parlour.

"Yes, in a way I have, Sir," I said uncertainly, as I propped myself up against the mantelshelf in want of any offer of a chair. "It's nothing very momentous, I'm afraid, but I felt that I ought to let you know about it."

"Well then, if you'll just let me have your written report I'll see that it's sent off," he responded curtly.

"I haven't actually made out anything yet," I replied evasively. "It would be better to wait, I think, until I have something more definite to impart. And to achieve this I was hoping that you might, perhaps, be able to assist me."

"Oh! In what way?" he interjected in sudden alarm.

"Perhaps I had better first tell you what has happened since I was last here," I said.

And, in as matter-of-fact a tone as I could, I then proceeded to give him some account of my further visit to the "Three Daws" and what I had achieved, being careful to omit, for I did not want to alarm him unnecessarily, any mention of my having been surprised by Cruden.

"Well, you must certainly see to it that the information doesn't get away," he said when I had finished. "But I don't quite see how you would need my assistance. Surely there would be no difficulty in obtaining the necessary authority to stop the ship sailing."

"No, I'm sure there wouldn't, but to adopt such a procedure could well have certain disadvantages," I said. And I then went on to state them.

"Yes, I appreciate what you say, Farrant," he said when I had finished. "But I don't quite see how you are going to tackle it any other way."

This was the lead I needed, and I at once proceeded to outline, not without, I might say, discouraging sounds from the captain, the plan I had in mind.

"No, no, it's quite unthinkable," he exploded when I had finished. "I could never for a moment even consider lending myself to such a scheme. It's quite preposterous!"

"I don't see why!" I said with some heat. "You would only be playing a part you must be perfectly familiar with. There would, surely, be no difficulty there."

"But I haven't been on the active list for years," he retaliated with vehemence. "Anyway, to impersonate a serving officer, as you are suggesting, would be quite unthinkable. I don't think you can realise what a grave offence I would be committing. No, no, Farrant. It's really absolutely out of the question. Quite unthinkable!" he added, with a finality which seemed to be irrevocable.

I was, none the less, determined not to give in without a struggle. For inwardly acknowledging his objections, as I did, they scarcely seemed to be tenable, when considered in the light of what we were out to achieve.

"But surely at a time like this, when the country's very future is at stake, such a trifling infringement of the regulations could surely be overlooked," I exclaimed scathingly. "You as an old serving officer must surely see that!"

That I had touched upon a delicate spot I could tell, as I watched him visibly writhing in the throes of his contending emotions.

"It's no use, Farrant," he cried out at last. "I'm too old to get involved in a scrape of this sort. Surely you must see that. Were I a younger man I . . ."

"Nonsense!" I interrupted. "You could manage it perfectly well. Anyway, I would be there to support you, and really, I can't see that you would be exposing yourself to any sort of danger. If, by chance, anything did go wrong, they would hardly be likely to get rough, with that frigate lying close by."

"I don't know what to say," he said at last, giving a groan of despair as he did so. "I'd like to help you of course, Farrant, and as I say, if I were a younger man it would have been different. But at my age I just haven't got the stomach for the sort of escapade you are proposing. Surely you must see that?" As he spoke, he gave me a look so pathetic in its appeal that I was almost inclined to relent. It was, however, no time for compassion, I decided, as I continued to press him.

"I can scarcely believe that!" I cried in a tone of assumed surprise. "Why, Lord St Vincent spoke most warmly of you. One of the most resolute and fearless officers he had ever had the privilege to serve under. That's what he told me." I was lying, of course, for he had said no such thing, but heaven, I knew, would forgive me for it.

"Did he? Did he really say that?" exclaimed the captain, his old wrinkled face suddenly lighting up with shy pleasure at the compliment.

"I can assure you that he did," I reaffirmed with conviction. "He recommended you to me most warmly. 'You'll find none stauncher.' Those were his lordship's very words," I said, enlarging upon the fabrication.

Moved by this flattering testimonial, as he clearly was, I could see that he was beginning to waver, and while he was still basking in the fullness of it, I continued, firmly, to press my petition. It was uphill work. Nevertheless, in spite of his misgivings, I managed, at last, to obtain his consent.

Having done so, and for fear that he might yet go back on his word, I lost no time in advising him of the hour and place of our meeting, which was, as Joe and I had already arranged, to be, by six o'clock, at the landing-stage a little way down river from Gravesend, where Joe would see to it that a boat would be ready to row us out to the brigantine.

All was thus settled, and with his firm reassurance that he would be there, attired in his old uniform, at the appointed time, I left him. Albeit not without some inward qualms, for, as I glanced back from the door, his hand, I noticed, was already reaching out shakily for the decanter.

Chapter XX

It was barely noon when I arrived back at the manor, so I had ample time to brood over the wisdom of the scheme we were to embark upon. Although, as it chanced, any such second thoughts were, at least for an hour or so, to be postponed as, owing to the indisposition of Miss Beauchamp, luncheon on that day, as I remember, was partaken in the sole company of Miss Catherine. I have indeed, special reason to recall the occasion, since it was then that there were first imparted, certain indications that my feelings towards her were, perhaps, not altogether unrequited; and that the dreams in which, I must confess, I was already beginning fondly to indulge, were not entirely without some hope of fulfilment.

This is all by the way however; and anyway, after withdrawing to the solitude of the library and having basked for a while in the rapturous felicity of such an awareness, my thoughts soon returned to the evening's escapade, and all its inherent imponderables.

In an attempt to divert them, I took up Dampier's *Voyages*, but it was to no avail, and having completed a chapter without really perceiving anything of its sense, I finally laid the book aside, and once again surrendered myself to the rueful contemplation of the undertaking upon which the three of us were shortly to set out.

To begin with, could we be absolutely sure that we had hit upon the right ship? The evidence, as I have said, certainly appeared to be conclusive enough. But if, by chance, we were mistaken, beside all the embarrassment of confronting some perfectly innocent master with possession of the incriminating document, it would have put paid, of course, to any hope of our recovering it.

And then, even if we were correct in our assumption, what sort of reliance could be placed upon Captain Wakeley? How, I wondered, was he going to conduct himself when it came to the touch? From what I had witnessed of his behaviour earlier that day, it was, I was afraid, only too easy to predict; and this was accepting that he would, in fact, hold to his word and keep the tryst, something of which, I must admit, I was becoming ever less optimistic.

In truth, as the afternoon wore on, and the shadows lengthened across the lawn outside, these, and countless other misgivings had so continued to work upon me, that I had, I must own, begun seriously to consider whether the venture was, after all, really worth the pursuing.

However, no sooner had Joe bounced in, as he shortly did, to confirm that everything had been arranged, and that a boat was lying there ready for us by the old landing-stage, that most of my qualms, so infected was I by his uninhibited enthusiasm for the jaunt, seemed somehow to evaporate.

Not, mind you, that he would, I suspect, have been any the less confident had we, instead, been just about to embark upon a design to capture Napoleon himself!

Anyway, all was now firmly resolved, and having made sure this time to arm myself with my pistol, the two of us duly set off for the riverside.

It was a blustery, raw night, and thankful I was for an old greatcoat of Sir George's which I had borrowed. The wind, I was relieved to see, still blew from the westerly quarter, which should, I imagined, at least ensure that the brig would be sailing.

Dark as it already was, and ever alert now to the menace that might be dogging me, I was careful, in spite of Joe's company, to keep to a good pace, especially as the path we had taken, being the shortest way to our destination, was the more solitary one bordering the marshes.

We were thus down there in good time, and so all we had to do now, as we stationed ourselves by the landing-stage, was to await the captain's arrival.

Thankfully, the frigate was still lying there at anchor some little way downstream, whilst the Dutchman, which Joe now pointed out to me, stood leeward of it and somewhat nearer to the shore.

Its upper yards were already crossed, I noticed, and from the sounds that echoed across the water, it was apparent that preparations were already under way for her departure.

That the tide was approaching the turn I could tell by the wash of the river against the shingle below us, and as the minutes passed and the agreed time of our meeting with the captain came and went, I began to be uneasy that even if he did keep to his promise, we might already be too late.

"'Fraid I can't see any sign of the captain, Sir!" said Joe, echoing my thoughts, as we peered anxiously into the darkness along the path towards Gravesend.

"Well, he gave his word. That's all I can say," I interjected impatiently. "But if he doesn't come soon, that's an end of it." For I could see that the brig's masts were now almost fully rigged.

"You wait here, Joe. I'll just walk along a bit and see if I can catch any sight of him," I then said, more in hope that any real expectation.

I had not gone far, however, when out of the gloom ahead of me, there emerged a tottering figure. Taking him to be some drunken sailor or other, I was, as he drew nearer, about to give him a suitably wide berth, when I realised that it was, in fact, the captain himself.

"Ah, there you are Fashant! I've been looking all over the plaish for you," he greeted me. That he was considerably the worse for drink, was only too apparent, for he was swaying like a pendulum. Indeed, more than once, as I made my way with him back to the landing-stage, I was obliged to catch hold of him to prevent him lurching over the bank and into the river.

"Are you sure you're going to be all right?" I said anxiously as he almost pitched over again.

"Wash you mean, Fashant? Corsh I'm all right. Now, wersh thish Dushman you told me about? I'll clap 'im in irons thash what I'll do!" he replied aggressively.

Faced with this new hazard, I had quickly to decide whether our scheme was now a practicable one, for, in the sort of state he was in, there could be no knowing how he was going to behave. There was, at least, one thing; Dutch courage as it might be, there could be no doubting his new found eagerness for the venture, and so, after a hurried consultation with Joe, I decided that we would take the chance, and come what may, proceed as we had planned.

And so, having managed, after several abortive attempts, to get him into the stern of the boat, we at last pushed off.

The tide had still not turned, and I could tell by the activity on the brig that it would, in fact, be several minutes before she was likely to sail, so I instructed Joe to take us downstream a little way and so make our approach from the direction of the frigate, and thus ensure, in case we were spotted, that we did, at least, appear to have come from that quarter. It would also, I thought, give the captain an opportunity to sober up a bit.

Not that there appeared to be much indication of this, when, having rounded the frigate, we eventually turned upstream and set course for the Dutchman.

"I don't much like the look of the captain, Joe," I said anxiously as he continued to lie there slumped in the stern with his head on his chest, and now snoring like a grampus. "See if you can stir some sort of life into him, will you?"

"I'll do what I can Sir, but he looks awful fuddled to me." And so saying, he gave him a sharp job in the ribs, which certainly had the desired effect, for giving an anguished cry, the captain all at once leaped uncertainly to his feet, and must have gone overboard had not Joe managed to grab hold of him.

That he had no idea where he was, or what we were about, was all too plain, and a deuce of a business it was, trying to get through to him any sort of clear-minded appreciation of the situation.

By then we were almost up to the brig and by the glow of the lantern in her forerigging, I could already make out the shadowy figures of the crew busy about their final preparations.

It was now or never I decided, and so having instructed Joe to bring us alongside, I shouted a "hello there" up to them. For a while there was no response, but after repeating the call, a member of the crew eventually came to the side.

"Captain Wakeley of His Majesty's frigate *Bellepheron* wishes to pay his respects to your commander," I said.

To this the fellow made some incomprehensible reply, and then disappeared, returning a few moments later with a companion.

"Vot ees it you vont?" cried this other, as he surveyed us with a lantern, which he held over the side.

"Vait a minute and I vil see," he then said, as I repeated my request.

The tide had now turned, and was running pretty fast, so that Joe, as we waited, was obliged to row to some purpose to enable us to hold our position; whilst I urgently continued to brief the captain with what was expected of him. To my relief he now seemed to be somewhat more sensible of what was happening, although he was clearly still pretty befuddled, and his speech so slurred, as to be almost unintelligible.

Just then, the crewman reappeared.

"Captain Zinkersen is most honoured, and would you please to come aboard," he said, and a moment later a rope ladder was slung down from the taffrail.

It was of the usual width, about a foot or so across, I suppose, and in calm water, and with one's wits about one, easy enough to negotiate. But with the brig heaving in the swell, and our own boat bobbing about like a cork, I could see that, with the captain in his present condition, we were going to have the devil's own job getting him up.

"We are now ready to board her, Sir," I said firmly.

"Wash that you shay, Farrant?" mumbled the captain hazily in reply.

"They have requested that we come aboard," I repeated with some impatience. "You must go first, Sir!"

With Joe keeping our boat as close to the brig as he could, I took hold of the rope ladder, and, having got the captain to his legs, we then managed somehow to manoeuvre one of his feet on to the bottom rung. No sooner had we done so, however, than our craft suddenly swung away, the captain lost his foothold and the two of us, with my feet clinging to the bulwarks, and my arms hugging his waist, were left suspended over the water. For one perilous moment, as I clung desperately to him, it seemed certain that we must go down; and would have done so, had not Joe dexterously swung the boat in again. Eventually, although not without a further near disaster or two, we succeeded in positioning the captain astride the ladder, with myself just below him in close support. Then, by much shoving and painstaking manipulation of his feet into each successive rung, I, as last, managed to heave him to the top.

Fortunately a couple of seamen came forward to help him over the side, otherwise he would, I am sure, have fallen flat to the deck before I was able to join him.

As I hurriedly did so, the commander, a swarthy, thick-set man of middle years, came forward to greet us.

"Thees ees an hounour, Captain, but you should 'ave given us warning so that we could 'ave prepared for your veesit," he said as he took the captain's hand. "But, as you see, ve sail very soon." For all his ingratiating reception of us, I could tell that he was puzzled by our visit, not, I am sure, that he could, anyway as yet, have suspected the purpose of it.

"Shorry to bother you like thish," responded Captain Wakeley. "Jusht a formality – Admiralshy's orders – paper of all neutrals mush be inshpected."

To my relief, and I must admit surprise, he had got it out much as I had instructed him.

"Ah! So I understand. Thees war, of course," responded the Dutchman. "But you vill find them all in order I theenk. Come with me, and I vill show them to you." And so saying he led us across the quarterdeck to the companion-way, whilst I guided the captain after him.

So far it had all gone better than I could have dared to hope. Even the captain's insobriety having some advantage, perhaps, in lulling any suspicions the Dutchman might have had of what we were really about.

"You vill find my – vot you say – quarters not so comfortable as you have on your naval ships," said the Dutchman, as he led us into his cabin.

It was indeed, the simplest of accommodation furnished with nothing but the bare necessities; a small circular table, a couple of chairs and a teak chest against one wall. The whole being dimly lit by a lamp, which swung from the middle of the deckhead.

"Seat down, gentlemen, and I vill find the papers you vant," he said. "But first let me offer you something to dreenk."

Having slumped into one of the chairs, Captain Wakeley already lay sprawled across the table, and, as the Dutchman turned away to fetch the refreshment, I was obliged to give him a sharp nudge to bring him to his senses again.

"I 'ope you will like thees. It comes from our island of Curaçao," said Captain Zinkersen with a certain pride, as he placed the bottle and glasses on the table.

"Curashao, did you shay?" cried the captain. "Exshellent stuff. Know the island well too – lay off there once – let me shee, when wash it? Sheventy-six or sheventy-sheven. You remember Fashant? The old *Dolphin* washn't it?"

"It must have been a little before my time, I think, Sir," I put in with due deference.

"Oh! Wash it? Yesh, I suppose it musht have been. Anyway, your very good health, Shir," added the captain, waving his glass with a wild flourish towards our host who had begun to move over to his chest.

"Wersh the fellow gone? Musht drink his health," murmured the captain.

"He'll be back with us in a moment. He's fetching the papers," I whispered, as I thrust him back into his chair, and at the same time contriving to drain his glass; for I was clearly going to have problems enough getting him away without his being more overseas than he already was.

"Thees are vot you vant, I theenk," said the Dutchman, returning to the table with a sheaf of papers.

"They are all in order you vill find," he then added, as he placed them before the captain, who, having stared down at them blankly for a moment or two, then impatiently pushed them over to me. "You look them over Fashant, I can't shee a damn thing in thish light."

Having made a pretence of closely examining them, I handed them back to the Dutchman. "They appear to be quite in order, Sir," I said, addressing Captain Wakeley.

"Thash all right then. Shorry to have bothered you Captain. Come along then, Fashant. We mushn't waste any more of the fellow's time," and so saying he commenced to stagger to his feet.

"You may remember, Sir, that there is just one other matter," I said firmly, and at the same time giving him a significant look, for it was quite evident that he had become wholly oblivious as to the real purpose of our visit.

"Oh! Ish there, Fashant?" responded Captain Wakeley blankly, as he collapsed into his chair again.

"You 'ave seen all the papers I 'ave," then put in the Dutchman. And for all that he did his best to conceal it, I could, I thought, detect a certain note of alarm in his voice.

"I 'ave nothing more to show you gentlemen. Unless you vish to see my log-book. I 'ave eet right 'ere."

"No, Captain," I said, as he made to move over to the chest. "That, I am sure, is perfectly in order."

"What ees it then?" he then said, and I could tell by the frightened look in his eyes that he had begun to suspect what we were after.

"No doubt you will understand what I mean," I said, as I began to finger the pistol in my pocket, "when I tell you that Nathaniel Cruden has been taken in charge, and has made a full confession." I was bluffing, of course, but he was not to know that.

"I don't know vot you mean. This, vot you say, Crooden! I 'ave never 'eard of 'im," expostulated the Dutchman. "There must be some mistake. You 'ave seen my papers. They are in order as you 'ave said. Vot else is eet you vant?"

So genuine did his refutation sound, that for a moment I almost began to wonder whether we were not barking up the wrong tree, and that he was, in fact, entirely innocent. However, it was no time to waver, and so, levelling my pistol at him I said, "Come now, Captain, it's no use pretending. As I have said, Cruden has told us everything so we know that you have the package."

Whether it was the sight of the pistol, or whether it was that he just fell for my bluff, anyway, he all at once capitulated.

"Ver' well. Yes, I 'ave some papers. I know nothing about them, or vot they contain. I vas told to deliver them, that's all. If you vait a moment, I vill get them for you," he replied, all meekness now, as he moved hurriedly back to his chest. Whilst I, for fear that he might have a weapon of his own secreted there, took care to follow after him.

"Thees ees what 'e gave me. As I 'ave said, I don't know what eet contains," he said, producing an oilskin-wrapped package, which he then proceeded to thrust into my hands with all the alacrity of someone disposing of a hot potato.

With our object achieved, and the package surely in my possession, I had now to turn my attention to the problem of getting Captain Wakeley safely back to our boat. Clearly no easy matter was it going to be, as he lay there slouched across the table, and now clearly insensible to all that was going one.

Having shaken him into some sort of consciousness, however, I managed somehow to get him to his feet and making sure, all the while, to keep the Dutchman still covered with my pistol, I succeeded in manhandling the captain over to the door.

"Now, there is to be no delay, you understand. I must insist that you weigh anchor, and set sail at once," I said addressing the Dutchman. "For if you don't, I can assure you that your ship will be impounded, and you yourself taken into custody."

"Yes, yes, ve sail at vonce. I vill see to eet," agreed the Dutchman eagerly, obviously relieved that we were intending to take no further action.

With this, I extracted the key from the lock, bundled Captain Wakeley out of the cabin, and, having followed after him, I then secured the door from the outside. It was an unnecessary precaution, perhaps, but I was determined to take no chances.

All that now remained was to get the captain off the ship; and no easy task did I have of it. Indeed, so helpless had he become by this time, that I was obliged virtually to carry him up the companion-way and over to the side whence, with the help of another rope ladder, and with the assistance of Joe and some members of the crew, we eventually managed to lower him down.

"Everythin' all right, Sir?" asked Joe anxiously, as we pulled away.

"It couldn't have gone better, Joe," I replied jubilantly.

"You got what you wanted then?"

"Yes, he was our man right enough. He tried to bluff it out at first and deny everything, but he handed it over all right in the end."

"'Ow about the Captain, though? 'Ow did 'e behave? From the looks of

’im I wouldn’t be thinkin’ ’e was of much help. Was ’e, Sir?” added Joe doubtfully.

“No, Joe, he wasn’t. And I’m afraid I can’t say that he did much to enhance the reputation of His Majesty’s Navy,” I added with a laugh. “Still he got us on board, and that, after all, was the main thing, I suppose.”

That the Dutchman was heeding my threats, and losing no time in getting under way, was soon evident, for as I looked back I could see that her sails were already beginning to billow in the wind.

“She won’t be long now, Sir,” cried Joe, as we made for the shore.

And indeed, as he spoke we could hear the sound of her anchor being weighed, and, a few moments later, I had the satisfaction of watching her glide away downstream, and gradually disappear into the darkness and towards the open sea.

It really did seem, I thought, as we regained the landing-stage and disembarked, that I had achieved what I had set out to do.

For, not only did I have the package securely in my possession, but with the brigantine safely upon her way back to Holland, there was the added gratification of knowing that Cruden would be quite unaware that anything had gone amiss with their plans.

My one concern was for the old captain, and the fear that he may have suffered some injury to his health. For, apart from all the rough and tumble to which he had, of necessity, been subjected, he had, as I was to discover when we helped him ashore, received a thorough drenching into the bargain.

However, having lost no time in hurrying him back to his lodgings, we soon fitted him out with a change of clothing, and after imbibing quantities of strong coffee, he was soon back to his old querulous self again, and all in all seemed, thankfully, to be little the worse for his ordeal. So, having entrusted him with the package, and enjoined upon him the importance of dispatching it to Atterbury with all urgency, Joe and I took our leave, and made the best of our way back to the manor.

Chapter XXI

Of the next day or two I have nothing of significance to relate, being content, as I remember, to remain within the confines of the manor, where apart from some further cataloguing, I beguiled the time away in a sort of ecstatic haze, as I continued to receive further intimations that my ever deepening devotion to Miss Catherine was not, perhaps, a hopeless one.

With my thoughts so joyously preoccupied, I was, thus, little disposed to reflect upon the problem of how best to further my mission. Anyway, as I have said, I really could not see how this was to be achieved; at least not without exposing myself to almost certain destruction, which, I might say, I was loath to do, having in that respect, I reckoned, already offered up more than sufficient temptation to fate.

In any case, I need not have worried, for as it chanced, I was very shortly to be so overtaken by, and involved in, events of such moment as to leave me little time for reflection of any kind.

These I will have cause to relate all in good time. But I must first give some account of my visit to the house of the old cripple out there on the marshes. Not so much for the occasion itself, extraordinary as this was, but rather the perilous nature of its sequel, in which, as you shall hear, I was to come once again so near to putting a period to my existence.

As I intimated at the time, it was with no little reluctance that I had accepted his invitation, and the intervening few days had certainly done nothing to lessen my disrelish for the jaunt. On the contrary, so further played upon by misgivings was I that when the appointed day arrived I was sorely tempted, I remember, to send Joe over with some concocted excuse or other. But somehow, when I came to put pen to paper, so reminded was I of all his kindness to me that evening, and the eager way in which he had pressed his invitation, that I felt I just could not bring myself to disappoint him.

Having thus finally pledged myself to the expedition, I bethought that it might be worth approaching Joe, to see if he could be persuaded to accompany me, at least for some part of the way. So having attired myself as presentably as my limited wardrobe would allow, and wearing the old greatcoat of Sir George's, I thus set off for the stables where, as Craddock had informed me, Joe was most likely to be found, adding sardonically, "And asleep I shouldn't wonder." Contrary to the old butler's aspersion, I found him, instead, to be hard at work grooming Bess.

"I'm sorry to interrupt you, Joe," I said as I leaned over the stable door.

"That's all right, Sir. Is there anything I can do for you?" he responded cheerfully, as he emerged from behind the horse's flanks.

"It's only that I have to go over to old Mr Fenton's, and I was wondering whether you would care to accompany me, for I don't think I'm quite sure of the way," I then asked him, albeit with some diffidence.

For that such a jaunt, especially with dusk about to fall, would have little appeal to him I had good reason to anticipate, knowing, as I did, of his superstitious fear of the marshes, and all the frightful apparitions which were popularly supposed to haunt them. There being one, in particular, of which he had spoken with particular dread. 'The Headless Horror of the Sea-Wall' I think it was called and which, or so he had grimly assured me, foredoomed an early death for anyone unfortunate enough to encounter it.

That such unpalatable reflections were, in truth, passing through his mind, I could tell by the obvious discomfiture with which he received my proposal; and even before he replied I knew what his answer would be.

"I should like to come along o'you, o' course, Sir," he said at last without looking up. "But I don't like leaving Bess, seein' as I've already started on 'er. She wouldn't like it, bein' only 'alf done as yer might say."

That it was nothing more than an excuse to cover his real reason, I could tell by the awkward manner in which he had come out with it.

Not wishing, however, to cause him further embarrassment by pressing my request, which I sensed would, anyhow, be quite useless, I simply said, "Yes, of course, Joe, I quite understand."

"But I wouldn't leave it too late if I was you, Sir," he interposed. "Once it gets dark it's not too easy to follow the tracks, and, if you asks me, I wouldn't dawdle either, Sir. There's some awful queer things 'appen down there of a night," he added darkly.

"Don't worry, Joe. I'll watch out," I said with an attempt at a laugh. And with this I left him to his grooming, and reluctantly set off down the driveway, and out on to the high road towards the marshes.

It was a heavy and depressing evening, with a bank of low-lying cloud overhead. Even so, in less unpropitious circumstances, I would have looked forward to the excursion.

As it was, I fear, my thoughts were filled with anything but pleasurable anticipation, when having left the manor grounds behind me, I looked down upon that desolate waste, and over towards the old recluse's solitary abode which, in spite of the fading light, was still just discernible out there in the far reaches of the marsh.

It was not, I must hasten to add, that I went in any dread of Joe's apparitions, which could be dismissed as just a lot of superstitious nonsense surely. My forebodings, as you can imagine, were founded upon something altogether more tangible; something of real flesh and blood. For much as I had taken care that I was not being shadowed, I was, nevertheless, still haunted by the chilling possibility that Cruden could somehow have got wind of my assignation with Mr Fenton, and that Crab Snade might already be lurking somewhere out there among the reeds.

Fortunately the light, as I have said, was still fairly good, and likely to remain so, I consoled myself; at least until I reached my destination, which was some four miles or so distant, as best as I could estimate. Although, to add to my disquiet, I could see that a low mist was already beginning to settle like a shroud, as it were, over the lower-lying ground.

That there was, in truth, something peculiarly eerie about the locality at such an hour, there could be no denying, I thought, as, having dropped down from the high road, I proceeded to set forth into the solitary expanse. Indeed, that anyone of an impressionable turn of mind could well be prone to all manner of ghostly imaginings, was not difficult to believe, and I could certainly appreciate Joe's reluctance to accompany me.

As I have indicated, my fears were, however, more substantially based, and open as the ground largely was, I was careful to approach any feasible means of cover with the utmost circumspection, being particularly wary when I came up to the flat-timbered bridges over the dykes, which, I should mention, intersected the marsh at irregular intervals, and where the reeds afforded ample opportunity for concealment.

That my path was not going to be as straightforward as I had imagined, I was soon to discover, as owing to the haphazard way in which the bridges had been situated, the path was very much a zigzag one, and not always easy to follow in the prevailing light, so that, more than once, I was obliged to chase up and down for some while before I was able to hit upon the next way across.

Eventually, however, and to my relief, for it was by then almost dark, I had negotiated the last of the waterways, and there before me, some few hundred yards distant, stood the old cripple's solitary dwelling, a gaunt square-shaped house of flintstone and brick, perched upon a low hummock of ground.

As I made my way up to the entrance, I could not but wonder, for all his gruesome appearance, that he could have chosen so isolated and bleak a locality in which to reside.

After the menacing inhospitality of the marsh, a welcome refuge it was none the less, and it was with something of an uplift of spirit that I took hold of the bellpull, and gave it a tug. Although I must confess that, in spite of what Joe had told me of the bizarre nature of the ménage, I was not a little taken aback when, in response to my ring, I was shortly confronted by a footman so extravagantly deformed as to make old Mr Fenton, who just then emerged at the far end of the hall to greet me, appear almost personable by comparison.

Of the evening I spent in that singular abode, there is no need to dwell at length. Suffice it to say that I soon found Mr Fenton to be as kindly and generous a host as one could have wished. Indeed, such was the sincere warmth of his personality, that I had not been long in his presence, before his terrible disfigurement seemed scarcely to be apparent.

What especially touched me was the affectionate, almost paternal, manner in which he treated his small band of male domestics, all of whom, like himself, being afflicted with some terrible disfigurement or other. That his devotion was equally returned by each one of them was plain to see when, during the course of the evening, they had occasion to wait upon us.

Of the interior of the house I will only say that it could scarcely have contrasted more strikingly with the bleakness of its surrounds, for inside all was light and magnificence, each room being furnished as splendidly as the next, although in differing styles. That of the main or drawing-room being essentially oriental in character, reflecting, no doubt, my host's extensive travels in that quarter of the globe.

The library to which we adjourned after dinner, although not as considerable as Sir George's was, even to my untutored eye, clearly a more scholarly and selective one.

Do my best, as I did, to conceal my utter want of connoisseurship, as with diffident pride he showed me some of the choicest items of his collection, he must very soon, I am sure, have realised that I was, in fact, the veriest ignoramus, although such was his courtesy, that he certainly gave no hint of his awareness.

Thus, all too quickly, the evening passed, and the time arrived when I felt that I could not, with propriety, delay my departure any longer.

Knowing my host's inclination for nocturnal rambling, I had been in some hopes that he would volunteer to accompany me upon my return to the manor. To my disappointment he made no such proposal however, and being shy of making any such request myself, I duly took my leave of that remarkable household, with all its friendly and bountiful hospitality, and set off out into the night upon my solitary journey back to the manor.

With such a sense of foreboding was I soon overcome, that I had not gone very far, I remember, when I was tempted to retrace my steps, knock up Mr Fenton and, upon some pretext or other, entreat his company. Unhappily a misguided sense of pride prevailed upon me to resist the temptation, and so summoning such resolve as I had left, I duly pressed on.

By this time it was well past midnight, and with the moon now obscured by cloud, the light was of the dimmest. Thus, with no real landmarks to guide me, I soon found that I was having even greater difficulty than before in keeping to the paths, especially as the mist had not only thickened considerably, but had also spread well beyond the confines of the dykes, so that it now enveloped a large part of the intervening stretches of marsh. Indeed, so impossible did I find it to keep to the true path, that more than once, I discovered myself floundering up to my calves in some odious patch of quagmire or other.

Every so often the plaintive cry of a seabird would break the eerie silence, and once, close by me, there came the sound of a cough so human in character, as to send my heart momentarily to my mouth, before I realised, as I reached for my pistol, that it must have been a sheep, the shadowy forms of which were wont, I might add, to loom up out of the mist, every now and then, to fill me with sudden alarm. Otherwise all was deathly quiet, and with nothing further occurring to alarm me, I continued to hurry on, until at last, and to my profound relief, I could dimly make out the high road on the ridge ahead of me, and, if my memory served me right, I must now, I reckoned, have only one further dyke to cross. I would then be virtually quit of the marsh, and the rest of the way back to the manor would, thankfully, be straightforward enough.

Encouraged by such a thought, and feeling altogether much lighter of heart now that the worst of my journey was seemingly behind me, I had sought out the bridge, and had just reached the far bank, when I was suddenly alerted by the sound of a faint rustling in the reeds beside me. Then, before I knew what was happening, or had time to reach for my pistol, I felt my legs being pulled from under me, as I was sent sprawling to the ground. Had I fallen absolutely flat all would, I am sure, have been up with me. In the event I managed somehow, as I landed, to twist myself on to one side, and this it was which undoubtedly saved me; for when the knife lunge came, my body consequently afforded nothing like so ample a target, as it otherwise would have done. Even so, it must have been a close enough thing, for it had, as I was later to discover, ripped up the front of my coat.

Anyway, before my assailant could lash out again, I had taken a firm hold, with both my hands, of his lethal wrist. Not that my plight was much less perilous, for he had his legs athwart me now, with his free hand pressing into my face whilst with its point wavering uncomfortably close to my heart, I was frantically endeavouring to fend the knife away.

He, of course, had the advantage of downthrust, while I had the use of both hands, and as well, I think, the edge in point of strength.

For an eternity, or so it seemed, the blade thus remained equipoised, neither of us yielding an inch. Then, of a sudden, and unwisely, for my arms were already becoming deadened with the fatigue of my hold, so that I must very soon have succumbed, he lost patience, and releasing his hand from my face, struck out at my head.

Anyway, as he did so, he must have overbalanced a little thus enabling me to twist him to one side.

By my manoeuvre, he had now lost something of his advantage, and although he continued to lash out with his free fist, I nevertheless managed to retain a firm hold of his knife-bearing right one which, from my better position, I was then able, by degrees, to force away from me. In so doing I sensed that his grip upon the blade was beginning to ease, and, as I continued to tighten my hold, his fingers suddenly went limp, and the knife slithered from his grasp.

Then, all at once, as we both struggled to retrieve it, with each still retaining a frantic hold of the other, the ground began to slip from beneath us and, before I realised what was happening, we had rolled over together into the dyke.

Impeded as our momentum had been by the reeds, it was into no more than three feet of water, I suppose, that we eventually came to rest. A depth nevertheless in which I, and doubtless my adversary also, was perfectly aware, either of us could easily be drowned.

I can still recall, with total vividness, the awful horror of the next few moments, as, scarcely visible to each other in the misty darkness, we sprawled and slithered together in that stinking mud.

More than once he had me floundering backwards, so that all seemed lost, and would have been, had I not clung desperately to him, and managed to swing his body to one side of me, as we sank beneath the water. There we lay, suffocating in a ghastly sort of embrace, before we were enabled somehow to heave ourselves up again.

Hampered, as I was, by my heavier build, as well as the encumbrance of my greatcoat, there is no doubt that I was having the worst of it, and I am quite certain that, had I gone down again, he would have prevailed. In the event it was sheer chance that saved me. My feet had quite gone from under me, as I remember, and having at the same moment lost my hold of him, I was sprawling helplessly backwards, when, of a sudden, I felt something hard strike across my shoulders. I had, in fact, as I quickly realised, come up against the side of the bridge.

Anyway, as he came for me again, and before he could have had any notion of what had occurred, I had a leg behind one of his, and using the bridge as a fulcrum, I had upturned him backwards into the water.

The unexpected dexterity of my throw so surprised him that he gave out a great cry, I remember, as he fell, and before he could recover, I had hurled myself upon him, thrusting his head backwards into the water as I did so.

He struggled for a while, his legs thrashing about in a desperate attempt to dislodge me, but it was to no purpose, for I held him too securely and, before long, I felt his body suddenly go limp and then sink lifelessly back into the mud.

So overcome by the exhaustion of it all was I, that, for several minutes, I remember, I just lay there in the water beside him before I was able, at last, to drag myself to my feet and, having first reassured myself that he was, indeed, quite dead, heave myself over the bank, whence I stumbled off upon the remainder of my journey back to the manor.

So preoccupied had I been with the sole aim of survival, that it was not until then that I came to give any real thought as to the identity of my assailant. Not that I was really in much doubt of it.

And, indeed, as I was to hear nothing further of him, it can safely be presumed, I think, that it was, in fact, Crab Snade, whose remains, for aught I know, still lie mouldering in that watery grave out there upon the marsh.

Chapter XXII

After that desperate encounter upon the marshes I was, I might tell you, irresolute of me as it may have been, even less inclined than ever to stir far from the manor. Having once again come so close to extinction, I was certainly in no mind to give that 'blind fury' another chance of wielding his 'abhorred shears'.

Joe, conversely, was imbued with no such craven inhibitions. Each morning, I remember, he would appear full of some wildcap scheme or other, most of them being of so perilous a nature as to send a cold shiver through me even to contemplate.

Indeed, so eager was he to be of assistance, that my great fear was that he might do something really foolhardy.

He had, in fact, although I had done my best to dissuade him, more than once taken it upon himself to shadow Cruden, when he had chanced to venture out of a night, and on one such occasion must, indeed, have come tantalisingly close to unmasking Cruden's co-conspirator. Upon the evening in question, he had apparently tracked Cruden as far as the old windmill, where, upon his disappearing inside, he had lain concealed as I had done, within the shadow of one of the ricks, on the off chance that someone else might appear.

"And perishin' cold it was too. I thought I should 'ave froze," declared Joe as he went on to describe his vigil. "For an hour or more Nat must 'ave bin in there, before I 'ears the door creak open, and out 'e comes down the steps, and makes straight for where I was lyin', or so I reckoned 'e was. My heart fair went to my boots thinking 'e must 'ave spotted me, and if I 'adn't bin so stiff and froze like, I would 'ave got up and scarpered, I don't mind tellin' yer. Instead, I jus' sticks me 'ead down and prays. And when I looks up again 'e'd gone."

"You didn't see anyone else, I suppose, did you, Joe?" I interjected hopefully.

"I'm just coming to that, Sir. As soon as Nat had gone, I was thinkin' I'd better look sharp, and make sure and be back at the 'Daws' before 'e did. Any'ow, I 'ad jus' got to my feet when, suddenly, I 'ears the door click open again. So down I goes flat, and looks to see who it could be. But what with the dark, and the mill behind 'im, it wasn't easy to make out much,

’specially as ’e was all ’uddled up like. And, anyway, ’e’d shot off over the other side of the ’ill towards the manor afore I could think of following ’im. I did try to, but ’e must ’ave got away awful quick, for ’e just seemed to disappear.”

“So, you’ve no idea whom it could have been then, Joe?” I said.

“’Fraid I ’aven’t, Sir. You see, ’e was all crouched and ’uddled up like, and as I say, ’e ’ad ’is ’ead stuck down in his greatcoat.”

“A pity. But never mind, Joe. You did very well,” I said doing my best to conceal my disappointment. “Anyway, perhaps you could give me some description of him. Was he short, tall, old or young, would you say?”

“I wouldn’t say ’e was short, Sir. But then, ’e wasn’t tall, leastways, I don’t think so. Broad-like and of middlin’ age, I should say ’e was. Anyway, ’e didn’t look young.”

“Did you notice anything else about him? Some unusual feature or other perhaps? Now think carefully, Joe, for it could be vital,” I added earnestly.

“Not really, Sir. Wait though, there was one thing.”

“Why, what was that, Joe?” I put in expectantly.

“Now I come to think of it, I should say ’e was gentry, or somethin’ of the kind anyway.”

“Oh! why should you think that, Joe?”

“Well, ’e ’ad that sort of walk, if you know what I mean, Sir.”

“But it wasn’t anyone you might have known, you don’t think?”

“I really couldn’t rightly say, Sir. But I wouldn’t say as it couldn’t ’ave bin.”

And although I continued to press him, that was as much as he could tell me of Cruden’s mysterious co-conspirator, or so I imagined he must have been. It was, of course, little enough to go on, but what there was, certainly had me wondering, I can tell you. Nor was I afforded much opportunity of speculating upon the identity of this shadowy personage, as, during the next couple of days, my time, as was the rest of the household’s, was taken up with preparations for a ball, which, as Sir George had suddenly announced, was to be held at the manor in honour of Sir David Dundas, the Commander in Chief of our anti-invasion armies, who was shortly to be in the neighbourhood for some military purpose or other.

It was to be no mean affair either. For, as Sir George had insisted, no expense must be spared, to ensure that the occasion paid ample tribute to our country’s brave defenders, and their commander.

Besides Sir David and his staff, some thirty couples or so had been invited, whilst, to my great joy, and I fear the major’s mortification, it was her father’s wish that I partner Miss Catherine.

As you can imagine the manor was in utter turmoil, especially as, on top of all the other arrangements, Sir George would have it that the main living-rooms must be entirely redecorated for the occasion. A service of which, one had to admit, they were certainly in dire need.

Come the day all was still pandemonium, needless to say; with a host of decorators, cooks, gardeners, cleaners and other assorted menials, still feverishly at work, in an endeavour to bring some sort of order out of chaos. Whilst Sir George, in an increasing frenzy of distraction, paced from room to room, exhorting all and sundry to ever greater industry.

Scarcely a minute seemed to pass before some new emergency would arise. First the dais which was being erected for the orchestra at one end of the library, was found to be too small, and so additional wood had to be procured. Then it was discovered that there were nothing like enough containers for all the flowers, which Sir George had seen fit to be delivered, and which lay about everywhere in such profusion, as if it had been Vauxhall that was to be decorated rather than a small manor house!

Then there was Miss Beauchamp, beside herself with distraction because the new gown which she had ordered had not arrived from the dressmakers.

First, she would have it, against all the evidence, that the parcel must in fact have been delivered, only to have become lost in the general confusion. So consequently, everything must be turned upside down in a fruitless search for it. Then, having been finally persuaded that it was not on the premises, she demanded that Joe be dispatched to Rochester to fetch it. While Sir George equally insisted that he could not be spared, declaring that he had more urgent business to attend to than the fetching of 'a silly bit of frumpery', and that anyway, she already had 'gowns enough to clothe an opera'. Which remarks, needless to say, provoked a long and vituperative altercation, until Sir George, realising that no peace was to be had unless he acceded to her request, finally relented.

Then, to cap it all, there came, during the course of the afternoon, the news that Lady Thurlow had somehow contrived to reach Portugal, and was expected to arrive at Dover by the Lisbon packet the following morning. Tidings which, in contrast to his daughter's great relief and joy, Sir George received with a dismay which, although he did his best to disguise, was, I fear, all too transparent.

Nevertheless, that it was his husbandly duty to set off for Dover at the earliest opportunity, consistent that is, with his presiding over the ball, all were agreed. The only question that had to be decided being how this could most expeditiously be achieved.

Sir George himself, and not unreasonably I thought, was of the opinion that the morrow would be soon enough. Miss Catherine, who was determined to accompany her father to Dover, would have none of this, however, insisting that they travei overnight so as to be able to greet her mother when she disembarked.

To this, albeit reluctantly, Sir George was finally persuaded to agree, and it having first been ascertained that two inside seats were still available, it was decided that they would set off by the night coach, which was scheduled to pass the manor gates soon after midnight.

Meanwhile, as I have said, the manor was a veritable bedlam, as all fell to work, family and servants alike, to get the final preparations for the ball completed.

By late afternoon, such was the disorder that still prevailed, that it seemed quite impossible that all could be got ready in time.

In the event, although scarcely before the first guests had begun to arrive, order was somehow achieved. The army of menials and their accoutrements vanished and, as if by a miracle, there everything stood revealed in all its new-found splendour.

On the ball itself there is little need to dwell at length. That the evening is one that will ever be hallowed in my own memory, you may believe, when I tell you that it was the occasion when my dear wife and I became betrothed; pledging, as we did so, mutual vows of eternal devotion which, taken all in all, we have continued to preserve these forty years.

That the evening was, as well, a triumph for Sir George, there could be no doubting. Magnificently attired, as I remember, in a military concoction of his own devising, he quite outshone the regular soldiery, and his evident and uninhibited enjoyment of it all set such a stamp of conviviality on the proceedings, as to infect the whole assembly. Save, perhaps, for the unhappy Major Fripp who, to add to his mortification was, as I recall, saddled for most of the evening with a partner who was as ungainly as she was plain.

Miss Beauchamp, splendid as she looked in her new gown, was another for whom the evening was, I am afraid, not without its tribulations, obliged, as she was, to endure the almost insistent and pot-valiant attentions of Captain Wakeley.

I had experienced some misgivings, as soon as he had joined the company, for it was clear that he was, even by then, already more than a few sheets to the wind. Anyway, as the night advanced, so liberally did he continue to refresh himself, that his behaviour became ever more intemperate, so that at last he was scarce able to stand; the climax being reached when, during the dancing of a quadrille, he overbalanced, and in so doing clutched hold of the unfortunate Miss Beauchamp, so that the pair of them were sent tumbling in an unceremonious heap to the floor.

Leaving Miss Catherine to placate as best she could the by now almost hysterical Miss Beauchamp, Dr Argent and I attended to the hapless Captain whom, although he much protested, we eventually succeeded in conveying to the seclusion of an anteroom, whence it was agreed that the doctor would see him safely back to his lodgings.

Thus the evening sped by, and all too quickly there came the time for Sir George and his daughter to join the night coach for Dover.

Needless to say, with the festivities still in full swing, this was something which Sir George was more than ever reluctant to do. So loath was he to depart, in fact, that in the end, I remember, we had literally to bundle him out of the manor and down to the awaiting coach which, in any case, had been obliged to be held up for several minutes to ensure that it did not proceed without them.

With the departure of Sir George and his daughter, the guests soon began to disperse save, that is, for Sir David Dundas and his aide-de-camp, who were to spend the night at the manor, and it was not long before Miss Beauchamp and I, the former's equanimity having, by this time, been restored, were waving the last of the carriages away down the drive.

On the plea of his grave responsibilities, Sir David soon excused himself and retired, leaving Miss Beauchamp, Major Fripp, the aide-de-camp and myself seated cosily around the fire in the library discussing the evening's events.

We were thus pleasantly disposed when, of a sudden, however, Sir David reappeared and, without any sort of ceremony, grimly requested that his aide-de-camp join him outside.

From his demeanour, that something had seriously disturbed him was evident, for he was, I should mention, the dourest of Scotsmen and not normally given, as I had observed, to emotion of any kind.

As it was, we were afforded little time to puzzle over what could have happened to cause his distress, for his aide-de-camp presently returned with the request that Major Fripp and I join them both in the drawing-room.

"I am sorry, gentlemen, to have to disturb you," Sir David greeted us sternly as we entered, "but something of the gravest consequence has occurred." Although he was doing his best to compose himself, his face as I could see, was quite ashen, and his hand visibly shook as he poured himself a drink whilst he spoke.

"To be brief with you," he went on, "I have just discovered that my travelling case has been rifled, and that documents of the utmost importance are missing. Documents which contain, I must tell you, such information as would certainly be of inestimable value to the enemy were they to get into their hands."

For a moment or so, the two of us were too stunned to speak, until the major interposed. "Are you absolutely sure, Sir, that they were there when you arrived?"

"Yes, quite certain," retorted Sir David sharply. "I was looking them over only this evening, so there can be no doubt that they were removed by someone after I reached the manor. Anyway, the question is, gentlemen," resumed Sir David more calmly now, "what are we going to do? Neither of you have any idea, I suppose, who might have taken them? It could, of course, have been any one of the guests, I imagine," went on Sir David in response to our unhelpful replies. "Or, one of the servants, I suppose. Or, again, someone could just have sneaked in from outside. I'm afraid almost anything's possible," he added ruefully.

"It would certainly be worth sounding the servants, don't you think, Sir?"

put in the aide-de-camp deferentially. "There's a chance they might have seen someone acting suspiciously."

"Yes, that's the first thing that ought to be done," agreed Sir David. "Perhaps we could leave that to you, Major, as you must know them better than any of us."

"Yes, of course. I'll see to it at once," agreed Major Fripp, as he hurried off.

What my own feelings were all this while, you can, I am sure, imagine. That such a thing should have occurred under my very nose, as it were, was distressing enough, but to make matters worse, I could not but feel that I was in some part to blame for what had happened, in as much as I should, with my special knowledge, have surely been alive to such a possibility, and have, consequently, warned Sir David of the danger.

It was too late to worry about that now, however. The damage had been done, and, although I had not the least conception how I was to set about it, it was plainly incumbent upon me to do what I could to retrieve the documents.

Anyhow, I ought first, I decided, to disclose to Sir David the real purpose of my being in Gravesend, as well as what I already knew of the enemy's espionage activities in the neighbourhood; and so, as soon as Major Fripp had left us, I proceeded, as briefly as I could, to do so.

"This, I fear, places an even graver complexion upon it," he declared solemnly when I had finished. "For, if, indeed, as now seems likely, an organisation of that kind is behind the theft, no time will certainly be lost in getting the information across to France. You have no idea at all then who might be behind it all?" he then added anxiously.

"No, I'm afraid I haven't," I replied in a tone of helplessness.

"It's even possible, I suppose, that, whoever it was, could have been at the ball tonight," he then interjected.

I could only agree.

"And if so," continued Sir David glumly, "he would, of course, have had every opportunity of slipping up to my room and removing the papers."

"Might it not be a wise move, Sir," interposed the aide-de-camp, "to have pickets placed at all the main roads out of Gravesend? There wouldn't be many travelling at this hour, so we might have a chance of intercepting him."

"Yes, you're right, that's one thing we ought to do," agreed Sir David. "Although I really can't imagine that it will do any good," he added with a heavy sigh. "For they're certain to go about it in a much more devious way than that, I am quite sure. Nevertheless, you had better get along and see to it, I suppose."

"Whatever else we do, the first thing, I am sure," said Sir David as the aide-de-camp hurried off, "is to have this innkeeper apprehended. Although it's most unlikely, it is just possible, I suppose, that he may have been entrusted with the papers. Anyway, it would certainly be worth interrogating him. I can give you the necessary warrant of course, so there's no problem there. And we've clearly no time to lose, so you had better get down there as soon as you can," he added, as he moved over to a desk to pen the authorisation.

"Cruden was his name, wasn't it?"

"Yes, that's right, Sir," I confirmed. "Nathaniel Cruden."

"Well, I can only trust, Sir, that you will be able to discover something," he said feelingly, as he handed over the warrant. "You'll need to take a couple of law officers with you, and make sure that you are armed. And, you'll report back to me at once of course if you discover anything."

And with this I hurried away to execute the commission.

What with the mellowing influences of the ball together with the blissful happenings attendant upon it, my mind was still in such a whirl of conflicting emotions, that it was not until I had reached the seclusion of my room, and could be alone with my thoughts, that I was able fully to comprehend the awful significance of what had occurred. There could be no doubting, from what Sir David had hinted, that the information which had been smuggled away was of the most vital nature, and that, were it to reach France, it could well be disastrous to our chances of repelling an invasion. The implications, indeed, were so appalling as scarcely to bear dwelling upon, especially as I have already said, I could not but consider myself to be at least, in some part, to blame for the whole sorry business.

It was, however, no time for self-recrimination, and having hurriedly changed into some more formal attire, I set off at once to organise Cruden's arrest and interrogation.

I had got no further than the hall, however, when I was intercepted by old Craddock.

"I'm sorry to bother you, Sir, but there's a girl below stairs, who says she must see you. I tried to argue with 'er seeing as it's so late, but she seems terribly put out, so I thought I'd best try and find you."

"A young girl!" I said completely mystified. "Do you know who she is?"

"I can't say as I do, Sir. But she's carrying on most distressful like."

"It's all very strange. Are you quite sure it was me she asked for?" I said, with some impatience.

"Yes, Sir. She says she must see Mr Farrant, that's all she'll say. It might help if you could see her, Sir, the way she's acting an' all," he then added earnestly.

Mindful of the extreme urgency of the errand I was set upon, I at first hesitated but, as it would, I thought, take no more than a moment or two to discover what it was all about, I decided that I ought at least to see the girl.

"Very well, all right Craddock, I'd better see her, I suppose," I said, still wondering whom she could possibly be.

"Shall I ask her to come up here, Sir?"

"No, that's all right, Craddock. I'll come to her." And with this I followed him down to the servants' quarters.

It was only then, as we began to descend the basement stairs, that it suddenly dawned upon me who the girl might be and, as it did so, there shuddered through me a dreadful premonition of what it was that had caused her to seek me out.

She was seated huddled over a table, in the consoling embrace of one of the maids as I entered the kitchen and, although her back was towards me, I knew at once that it was Sally Cruden. And when, as I continued to move over to her, she turned and I looked into that grief-stricken face, I sensed, with a terrible certainty, even before she had spoken, that my worst fears were to be confirmed.

"Oh! Sir! It's Joe! He's dead! He's been killed!" she sobbed out, before relapsing once more into the enveloping arms of her comforter.

Anticipated as it had been, when the dreaded pronouncement came, so stunned was I, that, for the moment, all I could do was to continue to stare blankly down at the pathetic bundle of despair slumped there beneath me.

Horrified and afflicted as I was by the dreadful news, even more agonising to bear was the awful awareness that I, myself, must bear a large share of the responsibility for his death, as, having little doubt as to how and why he'd met it, there could be no escaping the awful truth that he had been sacrificed in the furtherance of my own interests.

Signalling to Craddock and the maid to leave us alone together, I sat down beside the poor girl and, taking her hand in mine, attempted to offer what solace I could. Wholly inadequate as any such consoling words necessarily are, and always must be, upon such grievous occasions.

"I 'ope I did right, Sir, in coming to you," she said at last, doing her best to fight back her tears. "You see 'e said I was to, if anythin' should 'appen to 'im."

"You did quite right, of course," I said gently.

"'E must 'ave known, I suppose, that 'e was in some sort of danger. Though who would want to 'arm 'im, I don't know. Everyone liked 'im you see. Oh! Sir!" she cried, all at once breaking down again. "I don't know what's going' to become of us. 'E was always so good to me and the children. They couldn't 'ave 'ad a better father, even though we weren't proper wed like."

"No, I'm quite sure they couldn't," I put in soothingly.

Loath as I was to question her while she was so sorely oppressed, I felt nevertheless, that I must discover something of the circumstances of Joe's death, before I set off in search of Cruden.

"But, how did this terrible thing happen?" I thus cautiously asked.

"'E was in the water when they found 'im, Sir. Just along o' the shore from the 'Daws'. At first they thought 'e'd just fallen in and drowned, for 'e never could swim. But when they brought 'im in, they could see this wound in 'is chest where 'e'd been stabbed. It was a knife, that's what did it, Sir. But who could 'ave done it, Sir? Dear Joe, 'e was always so kind. 'E wouldn't 'ave 'urt a fly." And with this she dissolved into tears once again.

"When was it you last saw him?" I continued, when she had recovered her composure a little.

"'Bout 'alf-past ten, it would 'ave bin, Sir. When I went to bed. I'd left 'im tidyin' up, as 'e always does afore 'e comes up to the manor."

"You never saw him actually leave the inn, then?"

"No, Sir. But 'e must have done o'course."

Although I strongly suspected that he had not, anyway alive, it was certainly not the moment, I decided, to give expression to such a belief.

"But your uncle. He was still about, I suppose, when you went to bed?" I then asked casually like.

"Yes, Sir. 'E was still around then. But 'e must 'ave gone out soon afterwards for, when they went to 'is room to tell 'im about Joe, 'e wasn't there, and 'e 'adn't got back when I left, so I don't know where 'e could be."

"You've no idea where he might have gone, I suppose?" I then asked anxiously.

"No, 'fraid I 'aven't, Sir, but likely 'e'd be back at the "Daws" by now."

Whether he was to be found at the inn or not, it was essential that I delay my departure no longer, and so, with some further words of solace, I delivered the poor girl back to the care of the maidservant, and hurried out into the night, filled, as you can imagine, with a greater determination than ever now, to bring Cruden to justice. For that it was he who had murdered Joe, there could, I felt sure, be no reasonable doubt.

Chapter XXIII

My one fear, as I sped away from the manor, was that knowing that suspicion of the murder would be strong against him, Cruden may already have fled the neighbourhood. However, from what I knew of the man, the greater likelihood was, I thought, that he would have decided to stand his ground and brazen it out. In which case, if he had not in fact, already done so, the chances were that he would return to the "Three Daws" sooner or later during the night.

Anyway, with no other choice but to act upon this assumption, the first thing to do, I decided, was to go in search of the law officers, and then make for the inn where, if Cruden had not already returned, we would lie in ambush to surprise him when he did.

That, anyhow, was my intention; and with the wind howling among the elms in dirge-like accompaniment to my afflicted thoughts, I hurried up the driveway, and set out upon that now familiar path down to Gravesend.

Such an age did it seem since that evening of my arrival, when I had first trod that same road to go in search of the "Three Daws", that I could scarcely believe, as I looked back on all that had befallen me, the sequence of adventures I had met with, and the perils I had survived, that scarcely more than a month had elapsed. I must admit that in retrospect, it all seemed more like some hideous dream, and indeed, in the light of the disastrous happenings of the past hour, I devoutly wished that it all could have been.

The theft, under my very nose, of Sir David's papers, making such a mockery, as it did, of what I had managed to achieve, was mortifying enough, but this was nothing compared to the torment of remorse I was suffering over Joe's tragic death. This was something for which I could never forgive myself, and, however indirect my responsibility may have been, it would, I knew, lie heavily upon my conscience for the rest of my days.

So absorbed in these dismal reflections was I, as I sped on my way, that I was scarcely conscious of my surroundings. My gaze, in fact, had scarcely left the road in front of me, and what it was that compelled me, of a sudden to look back towards the hill behind me, for I was by then already more than half-way down, I really don't know. The intervention of fate perhaps.

Anyway, as I did so, I saw a light suddenly flash out from the darkness. At first so preoccupied with my thoughts was I still, that I didn't fully appreciate what I had seen, and it was only when there came, after a brief pause, a series of further flashes, that it sank into me what they surely implied. That Cruden must be up there in the windmill!

For some moments I stood there rooted to where I was, undecided what I should do. That my most sensible course would have been to proceed as I had planned and hurry on to seek the assistance of the law, I am quite certain. But, as I continued to stare up at the lights which were still intermittently flashing, and I thought of what he had done to Joe, a blind rage all at once possessed me, and, with it, the determination that, come what may, I would attempt to bring Cruden in alone. As I have said, in the cold light of reason it was an insane enough impulse, but just then I was in no mood for nice calculation, and so, without stopping to consider the wisdom of what I was about, I at once turned on my heels and set off hard bent for the hillock.

Aware that he might, at any moment, chance to emerge, I did at least manage, as I came up to the rise, to take a sufficient hold upon myself to approach the mill with some caution. But I need not have worried, for, as I reached the summit, there had still been no sign of him.

Even then, so beside myself with desire for vengeance was I, that I did not hesitate, and, instead of lurking in wait to accost him when he should appear, which would, of course, have been the sensible tactic, I decided that I would go in after him. And so, with my pistol at the ready, and having ensured that it was fully cocked, I crept on up the steps and cautiously raised the latch. Once inside all was, of course, quite black, or nearly so. The only light there was coming from the two small windows on either side. For a moment or two, I stood listening to see if I could catch any sound of him, not that I was likely to have done so, with the wind continuing to howl and roar about the old timbers.

As it happened, I had, as a boy, spent many a happy hour in the pursuit of make-believe adventures in an old disused mill near my home in Norfolk, so I had some familiarity with their way of construction, and knew that, about me, there would be two further compartments, it being from the topmost one, of course, that Cruden would have been signalling.

All the while, fearful that he might at any moment chance to descend, I then crept over to the first flight of steps. Here everything was perfectly dark, so I was obliged to tread with even greater caution now, especially as some of the boards had rotted away, and with every upward step that I took there was the added danger that I might stumble through a rift between them. Having thus reached the next floor, fortunately without mishap, my courage, I must admit, now began to fail me. So much so, that I came very near to funking it and was sorely tempted, I remember, to beat a stealthy retreat and embark, instead, upon my original plan.

In the event, I managed somehow to steel myself and, screwing up what resolution I had left, I thus continued to grope my way over towards the next flight.

With my heart in my mouth, and dreading, with every creaking step that I took, that he would catch some sound of my approach, for by this time, no more than a few feet could have separated us, I proceeded to inch my way up. I was still on the steps, when I caught my first sight of him as, dimly illuminated by a lantern which stood beside him, he crouched there on one knee against the aperture.

Just then he reached down for the lantern and, holding it up before the opening, began to manipulate the shutter. With his attention thus diverted, now was my chance, I decided, as step by excruciating step, I began to edge my way over towards him.

I had succeeded, I suppose, in getting within some three or four feet of him, when with an oath of impatience, he suddenly thrust the lantern down again.

As he did so, he must, I think, have caught sight of my shadow, for all at once he swung round. For a moment or two he just stared blankly up at me, with his body half twisted round, and his hand still over the lantern where it lay. Then, as recognition dawned, his look of astonishment all at once gave way to a sullen scowl.

"So, it's you, is it? I'd bin thinkin' it wouldn't be long afore we'd be meetin' up again," he growled. "Well it seems you've proper trapped me don't it?" he then added with a sneer, as, having moved over towards him, I thrust the barrel of my pistol hard into the small of his back.

"Stand up and just leave the lantern where it is," I said sharply, for I could see that his hand was beginning to tighten over it with the intention, no doubt, of plunging us into total darkness.

As he rose to his feet, I took hold of the lantern, and then started forthwith to prod him over towards the steps.

"Now, lead the way, and no false move mind, for I can promise you that there'll be a ball through your back if you do try anything," I said firmly.

To this he grunted something I didn't catch, and then, urged on by further prompting jabs from my pistol, he started off down the stairway, whilst I followed close behind, holding the lantern aloft in my left hand to lighten our way.

Promisingly as things had gone this far, I knew only too well that I was still going to have to proceed very warily indeed, if I was to come out of that windmill alive. For, knowing as he must, that, once taken in charge there would be little chance of his escaping the gallows, he was likely, I sensed, to seize upon any sort of opportunity to turn the tables upon me.

Anyway, I had managed to manoeuvre him down the first flight and we were, I remember, just approaching the head of the second one when, to my alarm, the lantern all of a sudden began to flicker and fade. And, with the realisation that in the complete darkness in which we must shortly be plunged, a good deal of my advantage would be lost, I at once began, in a desperate bid to get him out of the windmill while some light still remained, to urge him on more forcibly.

As to what happened next, I am not quite sure. Anyhow, we had, I think, taken no more than a couple of steps down the second flight, when, to my dismay, the lantern finally gave out. At the same moment I must I think in my panic have stumbled and fallen forward. Then all is blackness. Although I have a dim recollection of something hard smashing against my jaw. His elbow I suppose it was. For how long I lay there senseless I have no idea. All I know is, that when I eventually came to, so dazed was I that it was some while, I remember, before it dawned upon me where I was, and what had happened.

With this recollection, and the awful realisation that all must surely be up with me, my immediate impulse was to search frantically around for the pistol. Only then, as my hand eventually alighted upon it, did it occur to me that, apart from the howling of the wind outside, all was strangely quiet. Of Cruden, indeed, there appeared to be no sign at all. Mystifying as it was, I could at least comfort myself with the thought that, had he been able to, he must surely have dispatched me long before this.

As it chanced, my nose just then caught the whiff of powder, and, having given a confirmatory sniff over the end of the barrel, I knew, although I had no memory of doing so, that I must, in fact, have fired it, doubtless at the very same moment that Cruden's blow had struck. In which case, and this would explain his mystifying disappearance, the force of the ball could, I suppose, have propelled him forwards to the bottom of the steps where he might well, I imagined, still be lying.

Rising unsteadily to my feet, and, having taken care to reprime my pistol, for I was still taking no chances, I thus started to grope my way down. I had not gone far before I almost stumbled over him, where he lay straddled across the lower steps, with his head resting on the boards below. And so motionless and so cold to the touch, was he, that I imagined, at first, that he must be dead.

However, as I bent over him he gave a faint groan, and then made some attempt to raise himself.

"Don't try to move. Just lie quite still," I said, restraining him.

"What's 'appened? Where am I?" he grunted feebly in return.

"It's all right, you've just had a bad fall, that's all," I reassured him. Although that he had, in fact, been mortally wounded, I was in little doubt; and being so, I had plainly little time to lose, that is if I was going to extract any information from him. So, with no more ado, I urgently set about interrogating him.

Strenuously as I continued to question and cajole him, little sense could I get out of him, however. Indeed, from such little meaning as I could deduce from his incoherent mumblings, he must, I think, have imagined that he was back in the ring, and had taken the count.

Finally, in desperation, for I could tell that he was sinking fast, I seized him by the shoulders and, brutal of me as it was perhaps, not, as you can imagine, that I felt much compassion, I made a last frantic attempt to shake some sort of life into him.

At first, far from reviving him, he appeared to sink further, but then, of a sudden, he raised his head and started to mumble again.

"Now listen carefully, Cruden. And try to understand what I am saying," I almost shouted as, cushioning his head in my arms, I held my mouth to his ear.

"The plans that were taken from the manor this evening. You must tell me who had them and where they are."

For a while there was no response, and then I heard him trying to mutter something.

"Yes, yes?" I urged him still holding my ear close to his lips. But the only words I could catch were "The Dover coach. The Dover coach." And, with this enigmatic utterance, he fell back lifeless into my arms.

Chapter XXIV

It was only then, as I eased myself aside from beneath the dead weight of his shoulders, and climbed to my feet, that the full awareness of what I had done began to sink in. That I had, as a result of my ill-considered impetuosity, wantonly destroyed, perhaps, the one source via which Sir David's documents might possibly have been recovered.

Viewed dispassionately, as I was able to do now, there could be no denying that I had acted with the grossest irresponsibility. Joe's death had been amply avenged, that was certainly true, but only at a price that could well be incalculable.

So be it, there was nothing that I could do about it now, and with the awful sense of the blunder I had committed weighing heavily upon me, I ruefully made my way out of the windmill, and started off back towards the manor, with the unpalatable task of informing Sir David of what I had done.

I had descended the hillock, and was already some way along the lane which skirted it, when, as it chanced, those last dying words of Cruden's, "the Dover coach, the Dover coach," all at once came echoing back to intrude upon my dejected thoughts. At the time, in keeping with the rest of his mutterings, I must admit that I had dismissed them as being nothing more than the inconsequential ravings of a dying man.

Be that as it may, as I continued to repeat the words over to myself, I began to wonder whether, by this strange allusion, he might not, after all, perhaps, have been trying to convey something.

Taken alone it appeared to make little sense, but could it have been, I thought, with mounting excitement, that those incoherent mumblings which had preceded it had, in fact, contained a confession as to the identity of his co-conspirator, and that the final reference to the Dover coach had been meant to indicate that he was a passenger thereon?

Was it, I argued, as I continued to ponder the notion, really such a far-fetched possibility?

Delirious at the time as he may have been, it was surely, I thought, an odd sort of observation to have made if he had not been intending to impart something.

Anyway, the longer I continued to turn the notion over in my mind, the more convinced did I become that my hunch could well be right, and that whoever it was that had possession of the plans was a passenger upon the coach which was, at this very moment, bearing Sir George and Miss Catherine to Dover!

I was, maybe, catching at straws, but at least it gave us something to act upon, I consoled myself, as I hurried on towards the manor to acquaint Sir David with my belief.

That, anyhow, was my intention as I turned up the driveway. I had almost, indeed, reached the manor; when of a sudden, a more immediate, and altogether wilder scheme occurred to me. Why should I not take upon myself the responsibility of chasing after the coach? I was a tolerably experienced rider, and as good a start of me as it had, might I not, with a sufficient relay of horses, have a fair chance of overtaking it before it reached its destination?

Looking back now, with the hindsight of maturer years, it was, of course, on the face of it, the most hare-brained of resolves. With so much depending upon its outcome, I should never had entertained it for a moment. I should, of course, as I had first intended, have consulted Sir David who, with the resources at his command would, I am sure, have been able to organise some plan or other with a much greater chance of achieving our purpose.

I was however, I fear, no clear thinking, rational being at that moment, and no sooner had the idea presented itself, than I was determined to put it into effect. So, without any further thought and having first ensured that I had enough money about me, I at once sped across to the stables. In a trice, I had the old mare harnessed and saddled and before she could scarcely have come to her senses, we had trotted up the drive and were soon into a brisk gallop on the coach road beyond.

As I have said, it was a rough sort of night, with the high wind blowing as fiercely as ever. There was still a fair moon though, so the way ahead was clear enough, and with the advantage that, at such an hour, there would be little traffic to impede us, I was already becoming quietly confident, as the old mare stretched out towards Rochester, that, in spite of the considerable leeway I had to make up, I could indeed be up with the coach before it reached Dover.

In the event any such sanguine hopes were, I fear, shortly to receive an unwelcome check.

We had already swung up away from the marshes and, after a steepish climb, had reached a high point along the road, known as Gad's Hill, when, from out of the darkness ahead, a body of men suddenly sprang out to confront us.

Imagining that they must be a band of footpads, for which that locality had, I should mention, long since been notorious, I tried to swing Bess to one side in an attempt to hurtle past them. Before I could do so, however, one of their number had managed to seize hold of the bridle, and drag us to a halt. With muskets levelled at us from all sides, it was clear that instead of footpads, as I had at first feared, they were, as I could now see, a body of militiamen.

"It's orders, Sir. We've just 'ad 'em through. We're to stop and search anyone that passes along the road," declared one of them, no doubt their leader, in reply to my indignant remonstrations. Sir David's aide-de-camp had, it was manifest, certainly not been slow in organising the pickets.

"But I'm an agent of His Majesty's Government upon most urgent business," I retorted imperiously. "So just stand aside and let me pass. Now there's a good fellow."

"Ooah! We'll 'ave to see about that," drawled the yokel suspiciously as he peered up into my face.

"But it's true," I said. "I'm an emissary of Sir David Dundas, your Commander-in-Chief. Now, does that satisfy you?"

"That's easily spoken, Sir. But it don't mean to say that we believes yer now, does it?"

"But I am!" I cried with increasing exasperation, as the seconds continued to slip by.

"Well 'ow comes you're not dressed like an officer then?" he quickly responded, in a tone of triumph at his simple logic.

"Because I'm a government agent. We don't wear a uniform," I returned in desperation.

"If you're this government agent you says you are, no doubt you've papers then to prove it?"

"Papers?" I said. "I don't know that I have. You'll just have to take my word for it."

" 'Fraid we can't do that, Sir. Our orders is to search everyone, so if you'd just dismount." As there appeared to be nothing for it but to submit to his request, I was reluctantly just about to dismount when I was suddenly reminded of Sir David's warrant for Cruden's arrest, which, of course, I still had about me. It was not a very official looking document, but at least it bore his signature clearly enough.

"Wait a moment. Perhaps this will satisfy you," I said, as I withdrew the sheet from my pocket and handed it down to him.

With one of his companions holding forth a lantern to see by, whilst the remainder gathered round to gawp over his shoulder, he then proceeded to scrutinise it.

"Hurry up, man! The sense of it's plain enough surely!" I burst forth impatiently, as he continued to gape down at it.

"Well, I dunno," he said at last. "But I suppose it's all right. What's Nat Cruden been up to then?"

"That's none of your business," I replied curtly. "So now just stand aside and let me proceed." At this he released his hold of the bridle, and without more ado I snatched up the reins, and off we sped into the night again.

Unfortunate as the delay had been, at least it had given the old mare a chance of a breather, and, galloping on down into Rochester, we were soon over the bridge and, passing the old Norman keep on our right, had presently left the deserted streets of the old city behind us, and were out into the open country once more.

Although I had travelled the road upon two or three occasions, I was not really sure how far, in fact, it was to Dover. We had already, I supposed, covered some twelve miles, and there must, anyway as best as I could remember, still be a further fifty miles or so in which to overtake the coach.

That I was certainly gaining upon it there could be no doubt. But, was I doing so rapidly enough? Whatever the case, it was plain that I would soon be needing a change of horse. For, gamely as Bess had gone for me, she was now beginning to show such signs of distress, that I was sorely regretting that I had not made the change at Rochester. Still there would, I comforted myself, be plenty of opportunities at Sittingbourne, which, if my memory served me right, could not be much further along the road now.

Meanwhile, I had no choice but to sit and suffer, whilst doing the best I could to summon up what reserves of stamina the courageous old horse had left. In the event, I fear, I used her pretty harshly. But with so much at stake, and with every second saved possibly vital, it was no occasion for sentiment.

Anyway, we eventually struggled into Sittingbourne, and drawing up at the first posting-house, I hurriedly leapt off to go in search of an ostler. After much frantic shouting and knocking, a head at last appeared at an upper window.

"I want a horse," I shouted at him. "The best you've got."

"You'll be lucky," he drawled back sleepily. "Why, you might as well ask for the moon up there," he added pointing skywards.

"Come, man, this is a posting-house, isn't it? Surely you must have something," I urged.

"I tell you we ain't," he responded with a yawn. "The military gen'lemen 'ave 'ad 'em all. It's the same all along the road, as I've 'eard tell. Not an 'orse to be 'ad."

As he had been speaking I had, nevertheless, heard the unmistakable sound of a horse moving in a stable just along the yard.

"But surely there's one in that stable over there," I cried.

"Maybe there is, Sir. But that's not for the askin'. It's already bin spoken for. 'Fraid you'll 'ave to do with what you've got there."

"But she's all done in and my business is most urgent. I'll pay double your usual fee," I then added in desperation, as he started to move back from the window. "Look here, I'll give you five guineas and see that he's back later today. Now surely, that's fair enough."

At this he hesitated and I could see that he had already begun to waver.

"Make it six, Sir, and you can 'ave it. Though it's more than me job's worth, I can tell you," he responded. It was an exorbitant fee and not much less, I suspected, than the horse could have been purchased for outright. Even so, it was no time for haggling, and having been assured that he was "a right good goer", I at once agreed to his price.

"But look sharp," I added. "For I've no time to lose."

"I'll be right down, don't you worry, Sir," he replied, all alacrity now.

True to his word he was with me in a trice. The horse was quickly saddled and, having extracted his promise that Bess would be well watered, and comfortably bedded down, we trotted out of the yard and were soon in full career up the road.

As the ostler had said, the horse was plainly no ordinary hack. Indeed, such a charge of me did he take, that it seemed likely that I was going to be little more than a helpless passenger with no choice but to give my mount his head, and only pray that I would be able to keep company with him.

Knowing that I would have little chance now of obtaining a fresh mount until we reached Canterbury, which lay some fifteen miles ahead, my worry soon was, as our furious gallop continued, that unless I could manage to restrain the horse's impetuosity, and thus conserve his resources, we were going to be hard put to it even to reach that destination, let alone overhaul the coach.

At first my efforts were to no avail. The harder I endeavoured to curb him, the harder he pulled; and we must have travelled the best part of two miles with my arms, by then, quite limp with the fatigue of it, before I was able to settle him to any sort of reasonable pace. Meanwhile we must, I imagined, have been gaining ground fast. But at what a cost to the horse's stamina I could not yet tell. Anyway, for the moment, all was well, and for a further three or four miles our rate of progress was certainly brisk enough to keep my hopes alive.

But my optimism, I fear, was destined to be short lived. We had come to the end of a flat open stretch of road, and were commencing something of an incline when, to my alarm, the horse began to falter, and to blow so ominously, that, scarcely out of a walk as we soon were, I almost despaired of reaching the summit. By dint of much pressure to his flanks I succeeded, however, in getting him over the rise, and even into a trot down the descent on the other side. Nevertheless, it was now clear, for the moment anyway, that any sort of a gallop was quite beyond him.

I had some thought of trying to procure an exchange at the next village, but the only inn it boasted looked so unpromising that, in the event, I decided that, come what may, I would press on, and trust that by giving him 'an easy' the horse would get his second wind.

Meanwhile, at the pace at which we were now moving, it was woefully certain that any ground I managed to make up, was inexorably slipping away, and to add to my despondency, a signpost I happened to pass just then, indicated that Canterbury was still a further eight miles off.

With my mount unresponsive to any stimulus that I could apply, and becoming all the while more despairing, we thus continued to slow-jogtrot our solitary way along that dark and deserted road.

That my quest, even from the outset, had been a hopeless one, I was, of course by now, having ruefully to accept. For, upon any realistic assessment of the distance by which the coach must have had a start of me, it would, as I could now see, have required I don't know how many changes of horse, and the speediest at that, if the plan were to have had any chance of success.

So dispirited did I become that I was in half a mind, I remember, to seek a bed somewhere along the road, and continue on to Dover later that morning. However, in the belief that I might, perhaps, dispersed as the passengers would have been by that time, still be able to obtain some information or other, I decided that, belated as my arrival was going to be, the sooner I got there the better.

In any case, my mount was at last beginning to show some signs of reviving and, although he required a good deal of urging, I managed, at last, to persuade him into a gallop of sorts. And this I was able to maintain for some further three miles, before he, once again, slowed to a jogtrot.

Nevertheless, as we laboriously reached the top of an incline, I was at last afforded a glimpse of the old Norman tower of the cathedral, as it rose silhouetted again the night sky ahead of us.

Brief as it was, for the road soon dipped again, the sight of it did, at least, serve to cheer me a little, deceptively near as it might be, for Canterbury was still some three miles or so distant, as I knew, with the road undulating steeply for most of the way.

Nevertheless, after some merciless driving, and near to collapse as both the horse and I were by this time, we eventually came up to the old city wall, and having passed between the twin towers of its western gateway, we then continued to struggle on up that ancient and time-hallowed thoroughfare to go in search of a posting-house.

I had, in fact, drawn up beside the first likely-looking establishment, and was just about to dismount when, of a sudden, I was alerted by the sound of a commotion a little way along the street ahead of us. I had little to wonder what might be the cause of it, when there suddenly arose the cry of "All right," followed a moment later by the unmistakable sounds of a team of horses moving away on the cobbles.

And there, sure enough, although I could scarcely believe the evidence of my eyes, was the coach, its outline dimly visible in the glimmer of its red sidelamp as it glided away into the night, some hundred yards or so from where we had halted!

In no mind, just then, to consider what could have accounted for its being there, instead of at Dover, where, by the natural order of things, it should long since have been, I frantically shook up my reins and shouting to an ostler, as we shot past, to follow us and take charge of my horse, we just managed to get alongside the coach before the team were into a full trot so that I was able, almost in one and the same movement, to dismount, and grabbing hold of the rear rail, leapt up on to the back seat.

"The devil take it! What do you think you're doing?" exclaimed the startled guard, as he reached for his blunderbuss.

"It's all right. Don't be alarmed. I'm a government agent with some urgent business to attend to," I breathlessly reassured him. And, so saying, I slipped him a guinea by way of appeasement.

"Well I suppose that's all right then," he replied, his attitude all at once changing, as he pocketed the coin.

"You're bound for Dover then, I take it?"

"Yes, that's so," I said.

"Should 'ave bin there more'n an hour ago. Broken axle-tree. Coachman new to the road. Almost 'ad us over once," he then volunteered laconically, thus explaining the delay.

Apart from myself, there was, as I observed when I had collected myself, only one other outside passenger. He was seated up in front by the coachman, and clearly looked to be little more than a youth.

The inside, however, as I remembered, had been full when the coach had left Gravesend. There having been, as I had noticed, a youngish looking woman and three gentlemen besides Sir George and Miss Catherine, of course.

"Are there any others travelling?" I then asked the guard, impatient as I was to discover what he could tell me of the passengers that still remained.

"Aye, we're still full up inside."

"London passengers, are they?"

"Three of 'em are."

"Are they regulars do you know?"

"Two of 'em be. One's the M.P. for Dover. And there's Mr Coker. 'E's a lawyer."

"They've been with you since you left London then?"

"That's right."

"Do you know anything about the others?"

"Never seen 'em afore. One of 'em's with 'is daughter, Sir somebody or other. Never left the coach 'e 'asn't. Slept all the way," replied the guard, identifying Sir George and Miss Catherine. "They got on at Gravesend. And then there's a girl, travelling alone, she got on at London too."

I was thus left, it seemed, with but one last hope as a possible suspect. The sixth inside passenger.

"That leaves one other. Where did he get on?" I asked anxiously.

"Let me see," mused the guard. "Yes, that's right, 'e got on at Rochester. I remember now."

That anyway was significant perhaps, I thought with mounting excitement.

"Do you know anything about him?" I quickly added, scarcely able to contain my eagerness.

"No 'cept 'e was an elderly party. All of eighty, I should think. Took two of us to 'elp 'im in, I remember, so doddery like was 'e."

A description which certainly didn't appear to offer much encouragement, I thought dejectedly, unless, of course, his apparent decrepitude had been a clever disguise. It was a possibility, I supposed. Otherwise it now began to seem all too painfully obvious that it was nothing more than a fool's errand that I had embarked upon.

By this time we had left Canterbury well behind us, and had climbed up on to Barham downs, a flat open stretch of grassland across which the coach road runs for a mile or more, before dropping down into Dover.

Under normal, peaceful times it is, save for a farmstead or two and the herds of sheep grazing there, a somewhat bleak and uninhabited locality.

However, during those months of the invasion scare, it had been taken over by the military for the billeting of a number of reserve divisions, so that, at the time of which I am writing, the whole area was covered by a vast encampment of tents; their pyramid shapes just then becoming visible in the dim light of approaching dawn, as in serried ranks they stretched away on both sides as far as the eye could see.

As my gaze wandered across them I bethought of the great host of men slumbering there, and I was all at once seized with the grim reflection that I could well, by the sorry blunder I had committed, have forfeited the very lives of some of those among them.

It was an awesome realisation, made no less unpalatable by my growing belief that there was, after all, going to be no eleventh-hour reprieve for my folly.

Since, whatever Cruden's dying words may have meant, it had surely by now become apparent that I had misinterpreted them and, in catching at the flimsiest of straws, had wasted precious hours.

I was thus mournfully brooding upon my unhappy plight, when the guard happened to interrupt my thoughts.

"It's somebody on the coach you're after I take it then?" he said.

"Well yes. At least I was hoping that he might be. But it was nothing more than a hunch, I'm afraid, and it appears that I was mistaken," I replied gloomily.

"Of course, I don't know what your business is exactly, or what 'e's supposed to 'ave done, but I can't see as any of 'em look the sort of person you'd be after, unless it's the gentleman who got on at Gravesend with 'is daughter, or so I took it she was. I don't know anything about 'im except 'e was a late booking. Seems a proper gentleman though. Meeting 'is wife at Dover, or so 'e said."

It was Sir George to whom he was referring, of course, and for all my dejection, I could not forbear an inward chuckle at such a preposterous notion.

"Yes, I suppose it's just possible," I agreed, for I was in no mind to undeceive him as to the absurdity of his proposition.

Dear old Sir George; surely the very soul of honour, involved in a scheme of such surpassing treachery! It really was the drollest notion imaginable. And how he would appreciate the story when I came to relate it, I thought.

I was thus continuing to relish the humour of such a whimsical concept, when a ghastly thought suddenly struck me. Could it just feasibly be that there might be something in the guard's suggestion? Was it after all really so utterly ludicrous? So appalling was the possibility, and so shattering its implications, that I must admit that it was some moments before I could bring myself to evaluate it with any sort of calm objectivity.

Sir George was on the coach. There could certainly be no denying that. But then, he had a very good reason to be, and his being so was surely the purest coincidence. Unless, of course, his announcement of Lady Thurlow's expected arrival at Dover had been nothing more than a fabrication. It did not signify much, of course, but, to my knowledge, no one had actually seen the communication informing him of her homecoming.

But then, living under his very roof, and in such close association with him these past few weeks, could I really have been so blind? It was just conceivable I supposed.

And there was, of course, as I was now reminded, the slip of paper which I had found in that topographical book in the library. But what sort of evidence was that? And anyway, it could have been left there by any one of a number of visitors to the house.

Besides, what possible motive could he have had for involving himself in something so heinous as the betrayal of his country, that most detestable of crimes? Unless it be monetary gain of course.

That Sir George, when a young man, had had a reputation for prodigality I knew; and that he, indeed, still liked a gamble was clearly evident. There was thus a possibility it could, I supposed, be argued, that he was in the hands of moneylenders, and was being hard pressed for settlement. And if such be the case, it was certainly not unknown for men of the most honourable character to be driven to almost any lengths, when under the stress of a compulsion of that nature.

Be all that as it may, and even accepting that Sir George was in such a pecuniary predicament, of which I, anyway, had no concrete evidence, could one honestly believe that he could really bring himself to stoop to something so infamous?

As I have already said, what evidence was there to support such a terrible imputation? Not the merest shred, as far as I knew.

No, no, it was all quite unthinkable. Not only was the idea perfectly preposterous, I decided, but it had, indeed, been despicable of me even to have entertained such a suspicion.

Nevertheless, as the coach continued to rumble on its way towards Dover, a lingering doubt still persisted in haunting me.

Given such a doubt, and however remote the chance was that Sir George had possession of the plans, was it not incumbent upon me to ensure that he had not? Embarrassing, to say the least, as the prospect of such an accusation and subsequent search might be, could I, with so much at stake, really in all conscience, evade the issue?

As you can imagine, my predicament was an appalling one, for I really could not see how I was going to achieve my purpose without, at the same time, giving such offence as was likely to sour our relationship ever after. That is, if my suspicions, as I was of course quite convinced they would be, proved to be unfounded.

If, on the other hand, and perish the thought, he was discovered to have possession of the plans, our further acquaintance, I imagined, would anyway be of the briefest.

But what then of my hopes of Miss Catherine? Whatever the outcome they must surely be jeopardised. For that I had even harboured such a suspicion of her father would, in itself, be hardly likely to endear myself to her.

But what if my suspicions should prove to be founded? What of our betrothal then? Knowing, as she would, that I had been the instrument of her father's exposure and disgrace, justified as it might be, would surely put paid to all the blissful aspirations I had so fondly been cherishing. No, no, such an eventuality was too awful even to contemplate. Whatever happened, Sir George's villainy, if such was the case, must be kept secret. After all, if he did perchance have the plans, no one else need know. I would just say that I had found them upon Cruden. He, at least, would be unable to refute the charge And, above all, if it was managed discreetly, Miss Catherine need never know anything at all of her father's treachery.

So engrossed had I been in thus wrestling with my appalling dilemma, that I had, for the while, become quite unconscious of my surroundings, and it was only the sudden blast of the guard's horn to signal our impending arrival, that alerted me to an awareness that we were already approaching the outskirts of Dover, and would shortly be at our destination.

Meanwhile, the light had been steadily improving so that everything about me had become more sharply delineated. The coach itself, the team of horses, as well as the coachman on the box in front of me, instead of being shadowy and insubstantial as they had formerly been, were now beginning to emerge as sharply defined entities. Not that I was anything more than half aware of this, so absorbed was I in contemplation of the fateful crisis with which I was soon to be faced.

Indeed, it was by nothing more than the merest chance that my gaze, albeit unconsciously, happened at that moment to be fixed upon the back of the coachman.

So much a natural part of the whole equipage was he that I had, until that moment, scarcely given him a thought; and I would certainly not have done so then, had not something about him chanced to distract me. Even then it was nothing very much, only that he had all at once, and in quick succession, given three or four nods of the head!

At first, so abstracted was I, as I have said, that I didn't think any more of it; and it was only when some moments later the nods were repeated, that my attention became all at once riveted. For had I not recently been in the company of someone with that self-same trait? For a brief second or two his identity eluded me, and then, of a sudden, it flashed upon me. Dr Argent it had surely been, of course!

Chapter XXV

So startling was the recollection, that for several moments all I could do was stare, all agog, at the back of the caped figure seated there on the box in front of me. But was it really possible, I thought, as trying to contain my excitement, I proceeded to view the extraordinary concept as calmly as I was able? No, no, it was surely too preposterous. After all, there must, I argued, be many who were afflicted with a similar sort of twitch. So why should not the coachman be?

But then, as I studied him more closely, his build was much the same as the doctor's. Not that this was of much consequence. And besides, would he have been able to handle a team of horses in the way he had been doing? An achievement which required no mean expertise surely. On the other hand, it was significant, as the guard had intimated, that the coachman was new to the road, and also, from what I had gathered, that he had been making no very professional job of it. But then, what of the original coachman? By what means could he have been persuaded to relinquish his charge? Surely this was something which would have been very difficult to engineer. Although it could have been achieved, I supposed, by duress, or, and more probably, by the inducement of a substantial bribe. It would, after all, certainly be hard to imagine a more perfect cloak of identity. There could be no denying that.

It would, indeed, be virtually foolproof, for in such a guise he would have little fear of his being searched or interrogated, and he could, into the bargain, scarcely have devised a speedier means of getting to the coast.

Furthermore the doctor would, during the course of the evening, have had every opportunity of purloining the documents from Sir David's room and, by leaving the assembly early, as I now recollected that he had done, to escort Captain Wakeley home, he would have had ample time to join the coach, either at Gravesend or Rochester.

On the face of it then was it, in fact, really so wildly improbable? Anyway, all would soon be resolved, for by this time we were well into Dover, and it could not be many moments now, I imagined, before we reached our destination.

Indeed, just then an ostler emerged into the road ahead of us, and whilst the team were being reined back to a halt, he hurried over to take charge of the nearside leader, whilst our coachman, with no great dexterity, or so it seemed to me, and with his head now jerking like an automaton, proceeded to manoeuvre the coach into the inn yard.

As he did so, he was obliged for an instant to turn his head so that I was afforded a side view of his face, and brief as the glimpse of it was, there could be no doubt of his identity now. The features were, unmistakably, those of Dr Argent.

Before we had come to a halt, I had taken hold of my pistol, and was down. But quick as I had been, the coachman was equally so, and what with the steam from the horses, and the general commotion attendant upon our arrival, before I could get across to him, he had vanished.

Realising that in the time available to him, it could only have been through a door of the inn, which stood close by, that he must have escaped, I frantically brushed my way through the throng and burst in after him. Only to discover that the room was quite empty, although that he had only just been there was evident from the coachman's greatcoat which lay there in a discarded heap on the floor.

Faced with two other possible means of exit, the first door I tried led only to a small unoccupied taproom. The second one, however, opened on to a narrow passageway, along which I headlong sped to find myself, as I burst through the door at the end of it, in the dining-room of the inn, where a young servant girl was preparing the table for breakfast.

"Has anyone just passed through here?" I breathlessly asked.

"My! You did give me a start, Sir. Whatever's goin' on! First that other gentleman near scares the wits out o' me rushing through like 'e did, and now you comes."

"That other gentleman. Which way did he go?" I impatiently interrupted.

"I'm sure I don't rightly know, Sir. Afore I knew what was 'appening 'e 'ad gone. Wait, now I come to think of it, I think I seen 'im pass the window. Yes, I'm sure I did. So 'e must 'ave gone out, goin' a fair lick 'e was too, so you'll 'ave to 'urry if you wants to catch 'im."

At this I shot out through the entrance hall, and into the street beyond; where gazing anxiously in the direction which the girl had indicated, I was, to my relief, just in time to catch sight of him as he disappeared round a bed in the road, a hundred yards or so ahead of me. Fearful that I might yet lose him, I at once darted off in pursuit, and, happily, as I turned the corner there he was, although moving at such a pace that I had scarcely reduced the distance between us.

My main difficulty, as I could now see, was going to be in keeping sufficiently close to him, to ensure that he did not give me the slip, whilst at the same time, remaining unobserved until I was afforded a favourable opportunity of accosting him. And that, as you can imagine, with the light improving all the while and the street virtually deserted, promised to be no easy matter. However, whatever his destination, he had as yet given no indication that he was nearing it, as he kept steadily on at the same hurried pace, and without once looking around, which happily, I supposed, at least suggested that he had no sort of suspicion that he was being followed.

By this time we were well into the outskirts of the town and it was becoming more than ever a puzzle to me whither he could possibly be making, for, looking ahead, apart from a few straggling habitations, all that now lay before us was the old castle, with nothing beyond it but the open stretch of grassland above the cliffs.

No deviation did he make, however, as having skirted the castle, he proceeded to stride resolutely on towards the cliff top, whilst I, still keeping my distance, followed after him.

In contrast to the turbulence of the night, the day had broken calm and clear, I remember, with the sea scarcely showing a ripple as it flowed palely in the first rays of the sun, which was now beginning to emerge above the horizon over towards France. On the shore, far below, I could hear the gentle wash of the tide, and now and again, a gull would shriek overhead, but otherwise there was nothing to disturb the early morning stillness, as the fateful moment of our confrontation drew nearer. Just then, as he was approaching the highest point of the cliff, he suddenly stopped, and turning towards the sea, started to wave his arms.

Although I had, until that moment, scarcely noticed it, there lay anchored, some little way off shore, a small schooner, and it at once became clear that it was this to which he was signalling.

Meanwhile I had flattened myself into a slight hollow in the ground, from which vantage point I was able, unseen, to keep both the doctor and the vessel in view.

For several minutes, and with evidently increasing impatience, he continued frantically to wave; but without, as far as I could observe, any answering acknowledgement.

Indeed, I was beginning to wonder whether there had been a hitch in his obviously prearranged plans, when at last, I saw someone approach the ship's side, and wave back. At this the doctor dropped his arms, but nevertheless, continued to stand there with his gaze still fixed intently upon the vessel.

For a while nothing further happened, and then looking across, I could see that a boat was being lowered over the side.

No sooner was this evident than he hurried on again, and before I could get to my feet, he had disappeared over the rise.

With his purpose now clear, I set off in pursuit, only to discover to my bewilderment, as I reached the peak of the cliff, that he had quite disappeared.

Although I did not know it, at a point a little further on, a deep shaft with steps had been sunk into the cliffside, and it was down this, as I was shortly to discover, that he was hurriedly making his way to the beach below.

With the boat, as I could see, already fast approaching the shore, it was plain that I had no time to lose and so, firmly grasping my pistol, and with no thought of stealth now, I bounded down after him.

Even then he appeared to be quite oblivious of my presence and it was only when I had reached the shore, and he must have heard the crunch of my feet on the shingle behind him, that he looked round.

By this time there could have been no more than twenty yards between us, and although he quickened his pace, I was soon up beside him. For a moment or two he just stared at me with a look of blank astonishment. And then, all at once, he collected himself, studiously ignoring the pistol I was brandishing.

"Why, if it isn't Mr Farrant! What strange freak of coincidence could have brought you here to this lonely spot. And at such an uncivilised hour too. It really is most remarkable!" he said in the blandest possible way.

"I might as well ask the same of you, Doctor," I replied, as coolly as I could.

"Oh! That's very simply explained. I am here to meet some old friends who have just arrived from Cornwall. In fact, the good fellow in that boat, over there, is taking me out to join them. And you, yourself, if I am not being too inquisitive? Anyway, whatever it is, I am sure you must be finding it a welcome relief from that dreary old library of Sir George's," he added, giving me a quizzical look.

"I am sure you must know why I am here, Doctor?" I replied firmly.

"Should I?" he returned, his brows contracting in a show of puzzlement. "For the life of me, I really can't imagine. I fear that you have the advantage of me there, Farrant."

His cool self-possession, and air of complete innocence I was finding, I must admit, disconcerting. That he had possession of the documents, I was in no doubt. However, to search him then and there, situated as we were, was plainly out of the question. I would first, I decided, have to escort him back to Dover. And with the boat fast approaching the shore, it was clear that if I did not act soon, I could well lose command of the situation. And so, without more ado, I said, "I must tell you Doctor that I am a government agent and . . ."

"A government agent! Why, you do surprise me!" he interjected; and in such a tone of good-humoured mockery, as to leave me in no doubt that he had long since been perfectly aware of what I had been about these past weeks.

"I fear, Doctor," I continued, ignoring his interruption, "that I must ask you to accompany me back to Dover."

"Really, this is too absurd. Come now, Farrant, put that pistol away, there's a good fellow and tell me what all this nonsense is about," he replied in a tone of some impatience.

"I fear that I must insist, Doctor," I said firmly. "And if you should have any thoughts of resisting me, I must tell you that I shall have no hesitation in killing you here and now!"

He must have sensed that I meant it, as indeed I did, for, with an "as you wish," and without any further demur, he meekly turned back towards the cliff, whilst I kept closely behind him.

Meanwhile I had been concerned that the boatman might decide to follow us. However, to my relief, as I glanced back, there he still stood beside his boat, as he continued, in some bewilderment no doubt, to stare after us.

And so, without anything further being said, the two of us mounted the steps, and started back along the cliff top. As we did so, I could not help wondering about my companion, and what it could have been that had first set him upon the path of treachery. From what I knew of him, financial gain was surely unlikely. Did he, perhaps, I thought, harbour some deep grudge or other against his homeland, and this was his way of avenging it? It was possible, I supposed. Or, could it be that he was simply a French spy, espionage having, all along, been the purpose of his settling in Gravesend, his doctoring being just a convenient cover for his other more clandestine activities? His name certainly had a French ring about it, that was true. On the other hand, his accent was of the purest, bearing not the slightest trace, anyway that I had been able to detect, to indicate that he was anything but English in origin. Still that was an accomplishment many had achieved, and would anyway be a virtual necessity, I imagined, for anyone engaged in this sort of game.

I was thus musing over the enigma, when the doctor, of a sudden, broke in to interrupt my thoughts.

"I should be most grateful, Farrant, if you would be so kind as to tell me where it was that I slipped up, and how you managed to track me down here the way you did. For, I must admit that I find it all most puzzling."

So taken aback was I by his disarming and matter-of-factly spoken request, which, if only by implication, was surely tantamount to an admission of his guilt, that it was some moments before I could bring myself to reply.

"Well, I suppose there's no harm in my telling you now, Doctor," I said at last. "But it was Cruden who gave me the first intimation."

"Ah! So it was Nat Cruden. I imagined it must have been," he replied musingly. "He's an awful blackguard, of course, but somehow I would never have expected it of him. He was hoping to save his own skin, I imagine."

"No, to be fair to the man, I don't think he really knew what he was saying, for he was barely conscious at the time," I replied.

"It must have been you, of course, who jumped the coach at Canterbury?" he then said, after we had continued in silence for a while. "But, decked out as I was in that coachman's rig, and with my back to you all the time, I still can't see how you managed to recognise me. For Cruden could certainly not have known that I would be travelling under that guise."

Reluctant as I was to embarrass him by remarking upon a trait of such a personal nature, I hesitated for a moment before replying.

"I scarcely like to mention it, Doctor, and you must forgive me for doing so," I said, albeit with some diffidence. "But it was that trick you have of nodding your head every so often."

"Oh dear! So that was it!" he exclaimed with a laugh. "I was of course aware of it, but I certainly had no idea it had become so noticeable. Anyway, I really must congratulate you, Farrant."

At this we relapsed into silence again, whilst I could not but continue to wonder at the amiable and philosophical way in which he appeared to have accepted the situation. For, quite apart from the mortification of having such a masterstroke of espionage so untimely thwarted, he must also be perfectly aware of the awful fate which, following the due process of law, surely lay in store for him.

We were, just then, approaching the highest point of the cliffs, where the drop to the shore below must have been a couple of hundred feet or more; and although the path was situated some few yards from the edge, I was being careful, nevertheless, to keep to the doctor's starboard side. Partly as I have never had much a head for heights, but also because I was still wary that for all his apparent resignation, and closely covered by my pistol as he was, he might still attempt some desperate gambit or other.

Not that he had, anyway as yet, given any sort of a hint that he might be about to do so. In fact, for the past few minutes he appeared to have been quite lost in thought, with his gaze turned towards the coast of France, which had, indeed, by this time, become just hazily discernible upon the horizon.

What his exact thoughts were, as he did so, I had no way of knowing. Although they were not, I think, difficult to imagine, and I could not but feel a certain sympathy for the man at such a poignant moment.

We had not proceeded many yards further, however, when he suddenly broke the silence.

"As I imagine, Farrant, that we are unlikely to meet again, in this world at least, I feel that, for your information, I should tell you that that copy of Butler's *Hudibras* which Sir George has, is only a very late edition." So, as I had feared at the time, he had, after all, been perfectly wise to my dissemblement from the first.

Still, it was of no consequence now, and in keeping with the playful tone in which he had alluded to my gaffe I was about to make some suitably jocular reply or other in return, when all at once he swung round and hurled himself upon me.

As he did so I fired and the ball must have struck, for I remember seeing him flinch as he grabbed my lethal arm. Not, I imagine, such was the game fight he was to put up, that it could have been anything more than a flesh wound.

For all my advantage in years, it was, indeed, a devilishly close-run thing, I can tell you. More than once, as interlocked, we heaved to and fro on the verge of that awful precipice, and I caught a glimpse of that horrendous drop below, it seemed certain that my end had come.

How it was that I did not, in the event, accompany him upon his death plunge to the shore below is, I must admit, something that has always puzzled me. My memory of those last few moments is, it is true, somewhat confused. Nevertheless, that we were still close-grappled when he finally dragged me with him towards the edge, I am pretty certain. I can only believe that, in the realisation that he himself was inevitably doomed, he deliberately and by an act of compassion relinquished, albeit only in the nick of time, his hold of me, and thereby spared me from sharing his terrible fate.

Not that I was of a mind, just then, to dwell upon such a hypothesis, for I had still to recover the precious documents, and lose no time about it too, as I was fearful lest the fellow with the boat, who, as I had observed, had re-embarked and was already pulling back to his ship, may have witnessed our death struggle, and would elect to return in an attempt to reach the doctor before me.

Happily he must have considered discretion the better part, for as I sped back along the cliff to the steps, it was soon apparent, as he continued to make away from the shore, that he had no such intention.

The doctor, when I eventually reached him, was of course quite dead, and so, having gently turned his body over, I knelt down beside him, and then commenced to search through his clothes.

To my consternation, all I could find upon him were half a dozen sovereigns; some personal letters, a handkerchief and a gold watch. Of the missing plans there was no sign at all. In a frenzy of desperation I went through his clothes again, this time tearing the seams apart in the hope that they might be concealed somewhere in the lining. But to no avail.

The agonising thought now occurred to me that he must – although he had scarcely been out of my sight since leaving the coach – somehow or other have passed the plans over to a confederate, or perhaps have deposited them in some prearranged hiding-place at the inn, whence they could meanwhile have been collected.

To my despair, I had already persuaded myself that this must, indeed, have been the case, when I chanced to notice his boots which must have become dislodged as he fell, and now lay several yards distant from where he had pitched. Hurriedly retrieving them, I passed my hand into the right one, but there was clearly nothing concealed there. In the left one, however, I could, with a thrill of excitement, feel a distinct thickening under the lining, and as I ripped it apart, there enfolded within the boot's inner circumference, lay a sheath of papers.

After first confirming that they were, in truth, the missing documents, I carefully pocketed them, and then having arranged the doctor's body as respectfully as I could, I duly returned to the cliff top; and with such feelings of joy and relief, as can, I am sure, be safely left to your imagination, made the best of my way back to Dover.

Chapter XXVI

Well I suppose there is really little more that I have to tell. With Sir David's plans safely in my possession, and the archprotagonist of the conspiracy, as I could only imagine Dr Argent to have been, lying there lifeless at the foot of the cliffs, my mission, I assumed, must surely, and thankfully, have come to an end.

It was, as I have said, a truly blissful realisation. Not that my feelings of ecstasy as I plodded back to Dover, were wholly attributable to my deliverance, and the sense of what I had somehow managed to achieve, but had also, as I think I need hardly tell you, something to do with Miss Catherine, and the joyous prospect of our being, shortly, reunited.

When I arrived back at the inn, she and Sir George were just settling down to breakfast, at which, following some tender embraces together with exclamations of astonishment which, as you would expect, my appearance had occasioned, I was, I might add, more than ready to join them.

As soon as they had recovered from their initial surprise they were, not unnaturally, all agog to hear what I had been about, and would not be satisfied until I had given them some account of my misadventures, both of that night and of the preceding few weeks.

That Miss Catherine had guessed I was something other than the impecunious bibliophile I had professed to be, she was to own. Nevertheless we all had a good laugh over this, as well as much else that had befallen me, although, as you can imagine, much of the jollity was to go out of the occasion when I came, sadly, to inform them of poor Joe's tragic death.

Later that morning, we had, of course, all the additional excitement of repairing to the harbour side to meet Lady Thurlow, and pleasant it was to witness the unaffected joy with which the family were reunited.

To my surprise, not the least moved appeared to be Sir George, who I could swear, had a tear in his eye as he turned away from embracing his long-departed spouse.

Of our journey home by the afternoon coach, I have little recollection. Impatient as Lady Thurlow was to relate her own adventures, we were all, I fear, much too tired to give her the attention which she, no doubt, deserved.

By the time we had reached Canterbury, both Sir George and Miss Catherine were fast asleep; and I was not slow to follow them. Indeed, I did not reawaken until we reached Gravesend, to discover that Sir David was still at the manor anxiously awaiting my return. And so I was personally able, and a most agreeable task it was, to restore to him his precious documents.

Dr Argent, as I was later to discover, was in fact a true-born Frenchman. Whether he had been justified in practising as a doctor seems doubtful however. For, although it is believed that he had studied medicine in Paris, no record could be traced of his ever having graduated. Interestingly, it also came to light that he had, for a time, been a coachman on the Paris to Lille mail.

Before I conclude, you would, I am sure, like to know that having been granted some further leave from my ship, Miss Catherine and I were, within the month, joined in marriage, at the little solitary church which overlooks the marshes.

You will also be pleased to hear that, not many months afterwards, Sally Cruden was also wedded, to a local waterman, and an excellent husband and father to Joe's children he turned out to be.

They, indeed, still have tenure of the "Three Daws", and whenever I am in Gravesend, seldom a day passes that I do not repair to the old inn, where, seated in a quiet corner over a tankard or two of their prime ale, my thoughts are wont to wander back, not without a cosy shudder at times, to all that befell me during those fateful few weeks, now all those many years ago.

Whether it was all to much purpose is, of course, another matter. For as you know, the invasion never came, Old Boney, no doubt, deciding that the risks were too great to be hazarded. That, but for my chance intervention, his decision might just possibly have been otherwise, I do sometimes wonder, although, I must, in all conscience, truthfully say that I deem it to be very unlikely.